GIRL
MOST
LIKELY

Other Titles by Max Allan Collins

The Reeder and Rogers Trilogy

Thrillers

Nathan Heller novels

Mallory novels

The "Disaster" series

GIRL
MOST
LIKELY

MAX ALLAN COLLINS

Published by Thomas & Mercer, Seattle

www.apub.com

Amazon, the Amazon logo, and Thomas & Mercer are trademarks of Amazon.com, Inc., or its affiliates.

ISBN-13: 9781542040587
ISBN-10: 1542040582

Cover design by Shasti O'Leary Soudant

For the reunion committee

WELCOME!

Some call Galena, Illinois—near the Iowa-Wisconsin border and sixteen miles east of Dubuque, Iowa—"The City that Time Forgot," frozen in the 1800s. But its one hundred or so dining, entertainment, and shopping options are a present-day delight—the half mile of Main Street's shopping offers, free of charge, outstanding examples of assorted architectural styles—French Colonial, Greek Revival, Victorian, and more.

Galena is the birthplace of General Ulysses S. Grant, eighteenth U.S. president. His victorious post–Civil War return saw the town presenting him and his family with a house that, while no mansion, would become just one of today's many restored historic homes now open to the public—actual mansions included!

History buffs will take in with wide, appreciative eyes the exhibits of the Historical Society Museum in its magnificent Italianate setting. Named for its iron deposits, Galena was in its pre–Civil War glory days a mining boomtown. But you don't have to be into history to marvel at an underground tour of the Vinegar Hill Lead Mine.

Aboveground, myriad pleasures await—rolling hills, sweeping valleys, a golf resort, nearby ski lodge, trolley tours, an array of cozy bed and breakfasts and comfy hotels, hot air ballooning, magic shows,

antiquing, art galleries, artisan and craft shops, a dis-
tillery, breweries and wineries.

Events and activities every weekend await hon-
eymooners and families alike, who will wonder at the
stunning vistas of Greater Galena. Each year this city
of three thousand-some souls welcomes over a million
visitors. Be one of them!

Jerome Ward, *The Galena Visitor* (published twice year-
ly by *The Galena Gazette*)

ONE

The two girls would be there, of this much you are certain.

Two women, actually—"girls" ten years ago, but women now. Judging by their photos on Facebook, both are still quite lovely. Neither is married, interestingly. Well, married to their careers maybe.

And if they both attend—and social media chatter assures you they will—and see you, and start talking . . . what could you do? Stay home, you suppose. But even in your absence they might talk. And if they talk, and that talk spreads, what would become of *your* career?

The planning for the event took all year—the Galena High School Ten-Year Reunion has its own Facebook page, so keeping up becomes a daily thing. You have read all the posts, many from friends who pose no threat, others from kids you hadn't been all that close to; but the class is small—sixty-five, and maybe thirty or at most forty will show up . . . and a few are gone already. A car accident and two Iraq deaths.

Maybe something would come up and one or both girls would decide not to come. You keep tabs on them. Keep track.

Sue has shared her travel plans, has her plane reservations made and hotel, too. Like most of those coming, she takes advantage of the special deal Lake View Lodge is offering. That has been a big part of why the Class of '09 settled on a winter month—off-season rates. The lodge is geared toward golfers with its four courses. Travel isn't an issue for the other girl, whose parents still live in Galena.

That is how, six months before the reunion, you end up in Clearwater, Florida—not for golf, but because of the reservations Sue makes.

You don't know much about Clearwater. Your family has vacationed in Florida several times, but never Clearwater, which somebody told you is the Redneck Riviera. You can't argue with that. The main drag is littered with fast-food restaurants, including the very first Hooters, and traffic is awful.

You check into a Fairfield Inn paying cash, saying you lost your credit card, and will a cash deposit for incidentals do? It will. After your long day of driving, you cruise the main drag, in search of the kind of fresh seafood you can't find in the Midwest. That stretch is so brightly lit, you don't realize your lights aren't on till the cop pulls you over.

Turns out to be a kind of variation on a speed trap. When afternoon turns to dusk and then darkens to evening, that fast-food-littered four-lane is still bright as noon. That means a cop can pull over out-of-towners like you and reward them with a seventy-five-buck ticket. What a racket. Some people have no morality whatsoever.

And when you finally choose a restaurant, the seafood is awful— heavily breaded scallops you suspect had been frozen.

Back at the Fairfield Inn, you barely sleep at all. Can't shut your mind off with all you've got to do.

Next morning you locate her home, on a side street just a few blocks from the motel, which of course you already knew, thanks to Google Maps. You'd been able to view her street online, and already know what her house looks like. Shabbier in person. A pale green ranch-style that would have been nice back home, but the tropical weather's been tough on it here.

You drive around her neighborhood, and the surrounding area. That main drag is hard to get onto if you're caught at a side street stop sign—you need a stoplight, though even then it takes forever to turn green. But the light does change, and soon you have chosen your route. Getaway route, you think to yourself, and laugh a little at the absurdity of it all.

She is living alone. You watch from just around the corner, parked in your Ford Edge, as she walks from a side door to her Prius in the driveway under a carport awning. You almost don't recognize her. She had been curvy, very bosomy, and cute. She is a little heavier now, though still attractive. Wearing the blue blouse of her job at Best Buy, where she is assistant manager.

You are close enough from where you parked to get a decent look at her. The red hair—in cheerleader days, so full and shoulder-brushing—is now a pixie cut. Her makeup is a little heavy. It always was.

You follow her to work, keeping several cars between you. You already know the address of where she's heading, thanks to her Facebook posts and the Clearwater Best Buy website. You do not go in, though probably you could have done so, staying at a distance—she is behind the returns counter. Why would she expect to see you here? Still, it seems too much of a risk.

You return to your room and have a nap before checking out. In your car, you check your watch—she'd be fixing herself an early supper now. You drive to a diner not far from her place and have some yourself. Just soup, nothing heavy. It's after nightfall when you park around the corner in time to see her exit again from the side door to her car.

Now she has a professional look—burgundy silk blouse, gray pants, low heels. Purse with a strap over her shoulder.

Her second job is at one of several venues at Ruth Eckerd Hall, a 73,000-square-foot performing arts center (Google said), part of an entertainment complex that is definitely upscale compared to the rest of Clearwater. That is because the patrons are mostly from the nearby Tampa Bay area, plus plenty of tourists from all over, of course.

The Little River Band is tonight's attraction at Ruth Eckerd Hall. They have so many good songs—"Reminiscing," "Cool Change," "Lonesome Loser"—Pablo Cruise is on the bill, too, with "Love Will Find a Way," "A Place in the Sun," "I Want You Tonight."

You go to the box office and spend $45 on a ticket. Part of that is to check out the venue, to see if this would be the right place for what you have in mind—the parking lot, maybe. And of course part of it is that you thought the two bands sounded like fun.

After all, shouldn't you get some enjoyment out of this? Why not chill a little bit? Must everything be so darn serious?

And there is no chance of her spotting you, since she works the bar at the smaller Murray Theatre in the complex, and you are in the main hall. It is huge—four thousand seats, every one filled tonight—which tells you this is the wrong choice. That parking lot is packed, and endless, a sea of people and their vehicles.

No, her quiet neighborhood would be better.

The evening of music has relaxed you. But after driving back and parking in the diner's lot again, walking the dark, dank residential side streets with their droopy, mossy trees—some of these homes are really crummy—you feel your stomach twitch and jump. Can't help it. You are human. Anybody would be nervous in your place.

She isn't back yet. You'd had no way to research what her work hours are—she'd never been that specific on Facebook—so you just tuck yourself under the carport, toward the back.

Maybe that was a bad idea, because when she pulls in and her headlights wash over you, you can—despite the glare—make out her wide-eyed shock at seeing someone there.

When she emerges from the vehicle, you are the shocked one—she has a little pistol in her fist! She is firm-jawed and her eyes are narrow. Your presence hasn't stopped her from moving forward, the gun probably encouraging that. Then her expression turns puzzled, and she speaks your name, adding a question mark.

"I didn't mean to startle you," you say. You smile just a little and gesture toward the gun. "You really think you need that?"

"I'm a woman living alone," she says, adding your name to that, a decided—and you think quite uncalled for—edge to her tone. "What are you doing here?"

"I'm in town for a convention," you say. "Just thought I'd look you up. Say hello."

"Okay, hello. *Goodbye.*"

You raise your hands as if surrendering. "I know we left it in a bad place, all those years ago."

"We didn't leave it in a bad place. It was always a bad place. You really need to go."

You hang your head. "Okay. All right. The real reason I'm here? I want to make amends. I want to apologize."

"Little late for that."

You risk a tiny grin. "'Better late than never' is a cliché, I know. But they say all clichés are rooted in truth."

"Do they."

"Could we sit and talk?"

"Inside?"

"On your stoop, inside, outside, I don't care."

She studies you. She sighs. Nods. She always was a soft touch for you. She puts the gun away in her bag and fishes out her keys.

Then you two are sitting in her small, very clean kitchen. She makes coffee. You tell her about your life, your marriage, your kids, your job, and how much it all means to you. She mostly just listens.

Finally she gives you a cup of coffee and—her remembering you find touching—slides a sugar bowl over to you.

"And you like cream," you say.

No smile. She sits. She looks pretty, and pretty tired. "I like it black these days. Strong, even bitter."

"Are you seeing anyone?"

She squints suspiciously at you.

You say, "There is nothing in that but simple curiosity."

"What you did is wrong."

"You think I don't know that?"

She sips the coffee. Isn't looking at you. "I don't hold a grudge. I take ownership of my mistakes."

Is that what you are? A mistake? But you say, "You don't blame me?"

"I guess . . . I guess I blame us both."

You sip the coffee; you've sugared the bitterness out. "Going to the reunion, I see."

"How do you . . . ?"

"Facebook."

She pauses. Nods. "I am. You're planning to attend?"

"Well . . . yes. Why shouldn't I?"

Her eyebrows rise but her wide eyes look past you. "I guess if you don't know, I can't tell you."

". . . I just want to ask one small favor."

"You think you deserve one of any size?"

"No. But I hope you'll do it anyway. Please. What happened . . . can you please keep it to yourself? And not talk about it with anybody?"

The bitterness of the coffee touches her smile. "Not even . . . you-know-who?"

You swallow. "Nobody."

She shakes her head. "No promises. Look, it's nice that you have regrets. I like hearing you apologize. But I'm not sure an apology quite . . . cuts it."

"What would?"

You have thought about money, and she could clearly stand to have some; but that is such a bad road to go down. Anyway, Sue is a lot of things, but a blackmailer? No. You won't insult her.

"Nothing," she says. "Some things an apology can't make go away. I do appreciate the effort. The sentiment. And I have no intention of broadcasting what happened." She shrugs. "But if certain people bring it up . . . who can say? Some wine, some mixed drinks—who knows? No promises."

Your turn to nod. Your mouth twitches a smile. "I understand."

"Good. That's a start, right there."

You rise, smile again. "I appreciate being heard out. Sitting down with me, like a couple of civilized people."

She summons a little smile, nods once, then nods again, toward the door.

That is your cue. She works at a theater, doesn't she? She knows all about the theatrics of life.

You walk quickly through the muggy night—it is almost cold, despite being late summer—and the sidewalks, the side streets, are empty. You are back at the diner now. You look around—no one in the lot, just a few cars. People in the diner windows eating, but otherwise you are alone. And you are parked away from those windows.

You go to the trunk of the car, open it and put on the black hooded raincoat and rubber gloves. You know you probably look odd, with no rain even predicted, and the only bad thing is if someone sees you, they might remember.

Can't be helped.

You walk back, quickly. Walk past the Prius under the carport awning and knock on the kitchen door. Doesn't take her long to answer. Maybe she is fixing herself a little something.

Framed in the doorway, she looks out at you, with a startled frown, but very pretty still, blue eyes, red hair, and says, "What the hell?"

You begin stabbing her with the butcher knife, in the chest, surprised by how little blood gets on you, considering all your preparation. But after she falls, her mouth open in a scream that never finds its way out, when you step over her to go in and clean your prints from the coffee cup, you almost slip in the stuff.

TWO

Chief of Police Krista Larson pulled her dark blue Toyota into the reserved spot at the head of the slanted lot that started below on Main and ended just under Bench Street. She stepped out into sunshine that felt more like November than February, her tense expression belying what was an exceptional day for this time of year.

What awaited her on the upper floor of the rough-hewn limestone-block two-story building—which supposedly dated back to mining days, before it became a power company building and then city hall—was about as inviting as being called to the scene of a bad accident.

Krista at twenty-eight was a tall blonde (hair short though not mannishly so), her athletically slender but shapely figure somewhat hidden by the white blouse of her uniform—her long-sleeve polo (with badge-like insignia) a size up to downplay the natural beauty of her Danish genes. The weather required only a navy windbreaker today; her holstered .45-caliber Glock 21 rode high on her right hip, a badge pinned to her belt at left, her cotton slacks navy, her steel-toed shoes black.

She took the nine steps hugging the building up to street level, where a black wrought-iron fence separated the parking lot from a space for a couple of patrol cars. She went around front to the station's Bench Street door under the two-tiered white-pillared overhang, and stepped inside. In the entryway, she glanced left at the steps down to the PD's former quarters, which she and the other eleven officers still referred to as "the Dungeon."

Until two months ago, everybody had been crammed in down there, desks, files, records, before the Galena Police Department moved into a remodeled second floor when the city hall took on newer, bigger digs on Green Street. The Dungeon was now used for personal lockers—extra uniforms, coats, bags—and the caged-in evidence room.

She took the stairs up to the department's new home. At the top, she was greeted by a massive wall painting of a shield-style badge, its navy-blue background dominated by a solemn portrait of President Grant against a waving American flag as he loomed over a steamboat, back when the Galena River had been wide enough to accommodate such a vessel. Above him in yellow was

GALENA
POLICE

and below, just above the shield point,

IL.

The beige-walled reception area sported a pair of modern-looking chairs and a couch, fairly (but not too) comfortable, overseen by a bulletin board and a rack of tourist brochures. Facing this were the three office windows, with clerk-dispatcher Maggie Edwards at the center one. Slightly heavyset with big blue eyes and a head of curly red hair, Maggie—the chief's late mother's best friend and formerly an administrative secretary at Galena High School—was a doggedly pleasant person, perfect for the job.

Put it this way: an eleven-year-old Maggie had played the title role in a local production of *Annie*, and had been well cast. Even today, working in a police station with all its ups, downs, and tragedies big and small, she felt the sun would come out tomorrow. Maggie and Krista smiled and nodded at each other as the chief was buzzed into the bullpen area.

How different from the Dungeon! The first third of the space was barely taken up yet, except by a row of file cabinets along the left wall. Krista passed the short hallway at right, off of which were the doors to the two interview rooms and Detective Clarence "Booker" Jackson's office, then moved past the doors of the conference room and continuing-education classroom. At the Front Street end, facing her glassed-in office, were four desks for the uniformed officers, three men, one woman, each with his or her own generous space forming a collective U, joined by a common Plexiglas barrier.

Krista said her hellos to the four officers and went on into her office, which was a good-size area, with a small table and chairs at right and three windows onto Main Street under which was a low-slung file cabinet. In the corner at left was her L-shaped desk with computer screen and keyboard at its juncture. She kept the office neat, the desk only mildly cluttered, considering how much work passed through this place.

Maggie, as if the clerk didn't already have enough to do, came in and, unbidden, delivered a cup of coffee. Normally Krista would take care of that for herself, but she had walked by the table of coffee and snacks in a daze, distracted by the thought of what lay ahead, and Maggie had noticed.

A civilian employee, Maggie wore a light blue blouse and tan slacks, casual but not sloppy.

"Lovely morning," the clerk said.

Maggie had brought the chief a napkin, too, and a doughnut, unfrosted, out of which Krista promptly took a bite.

"Lovely morning," Krista echoed, chewing.

"Are you all right?"

"Now I am, thanks to this." She sipped the coffee.

When Krista began here—down in the Dungeon, anyway—she'd taken on Maggie's role. Unlike the older woman, she had used it as a stepping-stone to becoming a uniformed officer. Truth was, Maggie had one of the most demanding jobs in the department—part receptionist, part dispatcher, part file clerk; she even worked up certain monthly reports.

Maggie went to the door, paused there, and said, "They could have sent Ben, you know."

"He's mostly sports."

Maggie's understanding, compassionate smile was something Krista knew well, usually finding it comforting or at least benign. Today it mildly irritated her.

"Are you all right, dear?" Maggie asked. With no one else in earshot, at least, the clerk could get away with calling the chief "dear," having known Krista since childhood.

"Fine," Krista said.

"How's your father doing?"

"Fine."

"All settled in?"

Krista smiled and nodded.

"Big job, was it, moving all his things?"

"No," Krista said. "One U-Haul load. Everything else went at the tag sale."

"That must have been hard for him."

Krista just sipped her coffee.

Maggie smiled in a sad-eyed way. "I bought a few things myself. Just to remember Karen by. Your mother."

Yes, I know Karen was my mother.

"That's nice," Krista said.

Maggie closed the door, as if that would provide privacy for an office fronted with a wall of windows onto the bullpen.

The chief of the Galena police realized that her clerk would not likely go on and on so, if Krista would just open up to her a little. But even as a girl, Krista had not been one to blather, and in this job, she had emphasized that stoic side of herself even more.

If she were to be taken seriously, as Galena's first female chief of police, particularly at her age, she could convey nothing girlish. She must be steady, serious . . .

. . . like her father, when he was a cop across the river in Dubuque.

Her visitor wasn't due till eight thirty, so Krista got to work, going over the weekend's activities (this was Monday), starting in on approving completed reports on arrests made, tickets written, and so on. But by a quarter till nine, she was still at it, with no sign of her scheduled guest.

Then at a quarter after, she saw him moving along the edge of the long bullpen, a good-looking guy her age with dark curly hair, nice dark brown eyes, a purposely scruffy barely-a-beard.

Jerry Ward wasn't short but he wasn't tall, either—maybe an inch over her own five eight. He wore a black jacket over an untucked white shirt, distressed blue jeans and Chelsea boots, and moved with confidence and ease.

He knocked and she called for him to come in—in an uninterested, businesslike way, of course.

"Sorry to be late," he said, and flashed the James Franco grin. Not why—just "sorry."

She gave him a perfunctory smile, barely looking up from her work to acknowledge his presence. His existence.

He stood there, close enough for her to smell his Armani cologne, possibly waiting for her to tell him to pull up a chair, which she didn't. She finished reading the report, signed off on it, stood, smiled in as slight a way as possible and still have it register, then gestured toward the small square table with its several chairs on the other side of the room.

They sat across from each other. He set his Yamaha Pocketrak on the table, which she knew he'd gotten back at the *Des Moines Register*, before they downsized him. Being back in his hometown (he had frequently let her know) was just a way-station stop on his path to becoming a bestselling novelist.

Which he'd been trying to be as long as she could remember. They'd been in high school together; senior year, an item, before Astrid Lund came between them.

But that was a long time ago. Water under assorted bridges. The big city reporter had moved back in with his parents while he worked toward fiction-writing fame. Taking a job at the *Galena Gazette*—one of the nation's oldest established weeklies—was just another way-station stop. Slumming, he'd called it, one night after a beer or two too many at the Galena Brewing Company.

"Hope this is not a problem," he said, his smile in response to her stone face not anything near Franco level.

"No."

"How's your, uh, father doing?"

"Fine."

"Good. Glad to hear it. Always liked your father. But I don't think he ever liked me."

Not asking would have been rude: "And your folks?"

"Fine. Fine. Getting used to having me around the house again, I guess."

"Well," she said with a shrug, "you have your own entrance, anyway. Basement cold this time of year?"

"No, it's fine. I mean, it's a finished basement."

". . . So you had questions for me?"

"Yes! Yes. You're all right with the recorder?"

She nodded.

"I mean," he said, "it's better than note-taking. This way I can be sure to quote you right."

"Good."

"You understand this is not for the *Gazette*. It's for the *Telegraph Herald*."

The Dubuque paper. He was a stringer for them.

She nodded.

"And with luck," he said, "it'll get picked up on the wire. There could be national interest."

"Really."

His turn to nod. "After all, you're the youngest female police chief in the nation. Kind of a big deal. There's a younger one in Maine, but . . . a guy. You began as a clerk-dispatcher?"

He already knew that, but she said, "I did. I liked the work, I liked the people. Finally thought I'd see what life was like on the other side of the glass."

"It was a fast rise. Two years in your civilian role, then by twenty-five you're an officer, twenty-six the department's detective, and now . . . chief."

"Right."

"You cracked that big case, while you were a detective."

"Yes."

"Must have helped?"

"I guess so."

He sighed, sat forward. "Even so, some of your fellow officers, who've been here longer, must have felt passed over when you were selected."

"Most seem happy for me. Everyone's cooperative."

"Well, other than that one case . . . how did you land the position, over older, more experienced people?"

"I applied and the city council gave me the job."

"That was . . . six months ago?"

"Yes."

"You must have been at least a little surprised."

"Yes."

He sighed again. Shook his head. "Krista, meet me halfway here. Give me a little more to work with."

"Ask me better questions."

"Oh, is that the problem?"

"Give me something that isn't a yes or no."

He thought about that. Nodded, admitting she was right.

"So what's your typical day like, Chief Larson?"

"One can vary greatly from another."

"Uh . . . how so?"

She shrugged. "Today was pretty usual. Started with coffee and a doughnut."

He laughed. "So cops really do eat doughnuts?"

"Good cops don't allow themselves to be shamed out of one. This morning, before you got here, finally got here, I started in on my reports. After this interview, I'll gather my officers and talk about what's going on in town, for example whether the sheriff's office has arrested anyone, in particular anyone who we might've been looking at on an ongoing case."

"You work closely with the sheriff's office?"

She nodded, and gestured toward Bench Street, across which were the sheriff's office and courthouse. "We don't have any holding cells, for one thing. I meet with the sheriff on an almost daily basis."

"What else happens on an average day?"

"Sometimes I have a department-head meeting over at city hall. I return phone calls and take them. If an officer on duty needs help, I may lend a hand . . . nice to get out of the office."

"What kind of help?"

She shrugged again. "Traffic control when an accident causes a lane blockage. Ambulance call. Domestic situation, a fight, missing child, someone wanting to file a report—maybe complain about a neighbor. I cover for the clerk-dispatcher over her lunch hour. We all pitch in here.

We're twelve in a town of three thousand with a million-plus visitors a year."

He grinned. Actually grinned. "I just wrote that myself, for the next issue of the *Galena Visitor*."

"Well, you got it right. After my lunch break, I usually meet with my lieutenant, to discuss upcoming events, scheduling, various things . . . personnel issues, departmental needs. I work on policies, read law updates, help with training. Nothing too exciting."

"What if there's a serious crime?"

"Well, again, we work with the sheriff's office. We can pull in resources from surrounding communities and the state police. If it's a crime that requires interviewing witnesses or suspects, I'll handle my share of that."

"Because you were a detective yourself."

"Yes, but also because that's one of the chief's duties here. We're not just any small town."

"Of course, your father was a detective."

"Until he retired he was."

"Retired early—what, at fifty-something?"

"Yes. Is that part of the interview?"

He opened a hand. "I need background. It'll interest readers to know your father was a detective, well known in the area. Chief of Detectives on the Dubuque PD—no small thing. Medals of valor and various other commendations."

"I'm proud of my father."

"So, in a way, you went into the family business."

"In a way."

"Kind of funny, though, that he never figured out you were living with somebody."

She nodded toward the recorder. "Turn that off."

He did. "Funny that he never detected you were living with me."

"We've talked about this."

He was smiling, but something a little nasty was in it now. "You really think he would have moved in with you, if he'd known you threw your live-in boyfriend out to make room?"

She didn't look at him. "This is over, Jerry. Leave."

"I've respected your wishes, haven't I? You said, 'Don't call,' and I haven't called."

Now her eyes found him. "Jerry . . ."

"But you said you would call me. I guess I didn't get that what you were really saying was, 'Don't call me, I'll call you' . . . in the time-honored 'get lost' manner."

She pointed at the door. "Go. Now. Not appropriate here."

"Appropriate where then?"

She stood. "We're done."

"Is that the chief of police talking or Krista?"

"It's Krista. But I am armed."

He stood, too. Flushed. "I'll treat you right in the article. Don't worry about that. But we need to talk when we're not yelling at each other."

"We aren't yelling."

"We did when you threw me out, remember?"

"I didn't throw you out. I asked you to leave. Like I'm asking you now."

"No, you yelled. You were human. You were real. You weren't this, this law enforcement automaton you pretend to be at work."

He left.

At least he had the courtesy not to slam the door.

This time.

THREE

Karen had been gone six months now, but it felt like forever, and yesterday.

In a gray CUBS sweatshirt, jeans, and Reeboks, Keith Larson was in the kitchen of his daughter's home, at the counter, preparing things for the evening meal he'd promised her. The fifty-eight-year-old retired police detective, who had only moved in with his daughter Krista yesterday, had already made a trip back across the river to Dubuque. To get the makings of *frikadeller*, he'd needed to go to Cremer's Superette, because their fresh meat was the best in the area. Right now he was hand-grinding half a pound of veal and another of pork with an onion.

The kitchen was large, almost ridiculously so; but then the whole house seemed overlarge and always had. Dating to the 1890s, high on Quality Hill overlooking the downtown, the white-trimmed, gray-frame two-story with its quaintly covered porch had been the family home for Karen and her parents. Not only had Karen grown up here, but so had Krista, who like her mother had been an only child.

The place, with its lovely old woodwork, hardwood floors, and ornate wood-burning fireplaces, retained much of its historic look down to the leaded-and-stained-glass windows, pocket doors, and walk-up attic. The latter Keith thought could be remodeled into a good study or home office, but with so much space here—and just his daughter and himself to rattle around in it—that seemed excessive.

He'd met Krista's mother at the University of Dubuque in 1981. He was studying criminal justice; Karen was an elementary education major. The joke was, he was such a big kid and she such a sneaky little devil that they made a good fit. And she was on the small side, five three, and brunette, while he was a sturdy six-footer, with a head of blond hair worthy of a surfer here in farm country.

That hair now was thin as hell on top, and he had a slight gut that his exercise bike was not interested in doing anything about—of course he wasn't terribly interested in the bike, either. All his life he'd been told he *almost* resembled Paul Newman, thanks to those sky-blue eyes of his; but the emphasis was frequently on the "almost."

Karen had never looked like anybody but Karen, and that had been fine with him. Her big brown eyes, her dark curly hair, which she'd worn so big in the '80s, had seemed just right to him. She wasn't skinny, either, which he liked, but she'd fought with her weight until the cancer had brought it back down, last year. Ironic that for a few months she had been the slender girl he'd fallen for, as the real woman she'd become slipped away.

He'd lived in this house before, for the first dozen years of their marriage, after Karen's parents retired to Florida, generously making the young couple a wedding gift of the family home. For those first twelve years, Keith had driven to his job in Dubuque, starting in uniform, rising to detective. But when he landed the demanding Chief of Detectives role six years ago—making even a half-hour commute impractical—they'd gone looking on the other side of the river and found a perfect little '50s-era ranch-style on Marion Street.

They'd handed this big old place over to Krista, who'd still been living there—their daughter had commuted to Dubuque University to study criminal justice, much as Keith had, years before—when Krista landed the job as clerk-dispatcher on the Galena PD.

He stirred breadcrumbs into the meat-and-onion mixture. He wondered why the tag sale hadn't hurt more. Of course he hadn't been present for it—just walked away and later took the check from the auction house gal. But he hadn't wanted most of the furniture and none of Karen's clothing or jewelry, even the wedding rings. After he had Krista take whatever she wanted, all he held on to of theirs were the photos, a few framed, others in photo albums Karen put together.

Of his things, Keith packed up his clothes, a cardboard box of DVDs (mostly westerns—cop movies just irritated him), and another box of some books. When they'd moved to Dubuque, not so long ago really, he'd stored a lot of things here at the old homestead, as they archly referred to it. Now, after seeing what Krista had done with some of that stuff, unboxing it and salting it around to make him feel at home, he wished he'd gotten rid of that crap in the first place.

The move—moving in here—had been sudden.

Since Karen's passing—no, he wouldn't let himself say it that way . . .

Since the goddamn cancer killed Karen, he hadn't once taken the twenty-minute trip to Galena to see his daughter. She was busy with that demanding job of hers (which made him damn proud), so they had started having Sunday supper together on Marion Street. He would cook, and she would pop corn and they'd watch one of the westerns, or maybe sports if some event they both had an interest in was on.

Usually, neither father nor daughter was talkative. They both had Danish reticence in the blood. He liked to think they were so comfortable together that they didn't have to say much. But sometimes he feared the opposite was true.

Fathers and offspring who were much alike often had a hard go of it, he'd found.

Anyway, the Sunday evening before last, he'd been in the wood-paneled den of the ranch-style, selecting a DVD from the shelves of the stand under the small flat-screen TV. He was on his knees doing that when she came in, all chipper, with a big bowl of popcorn and two smaller empty ones; she was in dark blue leggings, a lighter blue tunic-style sweatshirt, and her bare feet. She put the popcorn and bowls down on the end table separating the old sofa from his recliner, then she went back out again, returning less than two minutes later with bottles of the Carlsberg Export beer they both loved.

He selected *Rio Bravo* and put the disc in the machine. Then he turned to go to his recliner, where the remote waited with his popcorn and beer on the end table. He stood staring at the recliner, as if the dark fake leather of it were fascinating.

"Pop?" she asked.

She always called him that. One of the few detective series he got a kick out of was the corny old Charlie Chan flicks, which he also had on DVD. Ever since they watched those together, she had (like Charlie Chan's various sons) called him "Pop" (and on rare occasions, "Papa").

She sat forward, the popcorn bowl in her lap. "Something wrong, Pop?"

"I was just thinking," he said absently, still looking at the chair. "About the last time I sat down here."

"Why's that?"

"No reason. Well. Last time I sat there . . . which was just this afternoon . . . never mind."

Now she leaned forward so far that the popcorn spilled a little. "What is it, Pop?"

He laughed. "I must have sat there an hour."

"Watching something or what?"

"No. No. It's just . . . it's a long time to have your gun in your mouth."

They hadn't watched *Rio Bravo*. They didn't even eat their popcorn. They did stay in the den, but on the couch. He did something he hadn't recalled ever doing in front of his daughter, even at the funeral. He wept.

"This house," he said, after a while. "It's full of her. I thought that would be a good thing. But it's not."

"You had some wonderful years here."

"Yes, but all the memories, all the ghosts, are of her last six months."

Her voice took on a firmness that sounded spookily like her mother's, in certain situations, like when he was being an ass. "You're moving in with me."

"Don't be ridiculous."

"This isn't a discussion, Papa. You're moving in with me. This house will sell fast, and you know how much room I have. It's lonely in that big old place."

"I'd just be underfoot."

"I said it was big, didn't I? You can reclaim your study. I never moved out of my room. Your and Mom's bedroom is waiting."

She paused, maybe thinking that was the wrong thing to say.

"Or maybe the guest room," he said, already capitulating. "But those aren't the kind of memories, ghosts that would bother me. Everything in that house was positive. Mostly things were positive here. But those last six months . . ."

He began to weep again and hated himself for it. Not as long this time. And her arm around him did feel good.

She talked about hiring a moving van for any furniture he wanted to keep, and that was when he suggested a tag sale. He knew some reliable people who could throw that together quick. He'd bring his own things with him, and rent a U-Haul if need be. He would move in a week from today. Would he be all right till then? Yes.

"How can I know that for sure?" she asked. She was holding his hand.

"Because I'm not going to do anything stupid."

"What . . . what stopped you this afternoon?"

"Really why?"

"Really why."

He shrugged. "Didn't want to take the chance that you'd be the one who found me. Wouldn't do that to you, honey. And pills? I might wind up a vegetable, and you don't need that in your life."

"There are other ways."

"I'm squeamish about blood."

"You? No you aren't."

"I'm squeamish about my blood."

She smiled and squeezed his hand.

"And," he said, "one time I found a guy who hanged himself. That didn't look like any fun."

She dropped her head and laughed a little. He could always make her laugh. A dark Danish sense of humor was something else they shared.

So it had all gone well. And now he was cooking his first meal in this house, and it would be a good one. He beat some milk, slowly, into the bowl of meat mixture, then egg, salt, and pepper. When the mixture got puffy, he shaped the mix into ovals. For now, he put the meatballs into the fridge.

That was when he noticed the bottles of Coors Light in with the Carlsberg.

He frowned at the interlopers. What were they doing in there, bringing down the property values like that? His eyes searched the shelves—was that yogurt? Dannon, which as a child his daughter had more than once described as "sweet snot," an opinion he knew she still held. *What was that vegetable—was that . . . oh my God, was that kale?*

His first thought was that Krista had lost her mind. But he knew she had a boyfriend, that would-be writer what's-his-name, who even back in his daughter's high school days Keith considered a nincompoop. But she had a right to a boyfriend, even that one, and Jerry (that was it) was just the kind of person who would like kale and yogurt.

"Maybe even kale-flavored yogurt," he said out loud. "Washed down with a Coors Light."

Keith shrugged to himself. So she invited Jerry over, sometimes. No harm, no foul.

Nonetheless, he checked the medicine cabinet.

Hair gel? Head & Shoulders? Krista never suffered a flake of dandruff in her life. Hugo Boss cologne? Axe deodorant for men? Musk fragrance!

He shut the medicine cabinet door and frowned at his own image, which didn't remind him one little bit of Paul Newman.

He forced his frown into submission, made his mouth nearly smile. She's twenty-eight, he thought. She has a guy in her life. Who stays over sometimes. She's an adult. She has a right.

The smile never quite taking, he sat on the lid of the toilet seat, leaning forward, hands folded, as if in prayer. He was trying to settle his mind down when he saw the stack of magazines on the little stand that was otherwise taken up by folded towels. He took the stack in hand and started flipping through: *Women's Health*; *Vogue*; *Cosmopolitan*; *Elle*; *WomenPolice* magazine; *Penthouse*.

His eyes widened. What was wrong with this picture?

Next he found himself in the garage, where he spread out a black garbage bag on its cement floor, then snapped the rubber kitchen gloves on before dumping the garbage can onto the waiting plastic. He ignored the food items and other garbage and focused on paper items, specifically mail. Most of it required unwadding. He found the name Jerome Ward, at this address, on various billing envelopes.

When Krista came home, just before five, he greeted her with a smile.

"Too soon to eat, honey?" he asked her.

"No! I'm famished. Smells wonderful!"

He already had the red cabbage going, the boiling potatoes, too—not that the latter was all that aromatic.

He said, "I'll start the *frikadeller* then."

"Oh, good! My favorite!"

She went off to change her clothes and he fried the meatballs in hot butter till they were brown all over. He was ready to serve her up when she returned in gray sweats, her comfy at-home clothes of choice this time of year. She ooohed and aaahed as he set before her the plate of meatballs, red cabbage, and small boiled red potatoes. He got himself a plate, then a Carlsberg, before opening and setting a Coors Light in front of her.

She didn't notice at first, digging into her food. He got started eating, too. The table was a big wooden farmhouse affair that could serve a party of eight; they sat at the end nearest the kitchen area. Finally she reached, rather absently, for the beer, and when she tasted it, her eyes got big and she held the bottle out in front of her, like somebody in a cartoon who accidentally drank from an ink bottle.

She stopped eating. Set the excuse for a beer down. Said, "All right, so Jerry stays over sometimes. Used to stay over. We broke up, if you want to know."

He must have wanted to know or he wouldn't have behaved this way. He felt slightly guilty—slightly—as he said, "If I'm going to stay, we aren't going to lie to each other."

"Okay."

"How long was he living here?"

"Living here?"

"We aren't going to lie, sweetheart."

She looked at the beer, still in her hand, and shivered. "Yuck. Who says he lived here?"

"The refrigerator. The medicine cabinet. The skin magazine. And the trash, with discarded mail to him at this address."

His blue eyes in her face goggled at him. "Jesus. Do you ever stop being a detective?"

"No."

She got up and went to the sink and began pouring the Coors Light down the drain. "He did live here awhile. I'm of age."

"I noticed."

"Well, you might have known, if you'd ever set foot in here after . . . you know."

"I know."

She got herself a can of Diet Coke from the fridge. Popped the top. Said, "We did break up. He stopped by the station today, supposedly to interview me, but . . . it was something else. Kind of really ending it."

"Must have been embarrassing having that happen at work."

She sat, shrugged. "Not terribly . . . Can we just eat now?"

"Sure."

They ate.

He cleared the table, gathered his pots and pans, put leftovers in containers and into the fridge. She was loading up the dishwasher.

He went to her. "You should call him. I can move in with Matt or maybe Leo till I can find someplace. I won't have you disrupting your life over me. I won't have it."

She looked back at him, still crouched to load dishes in. "Pop, it's done. He and I . . . we were heading that way anyway."

"You're not lying to me?"

"No. No more lies, you said. Starting with that."

"You were thinking of breaking it off anyway?"

"Yes."

"Will you tell me one thing?"

She stood and faced him. "Okay."

"Was it the kale?"

She started to laugh and fell into his arms. He was patting her back when she said, "That and the yogurt."

FOUR

The following Friday—still unseasonably sunny and not overly chilly for February—Krista met her good friend Jessica Webster at Otto's Place on the east side.

Dating to 1899, the two-story white-trimmed red-frame structure faced the side of the refurbished old train depot (now the local visitor's center) across Bouthillier Street. In front of the brick depot, and alongside the restaurant, ran the railroad tracks, beyond which the Galena River formed the dividing line of the little town's east and west sides.

Over the years Otto's building had been home to everything from basket shop to bakery, grocery store to furniture emporium, pizza joint to antique shop, even a record shop where her father said he'd bought his first David Bowie album.

Now it was a cozy breakfast and lunch spot, its specialties banana bread French toast and the daily quiche. For Krista and other locals, the restaurant was a nice alternative away from Main Street and the tourists the town depended on. Some of those visitors would be resourceful and adventurous enough to seek Otto's Place out.

The restaurant was only open till 2:00 p.m., and it was a little after one already—Krista had worked over the noon hour, as usual, to cover for clerk-dispatcher Maggie. But Jessy was already here, across the little dining room, perched at a chair at the counter facing the window on the kitchen, an open seat next to her. Jessy liked to sit there, closer to the wine on display.

Krista hung up her windbreaker, then slipped past the tightly arranged wooden tables and chairs, only a few of which were taken so near closing. Those who glanced up from their meals at the uniformed police officer moving among them were likely stray tourists.

The front of the place was all windows and sunshine streaming in, pleasant enough if you weren't sitting in it. Framed local art adorned the walls, and a wooden staircase at left yawned up to the secondary dining area. Right now a young blonde waitress in a T-shirt and jeans with a brown apron classing them up was coming down with a pot of coffee in hand. She nodded at frequent customer Krista, who smiled and nodded back.

Jessy was sipping a glass of what was almost certainly white zinfandel. As Krista slipped onto the chair next to her, Jessy smiled and said, "My first glass, officer. I swear."

"Public swearing is a violation," Krista said.

"No shit?"

Both young women laughed a little; it didn't deserve much more than that.

Jessy had been Krista's best friend in high school. She was not then and was not now a raving beauty, her nose a little big for her face, but she'd been very popular thanks to her big brown long-lashed eyes and great smile and curvy little figure, all of which she still had. When Krista had played basketball, Jessy—head cheerleader—had lobbied for the cheer squad to travel to out-of-town games to support the girls. Krista still loved her for that.

Now Jessy Webster was one of Galena's top real estate agents. She wore her dark brown hair short and wore dark suits and brightly colored silk blouses. Today was no exception. Orange blouse. Navy jacket and slacks.

"So," Krista said, "are you ready?"

Both women knew what she meant by that: the Class of 2009 reunion was this weekend—tonight, the casual get-together, tomorrow the more formal night out at Lake View Lodge.

"As I'll ever be," Jessy said, eyes widening before sipping the white zin.

The friendly blonde waitress in the brown apron was behind the counter now. Krista ordered the asparagus, mushroom, and Swiss cheese quiche-of-the-day, with a cup of black coffee (never too late for caffeine in the life of a cop), and Jessy had the chicken-salad-and-bacon club sandwich and a second glass of wine (something of a risk when the chief of police was having lunch with you, and you were driving).

"I wish I'd had time," Krista said, between sips of coffee, "to help you guys out on the reunion committee."

"Well frankly," she said, and sipped more white zin, "once Dave Landry stepped up, there wasn't much left to do. He's providing everything . . . and bargain-rate lodging."

David Landry was the general manager of Lake View Lodge, his father one of the owners of the lavish resort on Lake Galena in the rolling hills of Galena Territory—four golf courses, several indoor pools, and full-scale spa. And two hundred usually pricey rooms, sitting mostly empty in off-season, which likely had helped encourage Landry's largesse.

Krista smiled a little. "Like the yearbook said—the Boy Most Likely."

"Likely to inherit his old man's money," Jessy said with a smirk. Then she shrugged. "But, really—we're lucky to have him in the class. Not many high school reunions get this kind of royal treatment, with one generous classmate picking up most of the tab."

"Who's he trying to impress?"

"You coppers are so suspicious. But if I had to guess?"

"Guess, guess."

Jessy leaned toward her. "Remember how bad he had it for Astrid?"

Krista gave up a light laugh. "And why shouldn't he? She was the *Girl* Most Likely."

"Most Likely to Dump Him back then. Most Likely to Snub Him now."

Krista's brow frowned while she smiled at her friend. "Astrid isn't coming, is she? Would she really lower herself?"

Astrid Lund—class salutatorian, president of student council every damn year, president of Drama Club, editor of the school paper, *The Spyglass*—had looked like Kate Hudson only more beautiful. She seemed most likely to be a famous movie star. But instead she'd merely gone into broadcast journalism and a celebrated career—currently an on-air investigative reporter for Chicago's WLG-TV on the city's top-rated nightly newscast. She'd be anchoring on a network someday.

Astrid Lund was the single most famous person to graduate with their class. Also, the *only* famous person to graduate with their class. Well, maybe a few others rivaled her . . .

"I don't think she'd miss it," Jessy said. "The chance to lord it over everybody while she pretends to be nice? You should know better than anybody she wasn't the Ms. Goody-Goody-Two-Shoes she tried to pass herself off as."

"Should I?"

The big brown eyes got bigger and bored into Krista. "Didn't she steal Jerry away from you, senior year? If I may be so blunt? After all, she stole Josh from me, for a while. Greedy little buh . . . witch."

Josh was Jessy's husband. He ran the All American Popcorn Store on Main, a family business. They'd been married since shortly after graduation, and parents six months later.

Krista asked, "How many glasses of wine does that make?"

"Just two. My limit."

Their food arrived.

"You and me, we both got our revenge," Jessy said with a shrug, before biting into the club sandwich. "Didn't we?"

"How so?"

Jessy shrugged again. "I got Josh, and my girls, and you got Jerry back, didn't you? Took you a while, but . . . how's that going, by the way?"

Matter-of-factly, Krista told her friend about shooing Jerry out of the house to make room for a new boarder.

"Your dad's living with you now? Since when?"

"Since Sunday."

Jessy frowned sympathetically. "How's he doing?"

She nodded, smiled. "Good. Better than I expected. We're getting along. He's a better cook than me, that's for sure."

Jessy was studying Krista the way she might a water-damaged ceiling. "Does he know you booted Jerry out to make room for him?"

Krista gave her friend a condensed account of how Pop had played detective and brought her to justice. And how Jerry had dropped by the office, with an interview as cover, and how badly that had gone.

Jessy sipped white zin. "Weren't you going to the reunion with him?"

"I was. I guess I'm going stag now, or whatever you call a girl without a date."

"Call her a woman with possibilities."

They ate awhile. Even Jessy seemed to know having a date was better than possibilities.

Krista asked, "Who else is coming that you know of?"

"Reservations came in from quite a few out-of-towners. Chicago contingent includes Alex Cannon—would you believe it?"

Alex was a top defense lawyer who got lots of media.

"Mostly it's the Galena crowd, of course," Jessy said. "Ol' Fearless Frank, another of Astrid's conquests."

Frank Wunder managed a Buick dealership owned by his father-in-law, whose daughter, Brittany, was another Galena graduate, though two years behind Krista. Like Jessy, Mrs. Wunder had been a cheerleader.

"In fairness," Krista said, and touched a napkin to her lips, "I don't think Astrid made conquests in the way you might think."

"Oh, you mean she didn't put out? Maybe not, but she had enough on offer to have any boy she wanted. And she really got a kick out of taking a guy away from somebody else—particularly if it was somebody popular, like her."

Krista shook her head, chuckled. "Listen to us. We sound like we're still a couple of kids, talking trash in the cafeteria."

Jessy used her napkin and tossed it on the counter. "Nonsense. Like you, I'm a successful professional woman . . . and I can't wait to throw that in as many faces as I can!"

They both laughed. Like a couple of high school girls.

The blonde waitress, perhaps mildly amused at seeing the police chief and well-known Realtor behave this way, came over to see about dessert. The two successful professional women declined, but Krista had another cup of coffee while Jessy worked on her wine—she still had a little left.

Something passed across Jessy's face as she looked into the wine-glass, swirling the liquid, as if she were trying to read her fortune in it.

"Terrible about Sue," she said quietly.

"Sue? Sue Logan? What about her? Isn't she a manager at Best Buy somewhere?"

Jessy sighed and faced Krista with an expression turned suddenly grave. "You don't know? You of all people . . ."

"Know what?"

Now Jessy glanced around, as if someone might be eavesdropping and, if so, that would be disastrous.

"Sue," Jessy said very softly, and somewhat melodramatically (this *was* her second glass of wine), "got killed."

"You're kidding! When was this . . . ?"

Jessy's eyebrows went up. "Some time ago, actually. Her mother wrote the reunion committee, several months ago. I looked it up online. Her mother said only that Sue had been killed last August. We thought it might have been a car accident or something, but no. She was murdered."

Krista reared back. "Murdered? Sue?"

"I know. She's not the type."

As a police officer, Krista knew that there was no "type" when it came to homicide victims; but she let that pass.

Instead she asked, "What did you learn online?"

Jessy leaned close. Disturbingly, this felt even more like two silly girls talking in the cafeteria or maybe study hall. "It was terrible. Somebody stabbed her, a bunch of times. Left her bleeding on her own doorstep."

"Who did it? Did they catch him?"

Wrong to assume it had been a man, she knew, but that was what came to her lips.

Jessy shrugged. "No one knows. No neighbors saw anything. It's terrible. Horrible! And none of us knew till way later. No one could go down to the funeral . . ."

"Down?"

Jessy nodded. "She was in Florida. Clearwater. She did work at Best Buy, and also at some big theater down there. Not movies—plays and concerts."

Krista nodded, too. "She was into that. Always into that. Liked working backstage, remember?"

Jessy's chin trembled. "And we didn't even send flowers or anything."

Krista shrugged a shoulder. "We didn't know to."

But she also realized that none of them would have gone to Florida for the funeral, even if they had known. Maybe the class would have sent flowers—the reunion committee, that is.

Or maybe not. Life goes on. Death, too. More than life.

"I'll make a few calls," Krista said, like that would do any good.

"The police down there think it's some maniac."

You think?

Krista, straightening, asked, "Have we lost any of our other classmates?"

Jessy nodded. "Two in Iraq. One in that car crash, remember?"

Krista remembered, all right. She'd worked the scene.

"Well," Krista said, "we need to do a memorial for Sue and all the rest of them, Saturday night. Say a prayer or something."

"The reunion committee's doing that," Jessy said, just a little defensive. "We'll be releasing balloons with each name. We were going to do floating luminaries. You know, sky lanterns? But the fire marshal nixed it. Lot of trees out at Lake View."

The two women, their giddy girlishness turned glum, paid their checks and went out together. At Jessy's car, Krista asked, "Are you okay to drive? Do I need to have you walk a straight line or something?"

"No, really. I only had the two. I'm not lying. I have no wish for you to take me in a back room at the station and work me over or anything."

They smiled, laughed. Neither meant it. The discussion of death was lingering.

Still, Krista watched Jessy drive off, noting that her friend seemed to be driving quite normally. Then she got in her own car—she didn't make use of department vehicles on personal business—and within five minutes was across the bridge over the trickle of river and onto Main. Two minutes or so later she was pulling into the PD lot.

She got out of the car, locking it with her key fob, and took the steps up to the Bench Street sidewalk. Leaning against the gray rock wall near the front door, in the shadow of the overhang, his arms folded, his weight on one leg, was Jerry.

He was in a navy field jacket, light blue polo, jeans, and running shoes. He gave her an embarrassed grin, held his hands up in surrender.

"I'm not stalking you," he said, "I promise."

Now she was the one with folded arms, though she had her weight evenly distributed on her two feet. She said nothing.

"And I'm not going to make a habit," he said, "of ambushing you at the station."

". . . Good."

"I think maybe I've been kind of a dick."

"Maybe?"

"I've been kind of a dick. You're just trying to do right by your dad. That's a good thing. That's the right thing. So I'm sorry."

"Okay."

"I wondered . . . you haven't been returning my calls. Is why I came here like this."

"I didn't feel like talking to you," she said. No emotion in her voice.

His smile tried too hard; he gestured awkwardly. "Reunion starts tonight. Casual get-together . . . Will probably be more fun than the more formal thing tomorrow."

"Probably."

"How would you feel about still going tonight?"

"Well, I *am* going tonight."

He winced. "I mean, with me. I'll pick you up at seven, if you're up for it. Are you? Up for it?"

She nodded, and went in, leaving him there.

FIVE

After almost a week back home with his daughter, Keith Larson was already settling into a routine.

And "back home" was how he thought of it. He and his late wife had lived here for many more years than in the Marion Street ranch-style across the river. This was where he and Karen had raised Krista, and when the couple turned the house over to their daughter—what, seven years ago now?—they had left many of their things behind.

The big house was furnished mostly with Karen's hard-fought collection of mission-style furniture, particularly vintage Stickley things—chairs and a sofa and tables and cabinets with that distinctive stained oak finish, the metal fittings, the leather coverings, the boxy designs. To this she'd added touches—lamps with stained-glass shades, beaten-copper candlesticks, and hand-turned earthenware. Karen often said the contents were more valuable than the house.

He and Karen had been pleased when Krista restricted her additions to modern mission-style things, from her computer table to the TV stand in the den. And when she'd thought about upgrading the guest bedroom with a new Arts and Crafts–type, but more comfortable, king-size bed, Krista had taken it well when her mother asked her not to. The bed was real Stickley, and anyway (Keith had added), why encourage guests to overstay their welcome?

That was the bedroom he'd slept in the first two nights. But he'd had trouble sleeping, and found himself wandering in the wee hours into the bedroom he'd shared for so many years with Karen. Both nights he wound up sleeping on top of the covers. On the third night, he started out in that room and, at some point, crawled under the covers.

That felt better to him. That felt right. Was it odd he always seemed to end up on her side of the bed?

Yes, things were going well, but there was no question about it: Krista was trying a little too hard. His daughter had spent God-knew-how-much at Walmart buying a 65-inch TV, one of the new 4K models (whatever that was), for the basement rec room, specifically to encourage him to fix the space up as a man cave (awful term!) so he could invite his buddies over for Cubs, Bears, Bulls, and Blackhawks games—also Hawkeyes football and basketball, since so many of his old cop cronies lived over in Iowa.

He'd tried to get her to take the monstrosity back—it seemed ridiculously large to him—but she refused, claiming she thought it would be fun to watch movies on.

This was patently untrue, because the rec room was in no shape for regular viewing, and anyway they had a perfectly good flat-screen half that size in the den where the family had always watched TV. The room was cozy with a two-seater overstuffed couch that was definitely not Arts and Crafts, though the built-in bookcases were (albeit not designed for the collection of DVDs and Blu-rays that lived on those shelves now, Krista's British shows, and his own John Wayne–centric collection).

Anyway, Krista was clearly overthinking his circumstances, as if she were afraid if he wasn't kept busy, he'd stick the barrel of his Smith & Wesson M&P nine in his mouth again.

The very first day she had presented him with a list printed out on her computer. It said:

Things that need fixing (easy to harder):

1. bathroom faucet dripping (also tub)
2. wall switch in upstairs hallway
3. replace stained ceiling tiles in basement rec room
4. fireplace damper won't always close
5. add more shelves in the linen closet
6. replace old kitchen sink with stainless steel (cast iron too heavy and expensive, though it would look very nice—DISCUSS)
7. patch where the squirrels are entering the attic (you may have to get up on the roof—so BE CAREFUL)
8. repaint rooms that need it (check with me first on color!)
9. sand and refinish wood floors downstairs (later upstairs can be done)
10. re-caulk the outside windows (many need new glazing)

Going over that list, he didn't know whether to laugh or cry. Maybe suicide wasn't such a bad option.

But he would chip away at the list. He was up for all of it, although he might leave the sink and the squirrels to more experienced hands.

On Wednesday he'd put the Smith & Wesson M&P nine millimeter automatic in the top drawer of the guest bedroom where he'd at first been sleeping. On Thursday, he decided to move all his things back into that master bedroom he and Karen had shared for so long. When he first opened the drawer, to start the move across the hall, he thought Krista had removed the gun, maybe hidden it from him. But then he realized he must have covered up the weapon inadvertently, just getting into the drawer for his drawers.

He chastised himself for thinking ill of his daughter, but when he hefted the S&W, the weapon felt light. Upon closer examination, he realized it was unloaded.

And his box of nine millimeter shells, which he'd tucked in one corner among his underwear, was MIA. He searched the drawer and then, somewhat ridiculously, all the other drawers, even the nightstand ones.

So she'd left him his gun, but stolen his bullets.

He could confront her, of course—"Even Barney Fife got one bullet!"—and she would undoubtedly cave and give them back to him. But he would rather find them. If discovering her previous housemate's recent presence wasn't enough to convince her of his detective abilities, he would further demonstrate.

As George W. Bush had once said, "Fool me once, shame on you. Fool me—you can't get fooled again."

He tried her underwear drawer, figuring she might stash the cartridges where she figured he'd be too embarrassed to look. A cop should have known better than that. And maybe she did, because he found no bullets stored among her bras and panties and lacy unmentionables, leaving him with nothing but the red flush of embarrassment.

Still, he figured he was on the right track. An intuitive flash sent him to the upstairs bathroom near Krista's bedroom. He opened the supply closet onto shelves of towels, Band-Aids, Q-tips, bubble bath, hair spray, deodorant, toothpaste, bathroom cleaners, toilet paper, and . . . Tampax.

Three boxes, one in front of the other.

He just stared at them for the longest time—maybe five seconds. Couldn't quite bring himself to look inside. So he shook the first one. Nothing but a gentle, papery rattle. He shook the second one. The same. He shook the third, which had already tipped its hand by its weight, and heard a clunk.

The previously opened, and otherwise empty, feminine hygiene box contained his black box of 147-grain Speer Gold Dot nine millimeter cartridges.

He reclaimed them.

Then, with a smile, he went to his daughter's room, where she had a notepad by her nightstand phone, and wrote: *If you need to borrow ammo, just ask.* This he tore off the pad, folded, and put inside the empty feminine hygiene box.

If she'd found the note, it hadn't come up at any of their subsequent regular evening meals. Or at their breakfasts, which she was fixing, the same as her mother always had—scrambled eggs, toasted English muffin, butter not jam, and orange juice. He had never been a coffee drinker and she got hers at work.

As the week progressed, he settled into a routine. On Tuesday he'd arranged for a membership at the local fitness center, where he would exercise three mornings a week and swim any day he felt like it. He had always enjoyed the many restaurants a tourist town like Galena offered and would, unless he got tired of it, take lunch somewhere downtown. So far he'd tried the Victory Café, the Golden Hen, and the Green Street Tavern. Liked them all.

In the afternoon, he would chip away at Krista's list of things for him to do. And, so far at least, he would by midafternoon be preparing supper for his daughter and himself. He had planned the whole week's menu, and driven on Tuesday afternoon back to Dubuque for meat at Cremer's Superette, and Hy-Vee for everything else.

Today, he made *skipperlabskovs*—veal again, a pound and a half of it, onions, peppercorns, medium-size Idahos (peeled and cubed), chives, bay leaves, and plenty of butter. This would make more than one meal for them, and the smell of the stew was sheer ambrosia.

Oh, how nice it was to be back in this kitchen again. He could almost feel Karen peeking in to see how he was doing, or sense her creeping up on him to give his ass a friendly pinch. But she'd always known not to hover.

When Krista came home, she knew immediately from the warm, wonderful aroma what her father was cooking. He knew it was another favorite of hers, and a couple of times a year (after he and Karen moved across the river) they would have their girl over for the stuff.

"Sailor's stew!" she cried, coming in the kitchen door. "Fantastic!"

Keith, in a BEARS sweatshirt and jeans and socks, smiled as he stirred. "Faucets just needed new washers."

"Nice to have a man around the house," she said, just behind him now, putting an arm around his waist and squeezing.

He almost said, "You mean nice to have a real man around the house," but thought better of it.

"I'll change," she said, climbing out of her windbreaker, heading into the formal dining room they little used.

Don't ever change, he thought, and stirred stew.

She came back wearing a light blue terry-cloth bathrobe and he gave her a quizzical look.

"I have the reunion tonight," she said. She went to the cupboard for dishes. "I'm not dressing till after my bath."

"Thought that was tomorrow," he said, then tasted the stew. *Delicious.* "The reunion, I mean. Not your bath."

She smiled at that, setting the table now. "Casual night. At the Brewing Company."

They said very little as they ate. The food had their full attention, although several times Krista also said, "Delicious."

"A pity," he said, "so few know of my culinary genius."

"Few realize you know a word like 'culinary.'"

"Also true."

She shrugged without disturbing her latest spoonful of stew. "I don't mind having you to myself."

They shared a slice of cheesecake from Hy-Vee, just slivers. He'd made tea for them both.

Though she'd been pleasant before and throughout the meal, he could tell something was troubling her. Nothing overt. But he was her father.

"What is it, honey?"

She sighed. "Just some sad news."

"Oh?"

She nodded. "Remember Sue Logan?"

"Don't think so."

"She was in my class. Redhead, blue eyes, very cute. Busty."

"Cheerleader?"

She laughed. "I knew if I gave you the right clues you'd solve it."

"Something wrong where she's concerned? Not coming to the reunion?"

Krista shook her head. "She was killed."

He frowned. "Accident?"

A swallow. "Murder."

"Ah, that's terrible. Horrible. She didn't live around here, did she? Or we'd have heard about it."

"She was in Florida. Clearwater. This was months ago. August, I think. Jessy told me. Pop, it sounds like some . . . some maniac did it. I know that's silly . . ."

"No. Maniacs are a lot of things. Silly isn't one of them. What happened to her?"

"Somebody came up to her door and just stabbed her. Multiple times." She shivered. "Pop, I love being a cop. I really like the job, and I can handle the sad, even tragic stuff. Comes with the territory. Mostly you're helping people, and around here, people are nice to police. Most of the tourists, too."

"I know."

Her sigh came deep. "But something like what happened to Sue? I don't know if I could handle that."

"Sure you could."

"There hasn't been a murder on my watch. We have everything else—burglaries, domestic violence, fights, you name it—but not murder. And before that case I helped you on—and that was mostly on your turf—there hadn't been any murders in Galena in twenty years."

She was talking about a homicide case they'd wound up working together two years ago. That had been high profile and undoubtedly had led to her making chief at so young an age.

He reached over and touched her hand. "Don't you let it put a damper on the festivities this weekend. Every class has its tragedies. That's what makes reunions so bittersweet."

She was nodding. "I know. I know. Just one of those freak things. We already had a death with that car accident last year, and two boys in my class died in Iraq."

"Don't let any of that keep you from enjoying yourself. Class reunions are special. Your mother and I never missed one. Hers or mine."

Their arrangement, already set in stone, was that he cooked supper and she did the cleanup, including the pots, pans, and dishes, washing them off and rinsing them out and piling them into the dishwasher, although that ancient chugging machine needed replacing. He was surprised it hadn't been on the "To Do" list.

She was heading over to the sink with their dishes when he said, "Hey, I'll handle those. You go ahead and get ready."

"Thanks, Pop," she said, and kissed him on the cheek and scurried out.

He was watching the news on the TV in the den when she appeared between the French doors looking impossibly young and every bit as pretty as her late mother, which took some doing. Her short hair was different, fuller, with some waves in it. At work she didn't wear much if any makeup, but tonight she'd applied some, delicately. She was in a red sweater and dark jeans, with black-and-red cowboy boots.

"Uh, Papa . . ."

He muted CNN. "Yes, sweetie?"

"I'm going to this with, uh, Jerry tonight. You remember Jerry?"

He sat up in his recliner, the only piece of furniture he'd brought with him. "Jerry who until last week was living here? That Jerry?"

Quietly, leaning against a door, she said, "That Jerry. Yes."

He raised a palm. "None of my business. Have a good time."

She could only get half a smile working. "I just . . . he and I were already going to this thing together, so I didn't break the date."

"Nothing to explain."

"We kind of made a truce. Just for tonight."

He got up and went over to her. Put his hands on her shoulders. "Honey, he can move back in as far as I'm concerned."

"But you would move out."

"Right."

She laughed a little and the doorbell rang.

He followed her into the living room, but kept his distance as she answered it. Jerry, in a black jacket over a gray shirt and blue jeans and sneakers, stepped in and smiled at her, then noticed Keith standing half a room away.

"Mr. Larson," he said, the smile curdling some.

"Jerome. How's the writing coming?"

"The novel? Getting there."

Keith crossed the room, nearer now but not much. Not wanting to crowd his daughter. Or her date.

Keith asked, "What's it about this time?"

That reflected Keith's awareness of many abandoned Great American Novels of Jerry's that had preceded this one.

"Uh," Jerry said, "a coming of age thing."

"Can't wait to read it. Have fun, you two."

And Keith went back in the TV room.

He heard the front door close and got up and headed into the kitchen, helped himself to a Carlsberg, opened it, swigged twice, taking it with him as he walked through the dining room and around to his study, where he had a desk and a computer. He put "Susan Logan," "homicide," and "Clearwater, Florida" into Google.

He got a *Tampa Bay Times* account of the murder. A detective named Hastings had the case. Two follow-up articles indicated no resolution.

He called his friend Lou Ramos, a detective across the river who'd been his partner for a while, and asked, "You have pals in Florida, Lou? Police variety?"

"A couple."

Lou was active in the National Association of Police Organizations. He was always going to some NAPO convention, seminar, or conference. He and his wife didn't get along.

Keith asked, "How about the Tampa area?"

"I know a Tampa guy. Hell of a cop. You should see him drink."

"What about Clearwater?"

"That's almost the same as Tampa. But, no, nobody in Clearwater."

"Could you give me your Tampa friend's number?"

Lou did that, and Keith called the guy, who did sound like he'd been drinking. But friendly, and he knew Detective Hastings, who he didn't think would mind hearing from a fellow officer, even a retired one.

So within half an hour of Krista leaving, Keith was talking to the officer in charge of the Sue Logan homicide. Keith explained the victim was an old friend of his daughter, who by the way was the police chief locally. Did they have any kind of line on the perp?

"Some random nut, we think," Hastings said.

"Can you fill me in a little?"

"Well, we think the Logan woman may have known her killer. She lived alone, and she had a conceal and carry, which she got because she was carjacked one time. Made her paranoid, I guess, the guy who worked it told me."

"But not so paranoid she didn't open her door to her killer."

"Right. So she knew the killer, trusted him or her but probably him—it was dark, but the door had a glass panel—and she answered it."

"From what I read online, her killer attacked her right there in the doorway."

"Right. Eight deep thrusts of what we think was a knife blade, all in the chest. That's partly why we think it's a man—wounds went deep."

"But a woman in a frenzy could do that."

"Which is why we don't rule that out. So what's your interest in this, buddy? Or is it your daughter's, 'cause she's chief there?"

"Nothing except Sue Logan was a local girl. Sue and my daughter were in high school together, and this weekend's the class reunion. Thought if there was any news, any leads you might be able to share, her friends might like to know."

"Well, there isn't. Anything else?"

"No. Thank you."

"Nice talking to you," Hastings said, and hung up.

SIX

The outer area of the Galena Brewing Company on North Main was a big modern room with rustic touches, brick behind the bar, barnwood-trimmed doors, wooden tables and chairs, and—hanging from the open rafters—nostalgic posters. These hawked their house brews—General Grant for Uly's Dark, Carrie Nation for Anna Belle's IPA, and a weary Depression-era farmer for Farmer's Blonde.

This time of year the microbrewery was rarely hopping (or barley-ing either, for that matter). But this was a Friday, and fairly busy, so Krista was not surprised when she and Jerry were directed to the party room. Maybe thirty people were packed into the modest space with its own bar and rustic touches (here a barrel, there a pioneer picture), and half a dozen four-chair tables. On the edge of the bar, a phone in a speaker dock was giving forth with Lady Gaga's possibly prophetic "Bad Romance."

The word "casual" to Krista's female classmates hadn't stopped them from making an effort—around the room were colorful sweaters, ruffled blouses, and funky sweatshirts. Less thought had gone into the rest of their ensembles, which invariably ran to leggings or jeans. UGG boots and maybe her own cowboy boots were as fancy as the footgear got, with running shoes in the lead.

The guys had taken "casual" more literally, the room filled with flannel shirts and sweatshirts, nondesigner jeans, and even sweatpants, with running shoes winning the footwear event, male division.

But for the occasional selfie, the usual phones were tucked away, texting taking a back seat to actual human contact with these old classmates. It was better than Facebook.

Krista and Jerry, who on the brief car ride here had spoken very little, if politely, joined Jessy and her husband, Josh, at the table where seats had been saved for the less-than-happy couple.

"You look adorable!" Jessy said, standing and giving her a hug. "I love the cowboy boots!"

Josh, also on his feet now, grinned and said, "I thought you were the police chief, not the sheriff!"

He was a good-looking, friendly guy with dark blond hair and dark blue eyes, slightly overweight, in camouflage sweatshirt and khakis.

She laughed politely at Josh's greeting, not terribly interested in having her profession pointed out. Jerry said hello to everybody as they both sat down.

"Well, you look very nice yourself," Krista told Jessy, who—ever the professional—had on a crisp white shirt, open at the neck, with a tailored navy blazer, her makeup flawless, though her dark-washed jeans and flats showed less effort.

Krista added, "Love the purse!"

Jessy—the black Coach crossbody purse before her like a meal she was protecting from some hungry interloper—said, "Nabbed it at T.J. Maxx across the river. Where did you find those boots?"

"Online, I'm afraid," Krista admitted.

She and Jessy talked clothes for a while, and commented in hushed tones about the attire of other female classmates (mostly admiring, but a modest amount of cattiness creeping in). Josh and Jerry just smiled awkwardly at each other. They had nothing in common, Josh having typical male sports enthusiasms, Jerry a would-be hipster interested only in the arts.

Krista caught snippets of their occasional, strained conversation.

Jerry gestured to Josh's camouflage sweatshirt and said, "Didn't know you were into hunting."

"I'm not."

"Oh."

Josh shrugged. "Just thought it had a nice macho vibe."

Jerry nodded. "That it does."

"Don't want people to think because I'm in the food industry I'm some kind of . . . you know."

Jerry, who clearly didn't know, said, "Right."

And that, of the several things that got through her radar as she girl-talked with Jessy, was the longest and most interesting exchange between the two former classmates.

Krista asked Jessy, "Any sign of Astrid?"

"Not yet. I fully expect her to make an entrance. If she shows at all."

"Thought you said she was coming . . . ?"

Jessy nodded, her permed dark hair bouncing. "Yes, but we only took RSVPs for the formal night. We just informed everybody on our emailing that on Friday we'd meet casually here at the Brewing Company."

"Nice place for it. Did they charge us for the party room?"

"No. Not even for the bartender."

Of course, the microbrewery was obviously making out just fine. And that was cool with Krista, who liked their craft beers. Her particular favorite was the Farmer's Blonde. Noting that neither Jessy nor Josh had drinks yet, she interrupted the conversation with Jessy to take their orders, which she and Jerry rose to go over to the bar and get. They would buy the first round.

As they stood in line, Jerry said, "What the hell kind of aftershave is that doofus wearing?"

"Josh is very nice," she said firmly. "Anyway, I don't think that's aftershave."

"What is it then?"

"Maybe the new garlic caramel corn."

As they carried four beers over to the table, Miley Cyrus was singing "Party in the USA." Krista and Jerry distributed the beverages, giving an Uly's to Josh, an Anna Belle's to Jessy, with Krista keeping the Farmer's for herself and Jerry the can of Coors Light he'd disgraced himself asking for.

"You're kidding," Josh said, to no one in particular.

He was looking across the room where two guys had just come in. Both were noticeably older than Krista's classmates, which was as it should be, since Christopher Hope had been one of their teachers, and his significant other, Tyler Dale, was the longtime owner and operator of Galena's Own Artworks, where you could find paintings, prints, ceramics, and jewelry by local artists.

Jessy frowned at her husband and said, "Don't."

"I just think he has his nerve," Josh said.

Krista knew Josh meant Chris.

Jerry, not following, said, "What?"

"I'm no homophobe," Josh said, which was something that only homophobes tended to say, "but I don't think somebody like that should be teaching children. Much less . . ."

Jerry, getting it now, frowning, asked, "Much less what?"

Josh was looking somewhere else now. "Nothing."

But Krista knew. Chris and Tyler had adopted two children. Some people didn't like that. Most didn't care. She certainly didn't. And in her time on the PD, she'd seen four instances of barroom literal gay bashing that had made her sick.

"Excuse me," she said, somehow managing a smile, and rose and went over to Chris and Tyler, who were looking around for a place to sit, apparently.

Krista smiled big and took the hand Chris offered and she held it and squeezed. "I'm so happy to see you! I wish more of our teachers were here."

Chris, who was all in black—turtleneck, its long sleeves rolled up, dark-washed skinny jeans, and black dress shoes—had a slimly athletic build a quarterback might envy. He was in his late thirties and looked great, blond and chiseled, the kind of handsome gay guy that made a woman sigh in disappointment.

"You must be the best-looking police chief anywhere," Chris said, smiling and looking her up and down in a way most of the other men here couldn't get away with.

She laughed and thanked him, letting him have his hand back, not minding when Chris was the one invoking her job. She said to Tyler, "I was in the shop last week. I love the new things!"

Tyler—in a Tom Waits chapeau, black satin jacket, vintage Pat Benatar T-shirt, ripped jeans, high-top Converses, and fashionably scruffy beard—said, "I'm afraid the best things aren't selling like they should. And we're pulling in arts and crafts from all over the tristate area."

Chris gave his partner a sideways smile. "He means his paintings aren't moving as fast as he'd like. I told him he should do some more of those David Bowie images."

Tyler laughed quietly. "He wants me to pander."

"No," Chris said to him, "I want you to sell out!"

All three of them laughed, and Krista said, "You know, you really gave me a boost of confidence, back at GHS."

That half smile of Chris's was worth more than most people's full grin. "You mean that lead in *Into the Woods*? We were one of the first in the nation to do the high school version, you know."

That was the so-called "junior" edition that was mostly the first act. Krista had played Little Red Riding Hood.

"I was very shy before that," she said. "Kind of . . . inward."

"You were something of an introvert, yes. But now you deal with people all the time—at their best and their worst, I would imagine."

"Well," she said, "I hope you know how much you did for me. For so many of us."

Somewhat shyly, possibly a little embarrassed, he said, "You're very welcome."

"How are the kids?"

He gave her a full grin now. "Chloe and Liam are great. Nine and twelve respectively. Liam is in basketball and Chloe is into science. Not a speck of drama talent in either one of 'em. That will prevent a conflict of interest one day."

"I'm so happy for you guys," she said.

Chris looked around. "I don't see Astrid anywhere."

"I'm not sure she's coming tonight. But Jessy says Astrid put in a reservation for tomorrow night. She was your star, I know."

"Your costar," he said, referring to Astrid playing Cinderella in *Into the Woods*.

"Well, she had the lead," Krista said, "in every play you put on all through high school."

"I'm sure some of the kids resented that," he said. "But she was so very good. Talent will out, you know."

"Like evil," Tyler said.

Krista said, "I hope to see you two tomorrow night. Like I said, I wish more of our teachers were coming."

"Tomorrow a number are," Chris said, nodding. "Enough of us to reserve a table, anyway."

"Great!"

Several other classmates who'd been in drama came over and kidnapped the two men to come sit with them. On her way back to the table, Krista ran into Frank Wunder and his wife, Brittany. Frank had a can of Budweiser in a fist and Brittany a glass of wine in her more delicate grasp.

"You can arrest me anytime, Chief!" Frank said, good-natured but, as ever, a shameless flirt. Predictably he was wearing a Galena High football jersey, brand new but with his old number—69—which had been the source of much boring humor among his teammates.

Rugged, with short brown hair, Frank had a Woody Harrelson handsomeness undercut by those nice green eyes being set even closer together than Woody's, and a nose that had been broken a few times.

He was bound to start off by ragging Krista about not buying her latest car from him.

And he did: "How can the chief of police of an all-American town like Galena buy Japanese? I'll give you a better deal on that Toyota than you deserve, just to get you into the right kind of ride."

"Hi, Frank. Hi, Brittany."

Brittany had speared a page from her rock 'n' roll almost namesake, wearing a clinging black spandex top with the shoulders cut out, too-tight jeans with bedazzled butt pockets, and high-heeled black leather boots. This outfit would have worked better ten years and two kids ago, her long blonde hair sporting too much product, her makeup predictably heavy. But unlike many other women here, Brittany had given her entire wardrobe real thought.

"You look nice," Brittany said. She seemed sincere but not happy about it.

"So do you. Any of your classmates here?"

She nodded, sipped her wine. "A few married up like I did."

Brittany meant she'd been a sophomore who snagged the school's star jock. But it was her husband who'd married up—Brittany's daddy owned the car dealership that Frank managed.

Drake started singing, "Best I Ever Had."

Frank asked, "Any sign of Astrid yet?"

He was one of half a dozen guys who had been a boy toy of Astrid's back in his glory days. And bringing Astrid up in front of his wife like that was thoughtless, to say the least. And he wasn't even drunk yet.

"No," Krista said. "Not sure she's coming tonight. Pretty much for sure she'll be there out at the lodge."

Frank grinned, perhaps at the thought of seeing Astrid again. "Really cool of Dave Landry to roll out the red carpet like he is. Hell of a nice thing to do for his old classmates."

"Really is," Krista said, nodding, meaning it.

Some of Frank's old jock buddies were approaching, so she smiled and nodded at the couple—Brittany seemed in petrified misery—and headed back to the table.

But Jerry intercepted her halfway.

Whispering, barely audible above the Black Eyed Peas, he said, "What's the idea of leaving me alone with that homophobic fool?"

"Josh is okay," she said. "He's just a little screwed up in some areas."

"Yeah, maybe."

She leaned close to him. "Jessy is my best friend. Go mingle with some of your own friends—this is your class, too."

"I thought we came together."

She gave him a strained smile. "That's starting to feel like a technicality."

He gave her a dismissive wave, then moved away, not back to their table, rather taking her up on her suggestion to connect with some other classmates.

When she returned to the table, Jessy was sitting with another friend of theirs, Cindi Thomas, who was also on the committee. Krista went over and got a second Farmer's and, when she returned, Cindi was just going. Josh was across the room talking to a couple of guys from his old crowd.

Jessy leaned in and asked, "Are you back with Jerry?"

"Not really."

"Would I be out of line saying, 'Good'?"

"Not at all."

"Okay, then. Good. He was really a jerk to Josh."

"How so?"

"Well, he congratulated Josh on being the most boring, backward ass in the class. Was he trying to sound like a poet? Rhyming 'ass' and 'class'?"

"Dunno."

And Jerry wasn't completely wrong about Josh, but insulting him at an event like this, in front of the guy's wife, who organized the reunion . . . well. She drank some beer.

"Omigod, look." Jessy's eyes were on the entry between the party room and the outer brewpub. Sixpence None the Richer, with its girl singer, was doing "There She Goes," the old La's song.

Astrid Lund.

Pausing there as the world stopped around her. Tall, blonde . . . but then so was Krista. Attractive in her Nordic way . . . but then so was Krista.

But not like this. Not quite platinum hair stopping at her shoulders, classic blunt bangs. Wide-set ice-blue eyes. High cheekbones. Perfectly formed nose with a slight upward tilt. Mouth on loan from Charlize Theron. Slender with a narrow waist.

And the clothes!

Krista may have spent most of her time in uniform, but she had always loved fashion, getting lost in the chichi magazines. She consoled herself with the notion that fashion would be bad for her law enforcement image. Not that, in real life, she could afford anything that wasn't a knockoff or a T.J. Maxx castoff.

Apparently Astrid could afford it.

She was in a Burberry tan-and-black plaid shirtdress—knee-length with quarter-length sleeves and a sash belt. On her small, no doubt perfect feet were Burberry booties, the front half brown leather, the back half plaid cloth, wraparound leather strap, gold buckle. Casually from one shoulder hung a Louis Vuitton bag—brown-and-tan hobo with signature LV. Krista guessed that maybe her classmate had figured going all Burberry would have been a bit much.

The watch riding Astrid's wrist was an oversize Rolex. Her bare legs were bronze—product, tanning bed, or island vacation? Who could say? But all her exposed skin, face included (making that blonde hair pop), was that same bronze.

Krista was considering going up to her, but to welcome her, since everyone else was as frozen as the kids staring at Astrid playing Stupefyin' Jones in Mr. Hope's sophomore-year production of *Li'l Abner*.

What made Krista hesitate was thinking that if only that red sweater of hers had been cashmere, and not cotton . . .

But before Krista could get past that, Jerry ran up to Astrid like a lost puppy catching sight of its master. Or mistress. She took both his hands in hers and kissed him, briefly, on the mouth. And then they began to talk, Jerry fairly animatedly, and Astrid listening politely, making the occasional comment, as the rest of the party room thawed itself and got back to their conversations.

When Astrid and Jerry moved deeper into the room, Krista found her moment. She slipped out and headed home.

It wasn't much of a walk.

SEVEN

Keith was sleeping on the couch in the den when he heard Krista come in. He didn't remember stretching out, but at some point he obviously had—the last he remembered, he was in the middle of *Two Mules for Sister Sara* on the Starz western channel and now something with James Stewart and Audie Murphy was on the screen. He'd seen it before, but didn't remember the title. The TV was muted, which he must have done before flopping on the couch.

He sat up, quickly awake, running his tongue over his teeth in a not entirely successful effort to get rid of the sleep taste. The French doors were open and he could see Krista hanging up her fur-collared bomber jacket in the closet opposite the front door she'd just come in.

He checked his watch—not even eleven yet. What was she doing home so early? And what was he doing falling asleep like an old man in front of the television? Had he really slept through a car pulling up just outside his window, doors closing and good-night conversation included?

He wandered into the living room and he and his daughter met halfway.

"Wasn't expecting you yet, honey," he said.

She smiled a little. "Does that disappoint you?"

She sat on the sofa, which was one of Karen's favorite pieces. It had taken his wife some real convincing to get the antique leather cushions restuffed to make them as comfortable as they were now. That had been twenty years ago.

He sat next to his daughter, somewhat sideways, studying her. She was clearly upset, though not on the verge of tears. Like any father might, he hoped her unsettled condition meant she had finally dumped that louse Jerry. Never occurred to him that a Jerry might dump a Krista.

His daughter, in her red sweater, had looked very young before she went out tonight. Now she looked twenty-eight, and nothing wrong with that. Such a pretty thing. The Danish coloring and hair and eye color were all courtesy of his genes; the shape of her face and its beauty were her mother's Irish doing.

"This," he said, "is where a more sensitive father might ask, 'Do you want to talk about it?'"

". . . Nothing's wrong, Pop." She smiled but it was little pitiful, though not self-pitying. "It's just . . . I finally ended it for good with Jerry."

"Much drama?"

"No." She told him how Jerry had been boorish at the brewery, and had gone running up to Astrid Lund to make a fuss over the very girl who'd come between them, a hundred years ago.

He said, "Jerry doesn't sound very sensitive either."

"No kidding."

She shared the way he'd treated Josh and how that had irritated Jessy.

"The frustrating thing," she said, "is I agree with Jerry about Josh's stupid homophobic opinions. But Jessy's my friend, and they saved seats for us, and . . . let's just say I didn't think much of Jerry's social skills."

Keith knew that his daughter and her friend Jessica were on the opposite side of the political fence on some issues. Jessy was a conservative Republican and Krista was a very middle-of-the-road Democrat. He had voted straight Republican ticket all his life, till some of the choices offered him had made him sit out the last couple of national elections.

But Keith knew that Krista steered clear of certain topics with her friend—gay marriage and reproductive rights, for example. Jessy was a devout Catholic, and her husband was, too, Catholic anyway—Keith didn't figure Josh was devout about anything except maybe selling popcorn and fudge to tourists.

Krista was saying, "I kind of had a rude awakening."

"How so, honey?"

"Well." She sighed. "Do you know just how long Jerry was, uh . . ."

"Your houseguest?"

She nodded, smiled awkwardly. "I have a feeling you think him living here was a pretty recent thing."

"I guess I did."

"He lived here six months, Pop. I put up with that self-righteous, self-centered SOB for six months!"

That did surprise him. Almost shocked him. And hurt him a little, too, because it meant his daughter had been keeping something significant from him all this time. Not lying to him, but . . . not being honest either.

Of course he hadn't bothered once to drive the twenty or so minutes across the river to see his daughter during that same six months. There was plenty of mea culpa to go around.

She reached for his hand and squeezed. "I'm sorry, Daddy."

She rarely called him that.

He said, "You're a big girl, honey. You can make your own decisions."

"Jerry was a bad decision. I can't explain myself, really . . ."

"You don't have to."

She was still holding his hand but looking across the room. "I hadn't dated anybody in a while, and Jerry came along, hauling so many memories, mostly good ones. He's smart and he can be funny. We have a lot of shared interests. Do you know how hard it is to find a guy who isn't into sports and nothing else?"

"Probably pretty tough. Gems like me, who like sports *and* John Wayne movies, don't come along often."

That got a smile out of her, a brief one. "Jerry and I would go to concerts and plays and movies—movies that didn't have a single thing blowing up in them! We went to museums a couple of times. We both like the BBC-type mysteries, and would sit over in the den watching them for hours. I'd make popcorn, and . . ."

Was she almost on the verge of tears? He really couldn't tell. And it hit him that now he was the one sitting next to her in the den watching TV.

"I had no idea," he said quietly, "that you'd been in that relationship so long. That it was so serious."

"Pop . . ."

He held up a hand. "I would never move in and cause a breakup. Listen, I'm fine. Everybody has a bad day now and then, and since your mom passed, that's bound to happen. Particularly with us Nordic types. You have no responsibility, no need to babysit me, to keep me from blowing my stupid head off. I mean it!"

"I know you do," she said, looking right at him, her smile faint but loving. "I'm just being straight with you. You deserve that."

"I want that."

She was sitting sideways too, now. "You have to believe me, then, when I say this was coming. That Jerry was a bad idea. That the worst thing that could have happened was not coming to my senses about him. Okay? Okay?"

"It just wasn't my intention . . ."

"Stop it. Just stop it."

"If I thought I was a burden to you—"

"You want to do something for me?"

"Anything, sweetie."

"Do your own laundry."

He started to laugh. "Done deal."

She was laughing, too. "Also, go fix me some hot chocolate. I see you bought some Danish butter cookies. That'll be a good fit."

"Okay. Work me to the bone. See if I care."

Soon they were in the big kitchen with a little plate of the butter cookies and two mugs of hot chocolate.

"I hope," he said, "you got to spend some time with your high school pals, before you left Jerry in the lurch."

"Oh I did. Casual night was in the party room at the brewery—you know that little side room? And when I was on my way out, in the outer restaurant area, I ran into some overflow of my classmates, drinking, talking. I did some mingling before I walked home."

"Anybody I know?"

"Oh, you know them all. Jeff, Emily, Daniel, Jake, Nicole . . ."

He did remember them. Most still lived in the area.

She nibbled a butter cookie. "You know who everybody wanted to talk to me about?"

"Me?"

"Not hardly. Mom. She was everybody's favorite teacher."

Karen had taught third grade at Galena Primary till her illness forced an early retirement.

"She was my favorite, too," he said. Taught him more than he could say.

"They did ask about you, Pop. I mean, you're well known around here. After all, you made the papers a few times."

"Once with you," he reminded her.

She sipped hot chocolate. "Emily told me she thought I was the luckiest person she knew."

"Oh?"

"To have two great parents like you and Mom."

"Emily sounds very wise."

"She also has two really, really awful parents."

They both laughed.

He asked her, "Did you get a chance to talk to your friend Astrid, or did Jerry's bad conduct get in the way?"

Her forehead frowned while her mouth smiled. "She wasn't exactly my friend, Pop."

"She was for a long, long time. Going back to grade school."

Krista nodded, eyebrows up. "And in middle school, and through a lot of high school, too. Till she stole Jerry away from me."

"And that's a bad thing?"

Again they both laughed. Not hard. But they laughed.

Keith said, "I always felt a little sorry for Astrid."

Krista almost choked on her hot chocolate. "What? Are you kidding?"

"No. Remember, she was pudgy and kind of homely in grade school. Took her till middle school before she blossomed."

Krista's eyes popped. "And, brother, did she blossom!"

"Yes, but a person who starts out one thing and nature or puberty or whatever turns them into another . . . that can be tough. I always felt the homely little girl was still inside there, making everybody, oh . . ."

"Pay?"

"Maybe in a way," he admitted. "But some of the most confident, secure people on the outside are the opposite inside."

She smirked. "If you say so."

They talked some more. He was suddenly glad to be here in this house with her. No, not suddenly—he was already glad, but he just hadn't thought about it that way. He and his daughter were closer now. They'd always loved each other. But something like . . . friendship? Something like that had opened up between them.

They went upstairs to their respective beds. Krista took a shower first, and Keith got in bed, on his own side (knowing he would drift to

Karen's in the night), and began reading the novel he'd been working on since he got here.

One of the things his daughter had done, preparing for his arrival, was unpack some of the boxes of his books. In the guest room, where he'd started out, she filled a bookcase with his Civil War collection. He was less than a buff, but when he first came to Galena, the General Grant connection had got him started reading.

A local used bookstore, Peace of the Past on Main, had fed his interest. Nonfiction titles by Bruce Catton, Garry Wills, Shelby Foote, and more lined the shelves, with fiction by Foote again, John Jakes, and Gore Vidal, among others. As he settled under the covers, in pajamas Karen had bought him, he began in the nightstand lamp's glow to read the next chapter of MacKinlay Kantor's *Andersonville*, his second trip through the novel.

A knock at the door interrupted him just at the point he was about sleepy enough to put the book down. His daughter, in her blue bathrobe, had reached in to knock on the open door, her smiling expression somehow tentative.

"Hope I'm not bothering you," she said.

"Not at all."

"You always got along with my friends, right?"

He noted his place, closed the book, and set it on the nightstand. "Not as well as your mother did. And of course I loathed Jerry, or really any boy who thought he was good enough for you."

She smiled and came over and sat on the edge of the bed. "How would you like to say hello to some of the kids?"

"Why, are they going to drop by? Tomorrow, I hope. This day is over for me."

"Me, too. And I am talking about tomorrow."

He sat up straighter. "Honey, if you want to have some of your friends over, and want me out of here, that's no problem—"

"No. It's just . . . I don't have a date for tomorrow night, now. Since the breakup and all. It's a chance for you to see the kids, and . . . How about going with me? Filling in for a lousy no good son of a bitch?"

"I guess I could manage that," he said. "Maybe not the son-of-a-bitch part . . ."

"Good," she said with a little laugh. Then she noticed *Andersonville* on the nightstand. "Is that what you're reading? About a nasty Confederate prisoner of war camp?"

"Seems to be."

She slipped off the edge of the bed. "No wonder you almost blew your brains out."

She kissed his forehead, and went out.

EIGHT

The turn to Lake View Lodge was a left off Highway 20 West just beyond the Galena city limits. Krista and Keith Larson were in her Toyota and she was driving. She'd been out here countless times, but at night the irregular W leading to the lodge, seven slow miles through incredibly scenic landscape, could be a challenge, particularly on an overcast night blotting out the nearly full moon.

The thickness of largely leafless forest to her left, the rolling golf courses to her right, were mere suggestions, until the world brightened with floodlights upon reaching the lodge itself.

Lake View was a complex of intersecting modern buildings with rustic touches by way of olive siding and fieldstone chimneys. Its beautiful woodsy setting was in its skeletal winter phase, clumps of snow nestling half-heartedly here and there. Cars already crowded the parking lot—the cocktail party hour before the banquet had been going for half an hour—but out-of-towners had sought places near the front lobby. Krista found a place in the side lot, close to the adjacent convention center where the reunion was being held in the banquet hall.

They emerged from the Toyota ready for the "dress-up" night, but not ostentatiously so—her father in a nice dark gray suit from Men's

Wearhouse set off by a royal-blue-and-white-striped tie, the GHS school colors.

Krista was in a little black Ralph Lauren dress, picked up at a Nordstrom Rack in Oak Brook—half off the already discounted price. The black lace dress, with little cap sleeves, hit her just below the knee. The neckline was conservative, too, setting off her mother's pearls. Low-heeled, comfy pumps and a little pop-of-color red Kate Spade purse on a gold-chain strap completed the effort (half price at an outlet store).

Chic on the cheap!

For February, the evening was chilly but not cold, and she braved it rather than bother with a coat. Her father didn't wear a coat, either, the suit enough. They strolled the outdoor walk past the glassed-in indoor pool and went into the modest convention center lobby, where a few of her classmates were standing around chatting. Krista offered them a collective smile and wave as she and her father started up the wide stairs.

More classmates, women in cocktail dresses, men in suits (her father's cleverness dashed by frequent royal-blue-and-white neckties), were in the wide hallway outside the banquet room. Pop took her arm and guided her inside, where perhaps sixty people—classmates and significant others—were engaged in murmuring conversations that added up to a roar, many with phones out to share pictures of kiddies and grab selfies.

Round tables for six were everywhere in the high-ceilinged, modern, open-beamed banquet room, with a wall of windows onto the lake. No music was playing, but a small stage was set way off to the left, with a portable dance floor already in place. Food stations with servers were set up along the wall opposite the lake view—Italian, Chinese, Mexican, side dishes, meats for carving.

"Somebody's popular," Pop said, giving her a sideways smile. "Looks like three football teams huddling around one quarterback."

It did at that, and Krista had a good idea who the "quarterback" was. As they drew closer, heading for the table where Jessy and Josh

Webster were seated, chairs waiting for the Larsons, she got a glimpse through the wall of fawning classmates (male and female alike) gathered around the obvious belle of the ball.

Astrid Lund was smiling, laughing, listening, occasionally answering a question, but only granting a few words at a time, though generously posing for selfies. Tonight she wore a dress Krista remembered from last month's *Vogue*—a Dolce & Gabbana form-fitting red satin ruched number with spaghetti straps and a ruffled flounce hem.

Suddenly Krista felt like she was wearing a potato sack—a frayed one.

Galena High's favorite female alum was wearing impossibly high, pointy-toed gold heels—Christian Louboutins, as their red soles announced. Her clutch purse was iconic Chanel, quilted black leather with intertwined Cs on the front flap. The oversize Rolex of the night before had been replaced by a delicate diamond-studded wristwatch—Tiffany? Movado?

Astrid's hair, swept up in a French twist, a few carefully selected strands falling loose, made Krista in her short, styled do feel like the tomboy she sometimes feared she was.

They joined Jessy and Josh at the table. Her friend looked chic in a black tuxedo-style pantsuit, and Josh looked spiffy in a navy suit with, yes, a royal-blue-and-white tie. They both greeted her father warmly, and he and Josh shook hands. Pop, who hated small talk, held the chair out for Krista, putting her next to Jessy and himself between his daughter and an empty chair.

Jessy whispered, "Hope you don't mind. I invited Frank and Brittany to join us."

"That's fine," Krista said, not loving that, but not really minding either.

"It's just," Jessy said, "Frank was on the football team with Josh."

"Sure. You and Brittany can talk cheerleading and I can remember what it was like being unpopular."

Jessy grinned at that and slapped Krista gently on the arm.

When Frank and Brittany finally joined them, the jock-turned-car-salesman—that's right, Frank in a royal-blue-and-white tie—was nice enough to field drink orders for everybody, volunteering to take care of the first round. Krista and Jessy asked for white zins.

"Get me a zombie, Daddy," Brittany said to Frank, her eyes and speech indicating some pregame drinking, which had taken the plumply sexy blonde halfway to Walking Dead herself. She was trying a little too hard again tonight, hot-pink mini-spandex dress, plunging neckline, too much jewelry, too much teased hair, over-rouged cheeks, long fake eyelashes.

Still, Krista thought, most of the men in this room would be drooling over what Frank had at home. And, damn, those were some kick-ass motorcycle boots!

Pop and Josh got up to accompany Frank and haul back all those drinks.

Jessy leaned close. "Did you get a load of the Girl Most Likely?"

"Sure did."

"What do you make of that outfit?"

"I feel like I'm wearing clown shoes."

"Oh, sweetie, you look fantastic in that dress! But do you think our Astrid's all decked out in a knockoff?"

Brittany, empty chairs on either side of her, looked up with half-lidded eyes and said, "Don't think so. Bet that's five grand she's wearing easy."

Jessy said, "Oh, please!"

Krista said, "Astrid's on the top-rated news show in Chicago. She must be pulling in real money. Those shoes? A cool thousand. That little purse? Another five thousand."

Jessy rolled her eyes. "Maybe I should see if she'd like to buy a little Galena getaway and fight that big city stress. A modest million-dollar mansion, perhaps."

The men returned and distributed drinks to the women. Josh and Frank had carried beers over for themselves, and her designated-driver father was having a Diet Coke.

Various classmates dropped by to say hello, and pretty soon the guys except for Pop, who was sitting glancing around and taking things in, got up to mingle. Girlfriends of Krista's and Jessy's would come by and fill chairs for a few minutes, catching up, exchanging cheek kisses and the occasional hugs and selfies, saying they really should stay in touch, then scurrying off not to.

When the cocktail hour was over, everybody found their chosen tables and went to whichever food stations appealed to them. All the options smelled and sounded good to Krista, and both she and Pop had a little of everything. A second round of drinks, Pop's turn this time, were acquired to go with the food. It was all very pleasant. Fun. Nicer than Krista might have hoped.

At one point, Pop asked Jessy, "Is there any kind of program tonight? Nostalgia stuff? Slide show, video of graduation . . . ?"

Jessy shook her head. "We decided against that. Maybe next reunion. We just haven't been out of school long enough for that to seem a long time ago."

But it kind of was. Krista had the experience almost anybody did at a class reunion—seeing geeky girls who had blossomed into beauties, and beauties now overweight or otherwise gone drab, wearing the same hair and clothing styles as ten years ago. That seemed less true of the men, though now and then she would spot a guy who'd grown older than would seem possible—ex-military and farmers whose hard lives showed in lined faces and prematurely gray hair.

Brittany, who said very little and was on her third zombie—a potent drink Krista had tried only once in her life—said to Jessy, "Tell me about the band."

"They're from Chicago. The committee drove to a gig of theirs across the river and checked 'em out. They're called the Cover Band,

and that's spot-on. Play everything from Train to Maroon Five, Foo Fighters to Oasis."

Pop, listening to this, looked like a dog trying to figure out what the hell its master was saying.

Brittany gave up her first smile of the night. Small but easily discernible.

"Cool," she said.

Shortly after that, the band got started—two guitars, keyboards, bass, and drums, five guys in black stocking caps, dark sunglasses, black jeans, and matching jackets. This, apparently, was their version of "dress-up" night.

They were excellent, nailing every cover song while giving it something of their own, and the dance floor filled up right away. Soon only Krista and her father remained at their table.

"Cops don't dance," Pop advised her, with a raised eyebrow.

"Well, I do."

"You're a chief. You make your own rules."

"I bet you danced with Mom."

"She was chief of the household."

"Don't be so old."

"I try not to be. Starts with maintaining my dignity and never dancing in public."

They both laughed a little. The size of the hall, and the band restraining themselves, meant conversations like this were possible.

Pop was looking past her. "Look who found a date."

She glanced where his eyes indicated. Jerry, in a black sport coat, skinny tie, and black jeans, working hard at his hipster persona, was guiding a young woman toward the dance floor. Krista didn't know her, but recognized the girl as a waitress from a local Italian restaurant—a slender brunette in a dark green sweaterdress, lots of nice leg showing.

"Young," Krista said.

"Well, maybe he was confused."

"How so?"

"When he heard it was a high school reunion, he stopped by there and made a date."

That made her smile. One of her favorite things about her father was the way he could deliver a deadpan joke.

"You mind if I sit?" a female voice said, pleasant, polite. Alto. Well enunciated.

Krista turned her head and next to her, leaning in just a little, was the lovely face of Astrid Lund, those ice-blue eyes almost spookily beautiful.

"Sure," Krista said, with a smile so awkward it felt it might fall off her face.

Astrid settled herself and her probable five-thousand-dollar dress where Jessy had been sitting. She smiled across at Pop.

"Mr. Larson," she said. "Been ages. You look good."

"Thanks, Astrid," he said. "You don't look bad, yourself."

Her smile turned sad. "I was talking to somebody earlier, I forget who, and they said Mrs. Larson has passed away. I'm so sorry."

"Thanks," Krista and Pop said, overlapping.

"She was my third-grade teacher," Astrid said. "My favorite teacher ever. I think a lot of us felt that way."

They both smiled and thanked her for that.

"Could we talk?" Astrid said to Krista.

Pop started to get up. "I can go . . ."

"No," Astrid said, gesturing him back down. "Please stay . . . It'll just be silly girl talk you can ignore."

Pop got back in his chair and turned it some, to watch the band, as if he were really interested. Maybe he was, in some oddly sociological way. In the meantime, Astrid and Krista conversed in low tones, or anyway as low as possible with a rock band playing in the same room.

"I wanted to apologize," Astrid said, "about last night."

Krista frowned. "Apologize . . . ? Why? What for?"

Astrid sighed, perfect eyebrows flicking up and down. "Well, I understand you were there with Jerry Ward. And after he rushed up and monopolized me for a while, you slipped out, I heard. I felt terrible about it."

Krista couldn't resist. "As bad as you did when you went after him back in high school?"

Astrid flushed. Actually flushed, and with that Nordic complexion of hers, her cheeks seemed to flame. "I was awful to you back then. I don't know what I was trying to prove, and I'm not going to indulge in cheap self-psychoanalysis." A sigh. "I owe apologies to half a dozen women in this room, and maybe I'll get around to that . . . but I wanted to start here. With you."

"Why?"

"We were such good friends, once upon a time. I remember how . . . this was so very long ago . . . in first and second grade, we were BFFs, and then in third grade, they split us up. I was in your mom's class, but you were made to be in the other third-grade class."

"I remember," Krista said. "There was a section that was half third grade and half fourth, and I got stuck there."

Of course, it wasn't an effort to split the girls up—it was just that Krista couldn't be in a class taught by her mother.

"But the next year," Astrid was saying, "we were back together. All through middle school, and high school, too . . . most of high school. Till I got between you and Jerry, anyway."

"Maybe you did me a favor."

"Aren't you . . . back with him?"

Krista shook her head. "No. He's here with some girl who just reached puberty. My escort is my father."

Pop didn't react to that, apparently fascinated by the Cover Band, currently playing "Monkey Wrench."

Astrid frowned just a little; judging by the smoothness of her skin, she didn't do that much. "I hope I wasn't the cause of—"

"You weren't. Jerry being an ass was the cause."

That made Astrid smile. She nodded. "Okay. Good. Listen, I wonder how you might feel about me doing a piece on you. About you. For WLG—TV, not radio."

"Why would you want to do that?"

Astrid flipped a hand. "You're the youngest female police chief in the nation. I haven't checked it thoroughly, but you may be the youngest, period. Plus, Galena with its tourist trade is unique, and a place people in Chicago know of, even if they haven't been here. Would you, please? Let us bring a camera crew here?"

"Well . . . sure. I guess."

The reporter smiled big. "I'm staying at my folks' place. They're in Florida. Are you going to the class brunch tomorrow?"

"Not sure," Krista admitted.

"Me either," Astrid said. "Maybe you could stop over first thing in the morning—say eight? And we can talk over coffee. It's still the same address."

How many times, from grade school through GHS, had Krista been in that house? She had a sudden pang for their lost friendship.

"I'll be there," she told Astrid.

"Great!"

After they'd exchanged cell numbers, Krista sighed and smiled. "You really seem to be going places."

Astrid rolled her eyes. "I'd like to. It's a rough business. I've been promised a co-anchor spot this fall, and if I do well there . . . who can say?"

"Where do you hope to wind up?"

Astrid shrugged, the blonde hair shimmering. "A network, or one of the cable news outlets. Certainly something national. At my age, I need to get moving."

"Your age?"

"They turn them out young these days. And as big a market as Chicago is, there's still something small-time about it. Office politics, you know. And it's a scary town, too."

"Scary how?"

"Well, all the clichés are true. Crooked politicians, mob stuff. And a reporter who does investigative reporting, the way I've been doing, building a reputation on it? Let's just say when the phone rings, and it's a political call? They aren't always looking for donations."

"You don't mean . . . threats?"

"Oh yes. Even death threats."

"Death threats?"

"Comes with the job," Astrid said matter-of-factly. She leaned in. "Say, maybe you could help me with something for a story. Being law enforcement and all."

"Well . . . I'll try to."

"Is there a statute of limitations on sexually oriented crimes?"

Krista, blindsided, glanced at her father; but he was still wrapped up in the band, who were playing "Makes Me Wonder."

"Sexually oriented crimes," Krista said, as if she had to run that phrase through her mental computer before she could answer. "Like what?"

"Rape, for example."

"That varies state to state," Krista said, a little surprised a reporter wouldn't know this. Or just ask Google about it. "Ten years in Illinois. Only three years, if it hasn't been reported by then. But evidence collected at the time would be crucial. Be tough to prove a case without that."

Judging by her manner, Astrid might have been inquiring about movie times. "What about sexual assault, short of rape? Or even sexual harassment?"

"It's criminal in Illinois if it involves sexual assault, stalking, or any threat of sexual misconduct."

Suddenly Pop said, "Two years to report." Then he turned to the two young women. "No restriction for a civil suit. Ms. Lund, I'm retired now but I was a police officer for a long time. I would be glad to talk to you about this."

Astrid, staying very cool, said, "I may take you up on that, Mr. Larson."

"Ms. Lund," he said. "Is this really for a story or is it something personal?"

Astrid stood. For the first time her smile seemed nervous. "It's really for a story. So wonderful to see you both . . . See you tomorrow morning, Krista."

And the Girl Most Likely was gone, swallowed up in her admirers.

NINE

Keith turned to his daughter and said, "Astrid seems very nice. She sounds sincere."

Krista nodded. "Of course, she hasn't made it this far in the broadcast business without learning how to manipulate people. But I take everything she said at face value."

"Well, I do, too . . . almost."

Her eyes locked on him. "Why almost?"

"The idea that she's doing a story about sexual malfeasance just as a general topic of interest . . . no. Something personal's behind it."

Krista nodded again. "Yeah. I got that, too." She glanced past him. "Now that we've talked to the Girl Most Likely, here comes her male counterpart."

Heading over with a lovely woman on his arm was the classmate who'd made it all possible, including this free evening of food and entertainment. David Landry—with dark impeccably barbered hair and dark eyes and a Rob Lowe smile—looked six feet tall, but Keith caught the Italian heels right off.

The rest of their host's tailored apparel was more in tune with a successful executive on a night out—a notch-lapel number in dark gray, beautifully tailored. Keith had an idea his somewhat similar gray suit cost maybe a tenth of what Landry's had. No school colors for their host—his patterned tie was the same light blue as his shirt. Keith had heard his daughter refer to Landry having a trophy wife—not from their class, at least in the high school sense—and the vision drifting over with him was almost certainly her.

Her wavy long dark hair, with golden highlights, disappeared behind her shoulders, her face with its luminous brown eyes and bold, well-shaped eyebrows worthy of a fashion model. Like Krista, the apparent Mrs. Landry wore stylish black, but this form-fitting frock was nonetheless conservative-looking, high necklined, sleeves stopping at the wrists, hem almost to the floor.

Then he noticed the slit starting at her thigh.

Suppressing a gulp, Keith rose as Landry came over with his hand outstretched. The two men shook. They'd met in his daughter's high school days, when Landry and Krista had briefly dated.

"Mr. Larson," he said, in a well-modulated second tenor, "I'm so pleased you're here tonight."

Addressing him as "Mr. Larson" was a throwback to Landry thinking of him as a parent, the kind of respect grown adults would often show when running into his wife, who'd been their third-grade teacher—Mrs. Larson! How are you?

"You might as well call me Keith," he said. "Because I'm going to call you Dave. Unless you prefer David?"

"Dave is fine. This is Mrs. Landry." He gestured with his free hand, his other arm still being held on to by the lanky beauty.

She smiled, her mouth so lipstick red it was almost black, a wide, nicely toothy smile. "But you can call me Dawn . . . if I can call you Keith."

"Deal," he said. "This is my daughter, Krista, an old classmate of your husband's."

Krista was standing now, too. "No older than he is, of course."

"Oh, Dawn knows all about you," Landry said, coming around the table to Krista. "You're the one who got away."

Mrs. Landry's frown was barely perceptible, but Keith could spot the tiny daggers in the glance she gave her husband.

Krista nodded toward Astrid, caught between tables by a gaggle of admiring classmates. "Aren't you confusing me with somebody, Dave?"

Landry ignored that and, eyes going from Krista to Keith and back again, asked, "Do you mind if we join you for a moment?"

"You have your nerve," Krista said. "Think you own the place?"

Everyone laughed at that a little, and as they all sat, Landry said to Krista, "I'm just the manager of the joint. And even my father has some co-owners."

Krista touched her hand to Landry's. "Do I have to say you've been incredibly generous?"

"Listen," he said, "I'm glad to do it. Having so many of the ol' GHS gang in one place, it's really my pleasure."

Next to him, Dawn was smiling—a strained smile, Keith thought.

Krista removed her hand from Landry's and said, "I just had a nice talk with Astrid. She really seems to have her head on straight. You should talk to her."

Keith wasn't sure what that was about, but then Landry gave him a rough idea.

"It ended badly," he said, making a comic "ouch" face. "I think we probably ought to keep our distance, Astrid and I. But I'm happy for her. She's making a real success of herself."

Krista flipped a hand. "Why not tell her that?"

He shrugged a shoulder. "We'll see."

A slow song started in. Sounded pretty sappy to Keith, but at least it didn't remind him of a one-man band falling down fire-escape stairs.

Dawn stood up and her eyes were laser beams on her husband, and her smile had something bloodcurdling about it. "Oh, that's 'Thinking Out Loud'—Ed Sheeran! Come dance with me, sweetheart!"

Landry nodded his assent, but kept his attention for the moment on Krista, saying, "Did I see Jessica Webster and her husband sitting with you?"

"Yes."

"Well, I want to thank Jessy for everything she and the committee did."

"If you're headed for the dance floor, I'm sure you'll find her there. And she'll have plenty of thanks to heap back on you."

Landry and Krista exchanged smiles, and the couple headed for the dance floor, the host waving at, and exchanging quick pleasantries with, grateful classmates as they ran a cheerful gauntlet.

Alone again in the crowded hall, Keith said to his daughter, "He seems decent enough."

"Dave's a good guy. I mean, what he's doing for the class tonight is incredible, and he's done a great job out here at the lodge."

"You didn't date him long, as I recall."

"No. He was . . . no. Just didn't work out. And you know me, I'm not one to hold a grudge."

Keith knew enough not to ask why she might hold a grudge against Landry, but he did say, "No. You're not one to hold a grudge. You're one to caress a grudge. Nurture it through the long cold lonely nights."

Her smile made her chin crinkle. "You're a very bad man, Pop."

"And you're a terrible daughter. Really, just awful."

A girlfriend of Krista's (in the "friend" sense only) stopped by and asked her to dance. They'd been on the basketball team together. Krista excused herself and went off with her pal.

Keith had noticed a table of teachers—all still on staff at Galena High—and took the opportunity to go over and say hello.

"Nobody get up," he said, leaning in. "Just wanted to come over and see who was taking advantage of the free meal."

His hand was on the edge of a chair where Bill Bragg, longtime coach of Galena Pirates football, sat next to his wife, Kelly. Both were in their early fifties, Bragg a husky guy, undeniably handsome despite a butch haircut, thick wild eyebrows, and an eternal five o'clock shadow; Kelly an athletically slender gal with short brown hair, pretty hazel eyes, and a million-dollar smile. Bill was in a blue sport coat and a gold necktie—vaguely school colors—and Kelly a tan turtleneck sweater and tweed slacks.

English teacher Ken Stock, a more quiet kind of handsome but always somewhat dashing, wore a blue blazer with a red pocket square and a white shirt with no tie, while his wife, Mary—an art teacher, with short golden-brown hair, brown eyes, and an almost-under-control weight problem—wore a navy dress with a turquoise Native American necklace.

"Sit, sit," Bill said, gesturing to an empty chair beside him.

"Aren't Chris and Tyler sitting there?"

"Why," Ken said dryly, "are they invisible?"

Smiling, shaking her head, Mary said, "From the second the music starts up, those two are on the dance floor."

Keith sat. "I hate to give you reprobates any encouragement, but I guess you should know what a kick these grown-up kids get out of having their favorite teachers do them the honor."

"You said it yourself," Bill said, an arm around the back of Keith's chair. "It's a free meal."

Kelly said, "These are wonderful young people, really. Class of '09, always one of my favorites. Your daughter was a wonderful point guard."

The gym teacher also coached girls' basketball.

"Well," Keith said, "she was disappointed she didn't land a scholarship offer. Just not tall enough for college ball."

With a wry grin, Ken said, "So what do you think, Keith? Are you happy to have Krista join the family business?"

"She's a good cop," Keith said, "and she's making an excellent chief. She has a real sense of what Galena is about—that you have to keep the tourists safe and happy, but never forget about the local community."

"Karen must be so proud," Mary said. His late wife and Mary had been good friends, working together on several local charities, often through First Methodist.

"I'm sure she is," Keith said, though he hadn't been to church since Karen's death, and always harbored only the vaguest belief in an afterlife and a supreme being. For him this world was enough to deal with.

Serious now, Ken said, "You know, Krista was a good writer. One of my best on the school paper. I hope she's keeping a hand in."

Keith shook his head. "I know you tried to encourage her, but I think writing reports is about it."

Ken cocked his head. "Hasn't she been going with Jerry? I thought maybe they'd make a two-person writers' colony. He's very serious about his work."

"No," Keith told the English teacher. "That ship sailed or sunk or however a writer would put it. Look around—Jerry's here somewhere, with a girl who may be one of your current students."

Bill's shaggy eyebrows rose and he grinned like a friendly bear. "Yeah, I saw him with Jasmine."

"Jasmine Peterson?" Mary asked, frowning. "Isn't she a senior?"

"She graduated last year," girls' basketball coach Kelly said. "She's waitressing right now, saving up to go to college. She's a bright girl."

Keith smirked. "Not if she's dating Jerry Ward she isn't."

Everybody smiled at that.

Bill said, "You tell Krista we're proud of her."

Ken said, "I'll second that."

"Hear, hear," Mary said.

And Kelly was nodding.

Keith stood. "Can I stand you folks to a drink?"

Ken smiled. "Can you stand us, period?"

More smiles, but they accepted the offer. Keith took orders—pinot noir and chardonnay respectively for Mary and Kelly, a couple of Blue Moons for the guys.

The cash bar (their host wasn't that generous) had a line, so Keith took the opportunity to find the men's room. It was down a side hall. He was just about to go in when he noticed two figures down a ways, a pretty blonde in a red dress and a dark-haired handsome man, in heated, animated conversation.

Astrid Lund and David Landry.

Not close enough for Keith to hear anything, but the heat of it carried, all right.

When he emerged after a brief visit, neither Astrid nor David was around. Perhaps a momentary flare-up was over; or maybe he'd caught the tail end of a more protracted one . . .

Just outside the banquet hall, a short male figure in a dark well-tailored suit, which may have cost even more than David Landry's, approached Keith with a smile. If this was one of his daughter's classmates, the guy certainly looked older than most—he was bald on top and graying at the sides. His gray-blue eyes behind black-and-gray designer-framed glasses conveyed a seldom-blinking confidence.

"You don't remember me," he said. His voice had a radio announcer resonance.

"I'm afraid I don't. Are you sure you remember me? I'm Keith Larson."

"Krista's dad," he said, nodding. "I'm Alex Cannon. I was president of the Young Democrats."

Nodding back, Keith said, "I do remember you." Ten years ago, young Alex Cannon had dark hair down to his shoulders.

Cannon said, "Krista was my vice president one year."

Keith offered up his least smiling smile. "Yes, Alex, but I'm afraid you were too radical for her tastes."

He chuckled. "I'll leave it to others to decide whether I was ahead of my time or behind it. Anyway, now I'm an attorney in—"

"Chicago," Keith said. "I'm well aware of you and how successful your career has been. Congratulations."

"Thank you. You were always friendly to me, although I'm pretty sure you thought I was a little creep."

"Nonsense," Keith said, although that was spot-on. It was Karen who had been supportive of whatever her daughter's interests were, even when they had drifted briefly into radical politics.

"Well," the attorney said, with the kind of smile he no doubt gave a client right before billing him outrageously, "I just wanted to say hello."

The attorney was just going when Keith said, "We have a mutual acquaintance, Mr. Cannon."

"We do? And I'm still Alex to you, Mr. Larson."

Keith didn't offer his first name in return, saying, "I have a buddy on the CPD Homicide Bureau who collared a client of yours."

The rarely blinking eyes narrowed. "Your friend's name would be . . . ?"

"Barney Davis. Used to work with me over on the Iowa side. Your client was named Salerno, as I recall."

". . . That's right. I got him off. He was found not guilty."

"Which isn't the same as innocent."

"True. But the bottom line, Mr. Larson? I would appear to be a better defense lawyer than your friend is a homicide detective."

The smile, polite now—barely so—was followed by a nod, as Cannon shot into the banquet hall.

The line at the bar had thinned, and Keith made two trips, conveying the drinks to the teachers' table, including another Diet Coke for himself. For another fifteen or twenty minutes, he spoke to the educators about local sports and next year's prospects. Then some well-intentioned reminiscing about Karen, sparked by Mary Stock, made him uncomfortable.

He waited for the right moment, found it, and excused himself.

At their table, Krista was sitting alone, looking a little lost.

"You all right?" he asked, not sitting, just leaning in, a hand on the back of her chair.

With a pleasant smile and aching eyes, she said, "I think I've had all the frigging fun I can take."

"Where are Jessy and Josh?"

"On the dance floor, trying to be sixteen again."

"They'll pay in the morning. What about Frank and what's-her-name? The one who somehow makes 'sexy' annoying?"

She laughed. "They, too, are recapturing their youth. Me, I've been asked to dance once . . . by a female. Also, my father refuses to dance with me."

"Sounds like a jerk. You want to get out of here?"

She nodded. "Please."

Outside, as they headed for the Toyota in the nearby side lot, the temperature had dropped, their breath visible. They both added not wearing coats tonight to their lists of regrets. Krista was shivering as he got behind the wheel.

He asked, "You okay, honey?"

"Yes. I just . . . I'd so been looking forward to seeing those people, and I was happy to see them, even the ones I wasn't happy to see."

Such observations were what made designated drivers necessary.

She was saying, "I had a good time. I really did. So why do I feel sad?"

"I think you just defined 'bittersweet,' honey."

"Thank you for going with me, Daddy."

"Wouldn't have missed it. You were the prettiest girl there."

"Oh? Prettier than Astrid?"

"Astrid's pretty. But she doesn't remind me of your mother."

She leaned against him as he drove, taking the winding road out of the lodge's acreage slow and easy. "Part of me can't wait for the next reunion," she said. "Another part of me wouldn't mind never seeing any of them again."

Neither Keith nor his daughter could have dreamed that the reunion was just getting started.

TEN

You are proud of yourself for staying so cool at the reunion. No one would guess you are boiling inside, not even your "significant other," as the now all-purpose term puts it. And who knows you better?

You are friendly to one and all, not pushing it, and mostly just lie back, watching, watching, watching. What you will almost certainly be forced to do doesn't bother you—that part of it will be dispatched with a detached coolness.

But withstanding the buildup, the suspense of the uncertainty—and the threat of something happening here tonight, with so many people present, where it all could slip away from you—that is what drives you to the brink of madness.

You wonder if you did the wrong thing, not taking care of Astrid in Chicago. Before she even got here. But what had been easily accomplished in Clearwater would have been so very complicated in Chicago. And anyway, you hope you won't be compelled, *made* to do anything like that tonight.

So you watch her from a distance. With talk and laughter all around, which you participate in, as if you were part of the festivities and not apart from them. Isolated in your peril. Alone in what you might have to do.

Astrid seems very natural, at ease, unlike her rather plastic way in high school. Of course, when they'd been behind closed doors or otherwise by themselves, she had been different. Human, vulnerable, revealing that her self-confidence and friendliness as shown to the other kids was something artificial, a brittle candy coating.

Not a phony, exactly. But you know from your heart-to-heart talks years ago that she had been a homely, overweight child who had sprouted and blossomed but still carried that insecurity within an attractive shell. She'd always been smart but had seen the good-looking girls around her achieve popularity even before the boys had reached puberty.

In her high school prime, she seemed to pride herself on an effortless ability to snatch a boy from another girl, but not just any girl—only the pretty, popular ones, with the best-looking, mostly jock boyfriends. Yet she'd stayed superficially friendly with each girl she wronged, despised by them until they again admired her, even adored her. Those she'd betrayed would respond to her interest and flattery and not stay mad at her. It was all those unfaithful boyfriends' fault, right?

Wrong. But perhaps you are the only one who knew that. Well, no—Astrid had known. She'd revealed it to you, in your intimate moments together. You saw the pleasure, and guilt, of a onetime wall-flower's revenge.

But tonight, as she glides to a pause with this one and that one, here the center of a group, there in a private conservation—something seems different about her. Nothing plastic about her now. Or has she only learned how better to fake it?

She seems sincere, all right, and those she's engaging with one-on-one are listening with pleasant expressions, responding to her shy, sad smiles with nods and smiles of their own, in most cases. With a few of those she approaches, something else is engendered—a coldness, even held-back anger, resentment . . . what are these conversations about?

She isn't talking about you, is she?

You note that at first she's busy with these groups of former class-mates worshiping her. It takes a while, until well after dinner with the band starting in, for her to seek out individuals—and that is exactly what she's doing now, seeking them out.

And then it begins to make sense, some of it anyway. Those women she has singled out are in many cases the girls from whom she stole boys. Some are here with the men those boys became. Others have wound up with someone else. Maybe in some cases these women wish Astrid had stolen those boys away permanently. Maybe others are grate-ful Astrid was a thief of hearts, because they wound up with someone else, someone better, someone they deeply loved.

So. You have it now, you get it. Mostly she is making amends. She is apologizing for her long-ago bad behavior. Most of her onetime classmates are ready to fawn over her—she had been the class favorite, student council president, resident diva of chorus and drama. But for that handful of girls she had done wrong, Astrid was something else. Something dark, and—in a melodramatic high school way—evil.

This was good. She was in a frame of mind for making amends. Perhaps she would be receptive to them as well.

Late in the evening, you follow her from the banquet hall. Watch her go into the restroom. Wait for her, until she emerges, and just happen to run into her. You greet her warmly. She smiles, but there's a stiffness and her ice-blue eyes are cold.

"Could I have a word?" you ask.

"I don't think so."

"I just want to congratulate you on all your success."

". . . Thank you."

"And I want to apologize. Make amends."

She frowns a little. Still very beautiful—perhaps more beautiful as a woman than as a girl. So much perfect blondeness. Such high cheekbones.

"I sense," you say, "just observing . . . that you've been making a few apologies yourself. That you've been the one making amends."

She draws in a breath. Her breasts rise and fall.

"People don't always respond well to apologies," you say. "But a person has to try, right? I can tell your results tonight have been something of a . . . mixed bag."

She almost smiles. "That's true. We should talk sometime. But not here."

"I agree!"

"And, after all, you're not alone here tonight, are you?"

"No." You smile nervously—the nervousness is real, but not for the reason she may think. "I should let you go. We'll talk sometime?"

She nods. "Sometime."

You return to your table. Join the conversation. From time to time, '09 classmates come over to say hello. You dance a few times with your significant other, no one else. Then you leave the reunion.

In perhaps an hour, that significant other is asleep in bed next to you—you can hear the gentle snoring—and you go outside to your car. From the trunk you remove a grocery bag with some things in it. Otherwise, you don't need the car. You can go on foot.

The Lund home is on North High, not far from downtown. It's a milk-chocolate two-story frame house, circa early 1920s, nothing fancy but nice. Well kept up by Astrid's parents, who had for years operated the restaurant at the DeSoto Hotel. Retired, they were in Florida right now, wintering. The yard is fairly good size, the neighborhood quiet. At after one in the morning, it's really quiet.

You see Astrid's car out front—a silver Jaguar XF, as sleek and lovely as its owner. Lights are on in the kitchen downstairs—you remember the layout of the house well. You go around and peek in a side window. She is in a black silk robe at the kitchen table, sitting by herself, sipping coffee—or is it tea?

After pausing to leave your grocery bag of things behind a bush, you go to the front door. You knock. Nothing. You try again.

She cracks the door and looks out at you.

"You," she says.

"I'm sorry to disturb. I was out for a walk and saw the lights on. Couldn't sleep. And I didn't like the awkward way we left it. You said you wanted to talk. We could talk now, if you like."

Through your whole speech, she is looking at you through slitted eyes. When you're done, she's still studying you. But finally she opens the door.

"Why don't you come in," she says. Her hair isn't up now, rather hovering above her shoulders. "Just for a while."

She leads you into the living room—furnishings are mostly the same, nice, nothing special, wood-burning fireplace the best thing about it—through an archway into the dining room and beyond to the kitchen. You remember where the family room is and the laundry room. You were here several times. Not many times, but memorable ones.

The kitchen was remodeled in the '80s and has a lot of modern wood cabinetry with dated hardware. The round maple table has her cup, four place mats, a fake-flower centerpiece, and nothing else.

"Like some tea?" she asks at the counter, civil.

"I would. Thank you."

She pours hot water into a cup, drops in a tea bag. Puts the cup on a dish in front of you. Gestures to a chair, which you take. Sits across from you and looks expressionlessly across the fake flowers with those ice-blue eyes, so wide apart you almost have to look at them one at a time.

"Say what you have to say," she says.

"I'm apologizing for my behavior. Back in the day. It wasn't right. And it's . . . haunted me ever since."

It has, in a way. You often think of her lovely pale flesh and the ripe curves and what it was like with her. So perfect. So lovely.

"It wasn't right," she agrees. "And do you really think an apology covers it?"

"I suppose not. You were apologizing all over the place yourself, earlier, weren't you?"

She stiffens. "I was. But I don't think it was quite the same thing."

"No. No, that's right." You remove the tea bag, place it on the dish. Lift the cup and sip the tea. It's a little hot. Not bad. Nothing special. Not Earl Grey or anything. "Have you ever talked to anyone about us? About what happened?"

"Not a soul."

"Not even tonight? At the reunion?"

"No! Of course not."

". . . Is it something we can . . . put behind us?"

"You mean, can I forgive you? Give you a pass?"

"Something like that, yes."

"Maybe."

You frown. "What do you mean by 'maybe'?"

"You know what I do, right? How I make my living?"

"You're on the news. In Chicago."

"I specialize in investigative reporting."

"I'm aware."

She sips her tea. Her coldness turns somehow businesslike. "I'm doing a piece on sexual misconduct."

You say nothing.

"It's something of a major topic these days," she says. "Things that were acceptable once . . . you might say, things that people got away with . . . are now frowned upon."

"Isn't . . . isn't that putting it a little mildly? Aren't people being ruined?"

She shrugs a shoulder. "Some are. Some deserve it, wouldn't you say?"

You say nothing. Shrug, because some response is expected.

"I want to explore the way women . . . and girls . . . have been mistreated in this society. From harassment to abuse. From date rape to, well . . . you get the drift."

"I, uh, do. But you and I, we were . . ."

"In love?" She smiles. "You know, I thought so, at the time."

"I did, too. I still think of you . . . fondly."

Her expression seems to curdle. Disgust flashes across her lovely features, but then a businesslike calm returns.

"Even now," she says, "I could hurt you."

"I know."

"Perhaps destroy you."

"I know."

"Maybe you'd like to know how you could avoid that. Maybe there's something you could do to prevent me from turning your life upside down. After all, we were younger then. We neither one were making mature decisions."

You sit forward. "That's right."

"I would want an assurance from you that what happened between us was not a . . . pattern. That it was an . . . aberration, in both our lives."

"It certainly was."

"Good. Good. Because what I have in mind is this . . . I want to talk about what happened between us, on camera."

"What?"

"I want to talk to you on camera. I will use a small crew, all of whom'll sign confidentiality statements that you witness. I will sign an agreement with you that states your face will either be pixelated or in complete shadow, and your voice disguised."

You don't know what to say. Not at first.

But finally, as she stares at you, smiling with a terrible confidence, real confidence, you say, "But people will guess. They'll know who I am, because they know you, and—"

"No." She holds up a "stop" hand. "I won't identify myself as . . . the injured party. You will simply be someone I'm interviewing on the subject."

An offender. Confessing in the dark.

"I would have to think about that," you say.

"If you feel true remorse," she says, "you can be part of the solution and not the problem. You don't have to answer me tonight. I know how to get in touch with you."

She does?

"I'll let you know," you say. "I have to think it over."

"Of course."

You have finished your tea.

You stand.

She stands.

"You know the way out," she says.

She remembers, too, the times you spent here, in this house, when her parents weren't home, after her older sister went off to college.

"Goodbye," you say with an appropriately small smile and a little nod, and head through the dining room and into the living room. You realize she's following and is watching, from a distance, and she says nothing, obviously doesn't see, when you pat the piece of duct tape over the latch before you close it.

You walk around back, where the darkness conceals you.

You wait.

Within five minutes the kitchen light goes off. Your eyes go to the upstairs windows, where no lights are on. Your gaze bounces back and forth from the master bedroom window to Astrid's old bedroom, not sure where she will land.

The light in her bedroom window goes on.

You wait awhile longer, not very long, not even five minutes this time. The light goes out. No reading lamp light either, apparently, unless it's really weak. You figure it's unlikely she would read, as late as it is. She did have a few drinks, this you know from observing her at the reunion. She should go right to sleep.

You wait, and this is the hardest part, a good half an hour longer. You go from a certain reluctance about what must be done to an acceptance and even irritation, as what she suggested is a sort of blackmail. She's disappointed you.

Then you go back around to the bushes where you hid the grocery bag. You retrieve the bag and take out the black hooded raincoat and get into it. This is a new one. You threw the other one down a gutter in Clearwater, knowing not to wear it again. The blood would glow in the dark under certain light, if TV could be trusted.

You put on the fresh pair of kitchen gloves. Flex your fingers. As before, it's awkward but not terribly.

You have a butcher knife in the bag, but you decide not to use it. Maybe somebody could trace that knife to where you bought it, across the river. You leave it in the bag. You will collect it later.

You go in through the taped-latch door, removing that tape and pocketing it, before going deeper into the house. Returning to the kitchen, you withdraw a perfectly suitable butcher knife from the countertop wood-block knife set and smile to yourself. You glance at the two teacups on the table; you can deal with those on the way out. Then, because you are here, you go up the back stairs off the kitchen to the upper floor.

Kind of strange being back here after all this time. You feel like a ghost haunting the place. Outside Astrid's room—will it still have the Katy Perry poster, you wonder, and that Beyoncé one?—you pause and listen. Gentle snoring. Much like the snoring of the someone in bed you left behind.

You enter quietly. Some distant street light filters in, just enough to show Astrid on the bed. Funny—maybe she'd been a little drunk. You hadn't noticed that. Hadn't perceived it. But here she is, not under the covers, just flopped on top of them, though the room isn't warm.

Not cold, but not warm. She's on her side, still in the black silk robe. You gently move her onto her back, and she goes with the motion, not waking. Settling. Still sleeping.

That's all right with you. You loved this girl once. Maybe you still love her, a little bit. You don't want her to suffer. You're pretty sure she doesn't wake, although her body jerks and kind of convulses when you bring the butcher knife down again and again into her chest.

At this angle you hardly get any on the raincoat, but soon the ceiling is dripping.

ELEVEN

After showering, including shaving her legs and shampooing, and generally getting ready for her day, Krista had wardrobe considerations to deal with.

But as she stood staring at the contents of her bedroom closet, those contents stared back at her in bland indifference, as she asked questions of herself.

Uniform?

No. This was Sunday, her day off (though as chief she was always on call), and while wearing her uniform to the reunion brunch might be a nice way to quietly brag . . . no. That would just be sad.

What *about* the reunion brunch?

That was another no. She'd had a good time last night, perhaps short of a wonderful evening but she certainly wasn't sorry she'd gone. But neither was she anxious to spend any more time with her old friends.

The local ones she saw frequently anyway, at least in passing, and the reminiscing with out-of-towners had exhausted itself. Of course, the brunch had been set at 11:00 a.m., to give anyone who wanted time to go to church—and Galena was a big church town, historic ones lining much of Bench Street—but . . .

Are you even going to church?

Not today. She had gradually gotten out of the habit of attending regularly. She tried to make it once a month, out of respect to her late mom and, frankly, because her position in the community meant at least a little of that was expected from her. Since moving in, her father had said he'd go to church, "now and then," which meant maybe Easter and Christmas. Maybe.

Since you're going over to Astrid's, do you need to make a fuss? Select something special?

No. Already she'd decided not to do anything fancy with her hair. Why try to compete with the star of Chicago TV news? She would either fail . . . or succeed only by way of embarrassing herself.

She got into new jeans and a black pullover sweater. Also tugged on the snazzy red-and-black cowboy boots, not to impress but because they were comfortable. She snugged her pant legs over them. As was her off-duty habit, she snapped the holstered Glock 21 on her hip, smiling to herself, knowing Astrid couldn't compete with that kind of accessorizing.

Her father was still sleeping. That had been a late night for him. Usually she made breakfast, but she'd told him she was going to Astrid's this morning, and he'd have to fend for himself. She set out a couple of yesterday's muffins anyway, then got into her bomber jacket and headed out.

When she drew her Toyota up behind the silver Jag, Krista smiled and shook her head at the conspicuous success her friend and one-time rival had achieved. But that was momentary, because the sight of the ordinary brown-frame house—with its narrow sidewalk cutting through a modest rock garden to a one-step-up porch under an over-hang—took her back in time.

How often had she been here? As a grade-school kid? As a junior high girl? As a high school classmate coming over for a slumber party or an all-nighter before a final? Those memories made a warm blur and she felt such a wave of nostalgia for so many fun times, good times, that Astrid stealing Jerry away from her almost faded into nothing. Or almost nothing.

She knocked at the front door and got no response. She knocked again and still no response. She checked her watch: 8:00 a.m. Right on time. Thinking maybe Astrid's night had gone on longer than hers, she tried her friend's cell number. From inside the house, muffled but distinct, came a ring. And three more rings.

When the ringing stopped and Astrid didn't pick up, Krista figured her call had gone to voice mail. She knocked again, still nothing. The Lunds might have a landline, lots of older people did, so she punched in "Information," and Astrid's parents did have a number.

She tried that.

Again, she heard a ring, more distinct, somewhere on the first floor beyond the closed door. It rang ten times, an eternity, and then, faintly, came Astrid's mother's voice informing people (apparently *very* uninformed people) that they should wait for the tone before leaving a message.

A dozen dire things coursed through her mind, but she shook them away. It's hard for a cop to take things in stride. Probably Astrid had just slept through those cell phone rings, even if her phone had been on a nightstand table; and those landline calls were on the first floor. Krista knew the bedrooms were upstairs. Maybe her friend had slept through those, too, or hadn't heard them.

For about one second, she considered just leaving and trying later. Maybe there had been a misunderstanding about the time, or something had come up, or . . .

She started looking for a key.

Nothing under the mat. Nothing under the flowerpot on the porch. No magnetized tiny tin under the mailbox.

Where?

Her eyes looked at the rock garden near the porch to the left and right of the sidewalk. Usually a fake rock made a lousy place to hide a house key, but a rock garden did improve on things. It took Krista at least ten seconds to spot it.

She unlocked the door, opened it halfway, and called out, "Astrid! It's me! Krista!"

No response.

When she got inside, closing the door behind her, she repeated: "Astrid! It's me! Krista!"

Again no response, and she tried again, at the bottom of the front stairs, really yelling this time, and it echoed a bit. Rattled some things.

Mildly rattled herself, Krista—feeling a little foolish doing so— unlocked her Glock 21's holster as she went slowly up the stairs. Her hunch was that Astrid would have returned to her own bedroom, though the master bedroom might have provided more comfort.

The door to Astrid's room was open, but Krista didn't see her friend until entering, because the bed, a single, was off to the left, under the Katy Perry poster. Astrid was on her back, on the still-made bed, and Krista started to call out to her, but taking only two steps in gave her a view on what had become of her friend.

Conflicted, not wanting to contaminate a crime scene and realizing Astrid was surely dead, Krista nonetheless approached carefully and checked both her friend's wrist and throat for a pulse. Like the unanswered phone calls, indications were that nobody was home.

Astrid's chest bore half a dozen wounds, one-and-a-half-inch tears on the victim's black silk robe, a little crusty blood around them. That black silk was splotched and dotted with blood that had dried nearly as black as the robe. The coverlet was spotted some, too. Krista looked toward the ceiling and saw where the blood had geysered and streakily stained like a grotesque modern art mural.

Her Glock 21 in her right hand, she checked the room, under the bed, opening the closet door. Then, back in the hall, she considered her options. With any crime other than homicide or another major felony, she would have called the dispatcher.

But on Sunday the sheriff's office dispatcher took all calls and depu-ties were sent to the scene. Normally that would be fine, but with a seri-ous crime she preferred having her own officers answer the call. After all, it was her people who would be following through. Two were on duty right now, and the rest were likely at home. Policy was, if any officer planned to be away for even an overnight trip, she was to be informed.

All of her officers' cell numbers were on her phone, and she first called Officer Maria Cortez, who was on patrol with Wendell Clemson.

"Need immediate backup at a homicide scene," Krista said, and gave Cortez the North High Street address. She spoke softly, her back to the wall and the Glock 21 in hand, barrel up.

"You're working today, Chief?"

"Off duty. Stumbled onto it. Explain at the scene."

Then she called Officer Rick Reynolds at home. He answered right away. Toddlers were crying in the background, or anyway one was crying and another screaming.

"Yeah!" Reynolds said.

This was a landline and he'd obviously grabbed it without looking at caller ID.

"Larson," Krista identified herself. "I'm at a homicide with backup on the way but I need two more officers to help secure the scene."

"I can be one of them," he said, over the screaming, crying kids. "Judy can have all the family fun to herself for a while."

"Get yourself in uniform, drive over to the station."

"Okay."

"Wait there till somebody else shows. I'll try Deitch. But it'll be somebody."

"You bet, Chief."

She tried Earl Deitch, got him, and sent him to pick up Reynolds and a police vehicle.

With help on the way, she slowly made her way through the Lund house, making sure every room was clear, including the basement. A little gravel drive led to a freestanding garage; looking in windows on either side of the structure she could see no one, no vehicle either, just the expected yard tools, storage boxes, and so on.

She checked all around the house, front and back yards, her eyes on the ground as much as on the building, not wanting to disturb any potential evidence.

Satisfied that whoever had done this thing was no longer in the house or nearby, she stood on the porch and holstered her weapon, then called the state police number.

After identifying herself, she said, "Crime scene services, please."

Her twelve-officer department did not have forensics; neither did the sheriff's department.

Her next call was to the Jo Daviess County coroner's office in East Dubuque, which was on the Illinois side of the bridge. The officer taking calls could give her no idea when the coroner or an assistant coroner would arrive. It was Sunday, she was told.

With this vital information in hand, she called her investigator, Detective Clarence "Booker" Jackson, at home. Booker would likely be sleeping in—he played blues organ in a small combo who gigged one Saturday a month at the Grape Escape on Main. Last night had been this month's Saturday.

"Homicide, you say?" Booker said, his voice a mellow baritone, still a little sleep-thickened. "In our Galena?"

Booker got his name not from booking perps, but from Booker T. and the M.G.'s, the classic Memphis soul combo.

"Yeah," Krista said. "And a very nasty one." She told him backup was coming and briefly described the crime scene.

"Give me fifteen to get there," he said.

"Take sixteen if you need it."

Very shortly, a Ford Explorer pulled in, followed moments later by a Dodge Durango, both vehicles with lights flashing, no siren, each bearing the mostly white, dark-blue-trimmed GALENA POLICE markings.

Two officers emerged from each. After filling them all in, Krista directed the first pair—Reynolds, a lanky twenty-five, and Deitch, a baby-faced forty—to secure the scene, posting the former in front of the house, the latter behind.

Krista turned to the second pair—Cortez, twenty-six, stocky, pretty; Clemson, thirty-eight, mustached, a onetime GHS football tackle. She directed them to canvass the neighborhood for anyone who might have seen anything or anyone suspicious throughout the night—unfamiliar vehicles and strangers in particular, but any activity at all after dark.

Frowning just a little, Officer Cortez asked, "From what you say, Chief, it sounds unlikely the victim could have arrived home much earlier than midnight."

"Right, but someone could have entered the house before and been waiting for her."

Cortez and her partner headed left and right, respectively, to the houses next door.

A red Dodge Charger pulled up and Booker Jackson climbed out. The African American detective, bald with a close-trimmed beard, was about fifty and had seen everything twice. He was in a light gray suit and pink-and-white-striped tie, no topcoat. Had she caught him on the way to church? Maybe, but he always looked very sharp.

She met him at his vehicle. Booker leaned against the closed rider's side door, arms folded, and said, "Let's hear it."

Krista explained.

His big head tilted to one side. "Somebody killed the most popular girl in your class?"

"She was also unpopular," Krista said, "among certain classmates. But do you really kill somebody who stole your boyfriend away from you ten years ago?"

"Guy can get himself killed stealin' a woman some other guy met an hour ago. You have those funky cowboy boots on when you went in?"

"I did."

"Lot of blood?"

"Yeah. Seems confined to the bedroom where she was killed, ceiling and bed mostly, but the killer had to go downstairs and go out. Could have been dripping blood, though I didn't spot any on the front stairs. Didn't check the back ones."

"You did clear the house?"

She nodded. "Nobody in there. Not anybody alive."

"I'll trade you some slippery-ass booties for those crazy cowgirl boots."

"Deal."

The blue booties all the cops put on, on TV, were only called for when there was a lot of blood or other bodily fluids at the scene. This was borderline, but she knew Booker had a point.

He got the booties out of his trunk. They took turns using the Charger's front passenger seat sideways with the door open to get into them.

She showed the detective into the house, led him upstairs, and she waited in the hall while the big man went in for a look.

He came out, frowning, shaking his head. "Somebody crazy did that."

"I needed my investigator to tell me that?"

He folded his arms, leaning against the wall just outside Astrid's bedroom. He looked like a surly bouncer at a club that could use help like Booker. "No, but I can tell you where we oughta go from here."

"Listening."

One eyebrow raised. "Call in the state police boys right now."

She shrugged. "I've already called them for forensics."

"That's a good start. But you need, in my opinion, to get them in here right the hell now. Let them have this thing. Also you got other options."

Northwest Illinois Critical Incident Response—Major Case Assistance, her mind told her. Various other major case assistance teams.

"You don't think . . ." She almost said "you," but instead finished, ". . . we can handle it?"

"We could handle it. But, first, you knew the victim."

Krista shook her head. "She wasn't a close friend. And in Galena, if they aren't tourists, Booker, I'm going to know any victim."

He grunted. "Hasn't been a murder in Galena in twenty years."

"I worked a homicide not that long ago. Murder was across the river, but we wrapped it up here. Remember?"

"That hasn't slipped my mind, no. But, Chief—I'm tied up with those three child abuse cases, any one of which could stand my full-on attention. And tomorrow, I got a court date on that domestic. We need help on this one."

"You're out?"

The massive shoulders shrugged. "Well, that's your call. You want me to sideline those child abuse cases?"

She drew in a breath. Let it out.

"I'll think about it," she said.

"I know where you're comin' from," Booker said.

"You do?"

"You're a female."

"You noticed."

"You're younger than shit."

"You noticed that, too."

"You don't want to look like somethin' bad happens, somethin' big happens, you can't handle it. I understand that. But you're a damn good chief. Which I also noticed. You got nothin' to prove, young lady."

And yet he called her "young lady."

Firmly, she said, "If I can't handle it, Sergeant . . . if Galena PD can't handle it . . . then I'll call in help. But not till I feel we can't manage."

He nodded slowly.

"All I ask," he said. Then his eyes bored into her. "If you insist on taking this on yourself, we both know somebody you could call."

She nodded. "We do. Might be tricky."

"Might be worth it. Would be worth it. It's well within your authority to bring in a consultant, paid or otherwise."

She'd been thinking about making that particular phone call since the moment she saw Astrid's corpse. Now, standing in the hallway of the Lund home's second floor, the coppery smell of blood still twitching her nostrils, her dead classmate a few yards away, she thought about it some more.

Then she and her investigator went down the stairs and outside, where a silver state police crime scene vehicle was pulling up. With Booker at her side, she briefed the forensics team, showed them to the crime scene, and when they didn't need her anymore, she returned to the porch of the murder house, from which she made that phone call.

TWELVE

When Keith got Krista's call, he was already up and bathed and shaved, and in a blue Chicago CUBS sweatshirt and jeans and navy running shoes, which already gave him a vague if unintentional police-ish look.

In the middle of eating a slightly stale muffin she'd left him, he told his daughter on the phone, "Honey, I will be glad to head over there. But is it appropriate?"

She had already told him the basic, disturbing circumstances.

"My job description," she said calmly, "allows me to call in experienced consulting any time I feel like it."

She sounded very professional. He liked that, of course, but wasn't sure he wanted to put her on the spot. Fathers outranked daughters, after all, or at least thought they did. And with his decades on the Dubuque department, he might create an uncomfortable work environment for his little girl. For example, he might *treat* her like his little girl . . .

"Are you okay?" he asked her.

"We're on top of it here, but I can use you."

"Just to take a look at the crime scene and give you my thoughts."

"Pop, get over here, will you?"

She hung up on him!

He smiled at the phone. He liked that.

Parked in front of the brown two-story frame house on North High Street were two Galena police vehicles—a Ford Explorer and a Dodge Durango—and between them a silver Ford Expedition with ILLINOIS CRIME SCENE INVESTIGATORS over a state seal on the rear side windows. Down the street a ways was a red Dodge Charger.

His daughter stood on the porch talking with her investigator, Sgt. Booker Jackson. Krista wore her bomber jacket and jeans, Jackson his usual natty self in suit and tie (took a real man to pull off a pink-and-white four-in-hand). Both looked a little ridiculous in the blue crime scene booties.

Keith headed their way, exchanging greetings with the officer out on the front sidewalk, a tall kid whose name he couldn't remember, though they'd been introduced. Then before Keith got to the porch, a crime scene investigator in a blue jumpsuit came out of the house, apparently on his way back to the Expedition for something.

But the average-size guy—whose name was Eli Wallace, an African American CSI who used to work on the Dubuque side—grinned when he saw Keith. The two men met on the sidewalk at about the halfway point, and Eli—teeth very white under a thick black mustache—stuck out a blue-rubber-gloved hand. Keith shook it.

"Is that your kid?" Eli asked, good-naturedly gruff, wagging his head back toward Krista on the porch. She was watching them with a wary smile.

"Yeah," Keith said.

Eli exchanged the grin for a smirk. "She call Daddy in to help?"

"Just having a looky-loo. They don't have homicides in Galena every day."

"No, it'd discourage tourism. Aren't you on the wrong side of the river?"

"Aren't you?"

The grin was back. "Naw, I moved over here to the land of Lincoln for the better bennies. Your girl seems to have a good head on her shoulders. How did that happen?"

"Her mom, I guess."

Eli's grin vanished. "Yeah, I heard Karen passed. Sorry, man. Listen, that's some nasty shit in there. Somebody didn't like that girl."

"How many you got working it?"

"Two, plus me. We're just getting going. Give me a second and I'll show you around. I want to get out of these damn booties. I almost slipped on my ass in the kitchen."

"You always were a graceful thing."

Eli headed for the van and Keith joined Krista and Booker on the porch.

"Booker," Keith said.

"Keith," Booker said.

Keith said to Krista, "If you have this character, what do you need me for?"

But it was Booker who answered, "You worked way more homicides than I have, man. Anyway . . . I think your daughter wants to talk to you."

Keith looked at her and asked, "Is that right, honey?"

Krista nodded and led her father off the porch and into the nearby front yard.

"Talk to me about what?" he asked her.

"First of all," his daughter said, "don't call me 'honey.'"

That made him smile. "Even at home?"

That made her smile. He was glad to see she could.

"Home is okay," she said. "Look, Booker is working three, count 'em, three very bad child abuse cases. And there's an ugly domestic trial on the docket. He'll have to testify starting tomorrow afternoon."

Keith was nodding. "And you only have the one investigator—not counting yourself, of course."

"Not counting you. I want to enlist you for this investigation. As a consultant. Perfectly within bounds, considering you're retired law enforcement."

His eyebrows went up. "You think the city council will put up with nepotism like this?"

"Since you won't be paid anything, that's not a problem. This is strictly pro bono."

Eli was approaching them from the van, now in running shoes. "Hate to interrupt a family meeting, but Keith? You want the tour?"

"Yeah. Give me a minute."

Eli nodded and headed in.

Keith said to Krista, "I'm going to guess you don't want to accompany me inside."

"I will if you want."

He shook his head. "If I see something that needs calling your attention to, I'll come get you. Are you . . . are you doing okay?"

"You already asked me that. On the phone?"

"Astrid was your friend. You didn't come here as a cop, you came as a classmate, ready to have a scone or something. Talk old times. This can't have been easy."

"Pop," she said, "Astrid and I weren't that friendly."

"Don't call me Pop."

She grinned. Actually grinned. "That's what Charlie Chan said to his number one son."

"And his number two and number three. Okay, at home you can still call me 'Pop,' but honey—how are you doing? How are you holding up? Every cop who finds a dead body doesn't call their daddy, you know."

"They would if you were their daddy." She put a hand on his shoulder. "When I found myself in the middle of a crime scene, I stopped being friend and turned cop. It's where my head immediately went and where it still is."

He patted her hand on his shoulder. "Good girl," he said.

They both withdrew their hands. He let her take the lead and followed her back onto the porch, where Booker came over.

"Keith," the investigator said, "man, I wish I could do more, but I'm up to my ass in alligators. And they're hungry."

"Just give us today," Keith said, "and we'll be fine. If I might suggest?"

"Suggest away," Booker said, as Krista fell in alongside him.

"Chief," Keith said to his daughter, "if you haven't already, call David Landry at Lake View Lodge and tell him there is a serious police matter that we need his help dealing with."

Her eyes were narrowed. "Not tell him about the homicide?"

"No. Do you think it's got to social media yet?"

"Probably not. Although the neighbors know something serious has happened, obviously, and that much may be out there. Probably is."

Keith nodded. He glanced from his daughter to Booker and back again, pulling them both in. "Tell Landry all the guests are to be held. Have him announce, in no uncertain terms, that no one who attended the reunion will be allowed to check out by order of the Galena Police Department."

"Got it," she said with a nod, already getting her cell out.

"And," Keith continued, "have Landry tell them that, after the brunch, we'll be gathering all of them in that same room . . . assuming the brunch is in the banquet hall at the convention center . . . for 'informational purposes.' Don't tell him in regard to what. His guests are to be told 'a serious police matter,' nothing more."

She nodded again and walked off to make the call from the other end of the porch.

"You, my friend," Keith said, patting Booker on the shoulder, "will give us this afternoon, and we'll call it square, me covering for you the rest of the week."

Booker gave a single nod. "Fair trade."

Keith smiled and nodded back. He paused at the front door and from his coat pocket withdrew the pair of latex gloves he'd thought to bring along. Then he glanced over at Booker and asked, "How long have the CSIs been here?"

"Half an hour maybe. Show's hardly started."

That was an understatement. Ahead would be photographing and videoing the scene, including all possible routes of exit and entrance, diagraming and measuring any footprint, accessing any spatter, smear, or drop of blood, recording exact position of each. For the three CSIs present, as many hours of work lay ahead, and that didn't include recovering items for lab work or even dusting for fingerprints.

Keith opened the front door and went in. Eli was in the kitchen, facing away, as if he were showing off the bold CRIME SCENE TECHNICIAN logo on his back, the words curving above and below the state police seal. The CSI was at the kitchen sink, and when he half turned, in the blue rubber gloves, he looked like he was about to do the dishes—especially with the two cups and saucers down in there.

"What do you make of this?" Eli asked Keith, who came over.

The cups had been rinsed, but traces of brownish liquid lingered.

"Somebody," Keith said, "had a cup of tea. Actually, two somebodies."

"We have one victim," the CSI said. "And two teacups. Nobody else living here, right?"

"Well, this is the parents' house, but they're Florida snowbirds."

"So maybe the victim had a visitor before she went to bed?"

Keith thought about that. "Astrid Lund likely came straight here from an event out at Lake View Lodge. It's possible somebody stopped by for a chat over tea."

"Came straight from what kind of event?"

"Class reunion."

Eli let out a hollow laugh. "You ever been to a class reunion, Detective?"

Felt funny being called "Detective" again.

"A few," Keith said.

"And how many beers or drinks or whatever did you throw down at those reunions?"

"More than a few."

"After all that alcohol, you ever go have a cup of tea with one of your buddies?"

"No. But maybe women are different."

"There's a theory to run with. I'm just wondering if . . ."

Keith said, "If the perpetrator was a friend or anyway friendly acquaintance who turned out to be . . . not so friendly."

The blue-jumpsuited shoulders shrugged. "Of course, this tea might've been from earlier in the day."

"Might have."

Keith looked around, spotted a lidded wastebasket. He looked inside. Two used tea bags lay at the bottom of the black plastic bag lining the wastebasket. Nothing else.

"For the sake of argument," Keith said, "assume the Lund woman, who lives in Chicago, drove straight to the reunion, and came here to sleep in her family home afterward. That there's no other refuse here—knowing the parents are living elsewhere for now—would indicate this tea was consumed when she came here after the reunion."

"Reasonable," Eli said.

"Any indication of a blood trail?"

"Luminol says blood was dribbled from the victim's bedroom down the back stairs and trails off here in the kitchen."

"When you spray that sink, see if it doesn't light up like Christmas."

Eli frowned. "You think the killer cleaned up after himself?"

"Or herself, I do."

Eli frowned some more. "How does that play out? The victim and her guest drink tea, then go upstairs, the victim climbs in bed, and the killer stabs her repeatedly?"

"No," Keith said, and led Eli through the living room and into the entry area. He opened the door. He took a close look at the front door latch.

"I don't see anything, except maybe a bit of sticky residue," Keith said. "But I bet you find evidence that this door latch was taped not to lock."

Eli had a closer look. "Real possibility. You think a friendly cup of tea was followed by the guest leaving, but on exiting, making sure he . . . or she . . . could easily get back in?"

"That's it. Or maybe it is, if you say so, after you've done your magic. Did you notice that wood-block knife set on the counter?"

"Noticed it, but so what?"

"One knife is missing. The largest one. Have you found a murder weapon?"

"No."

"Well, that may identify it for you even if you don't find it."

A little hurt, Eli said, "I'd have noticed that eventually."

"I'm sure you would," Keith said, not wanting to rub it in. "Has the coroner been here?"

"No." Eli shrugged. "You know Sundays. Want a look upstairs?"

"No," Keith said. "But show me."

At the top of the stairs, gesturing toward a room with an open door, Eli said, "Best guess is murder happened around midnight. Rigor has set in everywhere. Based on lividity, she died in bed, maybe asleep."

The two CSIs working the room had not just their bodies covered in white plastic, but their faces and heads as well, and both wore their blue booties. One investigator seemed to be a man, the other a woman; both were white but that's about all Keith could tell.

Eli stayed in the hall, but called out, "This is Detective Larson. He's working with the Galena PD."

The ghostly figures nodded and went back to work, gathering blood samples at the moment.

Keith stepped inside.

The lovely girl he'd seen last night was still lovely, her face anyway, but her chest bore a massive wealth of wounds, a black silk robe torn at every entry point, crusty black blood framing each wound. Even worse, the blood had sprayed the ceiling and it clung up there in ghastly streaks, with heavier areas looking like horrid black stucco.

He exited the bedroom.

He felt the tears well up. His daughter, so much younger than himself, with so much less experience, had held together, stayed cop, emotionless, professional. But he had to fight it. That young woman . . . that girl . . . his daughter's classmate . . . all he could think of was, *That could be her in there!*

He shook it off, but first it had shaken him.

Eli led Keith down the front stairs, which took them near that front door again.

Keith said, "I believe this is a killer who has struck before. A classmate of the girl upstairs . . . a classmate of my daughter, Krista, that young chief of police outside . . . was murdered in Clearwater, Florida, last August. In much the same way. I'm going to contact the detective working the case, whose name is Hastings, so if you receive a call from somebody of that name in Florida, take it."

Eli nodded. "We dealing with a serial, you think?"

"Yes and no. I think these are specific, not random murders. But the method . . ."

"Is madness," Eli said. Sighed.

And headed back through the living room and dining room into the kitchen.

Outside, Keith told Krista he needed to make a call. She was still keeping an eye on things from the porch, in Booker's company.

Walking down the sidewalk, somewhat away from the murder house, Keith looked for the number in the phone. Then he called it.

"Yeah, I remember you," Hastings said. The sound of a basketball game on the TV, turned down a little, was nonetheless noticeable.

Keith said, "I hate to bother you on a Sunday."

"Yeah, no problem, what is it?" All run together.

"That Sue Logan homicide you're working . . ."

"Yeah, nothing new since we talked."

"I have something new."

"Oh?"

"A similar homicide. Young woman the same age as Logan. And a classmate of hers. Murdered. Stabbed repeatedly in the chest."

"Like our victim . . ."

"Just like your victim. Could you send me the entire file on the case so far? I'll give you my email, and—"

"Yeah, okay, but you said you're retired or something. It's your daughter? Who's chief of police, there? Where?"

"Galena, Illinois. I am retired, but I'm consulting. They haven't had a homicide in twenty years, but I worked my share on the other side of the river. In Dubuque."

"Okay. I can do that. Need to clear it, but . . . pretty sure I can do that."

Keith gave him the email address.

He had just slipped the cell phone back in his jacket pocket when he realized his daughter was approaching.

"Everything's set out at the lodge," she said.

"Good. We'll take Booker along. Pick your best officer here on the scene and put them in charge. The forensics team is just starting."

"You look pale, Pop."

"Let's get going before I embarrass you."

"You don't embarrass me."

"If I hugged you like I want to, I would. Let's get the hell out of here."

They did.

THIRTEEN

Though she'd lived in Galena all her life, Krista never failed to marvel at the ride out to Lake View Lodge—by summer, a shimmering, rolling tapestry of green, in fall a sea of brown, gold, red, and shades between. Yet somehow the skeletal gray of countless trees reaching bony fingers skyward had its own singular, haunting beauty.

Krista was driving the department's unmarked car, a dark blue Chevy Impala. Her father was behind her in the Toyota as they pulled up to the lodge, to start questioning reunion attendees.

She and Pop had gone home briefly for her to get into her uniform—she thought that was a must with what lay ahead—and her Pop thought it best to get himself in a fresh button-down shirt, tan sport coat, brown slacks, and brown-and-yellow tie himself. Then they headed to the station to make a quick stop.

On the way there, Pop had told her he was getting the files on the Sue Logan homicide from the Clearwater PD. Of course she'd immediately made the connection herself—even though she didn't have details about Sue's murder, what she did know tallied with Astrid's. Two classmates slain so similarly was a coincidence she could hardly shrug off.

At the station, she'd unlocked the door at the Bench Street entrance and gone up to her office to get the keys to the Impala, then had another thought.

From a desk drawer she took her old badge, which said

GALENA POLICE

OFFICER K. LARSON

and went back down to the street, where her father was leaning against the Toyota.

She gave it to him, saying, "In case anyone asks for your identification."

He took it with a nod and approving smile and pinned it in his wallet, where his Dubuque PD badge had once lived.

Outside the sprawl of Lake View Lodge's interlocking modern buildings with their rustic touches, the front parking lot had its first several rows filled, despite off-season. In the next row with open spaces, Krista pulled into one and her father found another a few spots away.

She waited for him and they paused for a moment. He gestured around.

"Mostly local plates," he said.

"I'd be surprised if any of my classmates hadn't returned for the brunch," she said. "Anybody from our class just has to show up for a complimentary breakfast."

"That's a break for us."

As they headed for the main lodge building, Booker came ambling out and met them as they stepped up onto the outer walk.

"I told everybody they can't leave," Booker said. "They don't seem happy, but the free food helps."

"Yeah," her father said, "but what happens when breakfast is over?"

Booker spread his hands wide. "Well, it's not over yet. And I'm about to serve myself up. Our host says to help ourselves, and I grabbed us a table."

Krista and her dad shrugged at each other. She didn't have any appetite that she'd noticed and Pop didn't seem very interested, either. But this day had already been long and fueling up wasn't a bad idea.

They went in the front way this time, the lobby seeming almost as sprawling as the lodge itself, with some business offices to the left and right as they entered, the front desk up ahead with very modern furnishings scattered among lodge-like trappings, including a sitting area complete with stone fireplace.

David Landry materialized from somewhere, his attire like the lobby, half-modern, half-rustic—a stylish olive jacket, fat-knotted dark green tie, but a V-neck brown nubby sweater, fashionably worn-out jeans, and cowboy boots with (as usual with David) uplifting heels.

The resort manager came over quickly and shook first her hand and then her father's. David and Booker nodded at each other; they'd already been consulting, about breakfast anyway.

"Now can you tell me," David said, perhaps a shade of irritation in his voice, "what exactly is going on?"

"Astrid Lund," Krista said, "was murdered last night. At her parents' home after the reunion. It was a brutal crime and we're dealing with an unknown party who is dangerously violent."

David's mouth had dropped open and his eyes were almost comically wide; the blood had drained from his face. He was not likely to surprise easily, she supposed, considering the kinds of things he faced in his job. But this was a rather special circumstance, wasn't it?

"My God," he said. "Oh my God. She was so . . ."

"She was a lovely girl," Krista's father said. "We thank you for what you've already done. But we need more."

"Any way I can help," David said, "you've got it."

Krista asked, "You wouldn't happen to remember when Astrid left the reunion?"

"I do, actually. The band was just starting a break and I glanced at my watch as Astrid was making a few goodbyes near the door. Right around ten thirty."

Not long after she and her father had left.

Krista gestured toward the connecting hallway to the convention center. "Let's walk and talk. The sooner I can get in front of our . . ." She almost said "suspects," then considered "witnesses," before finally settling on: ". . . classmates, the better."

They walked, David between her and her father, Booker bringing up the rear.

Krista said, "We'll need access to your security-cam footage."

"Anything you need," David said.

Her father asked, "Where are your cameras?"

"We have one that captures perhaps the front third of the parking lot, another on the entrance. All of the halls are monitored. Front desk. Indoor pool."

"How about the side parking lots?"

"I'm afraid not."

"Anything on the various sides of the building?"

"Just the entrance, I'm afraid."

Krista said, "What you do have will be helpful. As I recall, your bar closes at one a.m., right?"

"Normally. But with the reunion, we extended to two."

That was another nice break. Her dad had told her the time of death—though hardly official—was around midnight. And by tomorrow they'd have something more definitive from the coroner.

Krista said, "We'll need all the bar receipts that were charged to rooms. I assume your generosity didn't extend to giving everybody free bar tabs?"

David let out a little laugh. "No. We lowered our room rates rock bottom, but we required credit cards at check-in, for incidentals, as usual. We provided food and entertainment last night, and the breakfast buffet today. But as you'll recall, that was not an open bar last night, and this morning we've taken orders for mimosas, Irish coffees, Bloody Marys, and champagne cocktails."

Behind them, Booker said, "You're makin' me thirsty, Mr. Landry."

Krista smiled back at him. "Too bad you're on duty."

David brushed back dark hair that didn't need it. "How long do you think you'll be wanting the out-of-town guests to stay around?"

"With luck," Krista said, "we'll be able to thin this group considerably by tomorrow some time."

"So just one night."

"Yes. Except for any who might become persons of interest."

"Suspects you mean?"

"Not necessarily. We just have some checking to do before we can clear them."

Her father said, "And some won't be completely out of the woods. We'll have to make sure they know—if they go back to their homes elsewhere in the state, or out of state—that they may still be hearing from us."

"I can tell you right now," David said, "that a few people who were here last night did not come to the brunch."

Krista asked, "Do you know specifically who that might be?"

"Oh, yes. The free brunch was offered only to our GHS 2009 classmates and significant others. For nonclassmates, it was only ten dollars. But the handful who weren't in our class mostly took a pass—the table of teachers, for instance."

Her father shrugged and said, "They're all local. Easy enough to find."

"As I mentioned," Krista said, "this is a thinning process."

David nodded as they walked along the sun-flooded hall with its wall of windows at left. "Is there anything in the city budget to allow for lodging these, uh, persons who may prove to be of interest?"

That locution made Pop smile. "No, Mr. Landry," he said, "I don't believe there is. Your out-of-town guests are a captive audience for us and the lodge."

David was frowning in thought. "Look, we'll comp them for a few days, if need be. It's off-season. Maybe that'll help you out some."

"That would be great, David," Krista said.

Behind them, Booker said, "You got a spare whirlpool room I could use? Just so I got somewhere to work out of."

Krista looked back at him, amused. "We only have your services for today, Sergeant, as I recall. Your court date tomorrow?"

"Earliest I'll testify is afternoon. Maybe I can help tomorrow morning. Lotta folks to sort through."

Krista told the resort manager, "Sergeant Jackson will be sleeping at home tonight, David. He's just kidding."

On the square.

David's forehead frowned though his mouth smiled a little. "Well, I'm sincere about the offer—for extending stays and comping anybody you need access to."

Her father said, "Very generous, Mr. Landry. I think we can move this along quick enough to not wear out our welcome."

They were just outside the banquet hall now.

David asked, "Anything else I can do?"

Krista said, "Do you know of anyone who checked out early?"

"I don't think anyone did, but I can look into that."

"Please."

"You mean . . . now?"

Her father gave David a single nod.

"Uh, anything else you need?" The resort manager was just starting to look like maybe they were pushing it.

Her pop said, "Yes. Keep taking drink orders. It'll help us both."

David grinned, nodded, and headed back the way they'd come.

When the trio entered the open-beam-ceilinged banquet hall, all eyes went to them, none very friendly. Many attendees were still eating. The tall windows onto the lake were streaming sunshine, but the murmur among the guests was like the rumbling that threatens thunder.

Again, tables for six were scattered around the room. Everyone seemed to have dressed for the church services they skipped.

Krista positioned herself before them and said, in a loud, clear voice, the murmuring cutting off as if a switch had been thrown, "Please go on with your breakfast. We'll be with you shortly. Thank you for your patience, and your cooperation."

The murmuring switched back on, perhaps a little softer.

Booker was already at the breakfast buffet. She and her father joined him. The big man was piling on the scrambled eggs, French toast slices, hash browns, and sausage links. Krista took a bagel and a dollop of cream cheese, then got a small orange juice and some coffee. Her dad took the same as Booker, only about a fourth of the quantity. He got himself some iced tea.

Booker led them to the only remaining empty table, just inside the door. Krista was happy not to be stuck in that bright sunshine. This might be technically a beautiful day, but not really.

As they ate, her father asked, "Have you got in touch with Astrid's parents yet?"

She shook her head, using a butter knife to spread the cream cheese on the bagel. "No. I don't have their number in Florida. Maybe the forensics team will find it on her phone. I'm hoping someone in this crowd has it right now."

His tone went fatherly. "You don't want them to hear it from the internet or anything."

She sighed. "They may already have."

She'd had to make such calls—in person—to the parents or wives or husbands or children of accident fatalities. Nothing in her job had ever seemed tougher. Now she faced something even worse—telling the parents of a talented, lovely, successful young woman with an incredibly bright future ahead of her that all of that had been snuffed out, like a candle on an altar.

"And," her dad said, "you still have the media to deal with."

"Jerry's date may not be here," she said, glancing toward the table where her ex had just joined two couples, "but he is. He can give his scoop to the Dubuque paper."

"Yup," Booker said, spearing a sausage for what looked to be one bite. "*Galena Gazette* is a weekly. That don't cut it."

A waitress in black bow tie, white shirt, and tuxedo pants stopped by to see if the constabulary wanted a mimosa or one of the other break-fast cocktails. All of them wanted something. None of them ordered anything.

Her father was poking at his small plate of food. He asked Krista, "How many of your people can you pull in here?"

"We only have two shifts of a single patrol car today," she said. "That leaves everybody else."

"Let's get them out here," he said. "The sooner we can thin this crowd to our best suspects, better off we are. We need two pairs of eyes on those security tapes, and everybody else asking questions."

She was glancing at the dozen tables in the big room. Nobody seemed to be eating now but the cops, who were almost done, even Booker. Waiters were out there busing. It was time.

His plate empty of everything but syrup traces, Booker seemed about to get up but she put an arm on his sleeve.

"No seconds for you, young man," she told him.

He made a face but it turned into a smile. "Yes, Chief Larson. I will struggle by on a single serving."

"Stay here, you two," she said to her pop and her sergeant.

Krista rose and positioned herself at the front of the room, with the buffet at her back, the opposite end from where the Cover Band had played. She looked across at the many faces where confusion and irritation were mounting.

"I think you all know me," she said, in a loud, businesslike, but not unfriendly voice. "It was a pleasure last evening to spend some quality time with old friends. I'm sure you all agree."

Forced and/or uneasy smiles met her.

"But it is my unpleasant, and official, duty to inform you that last night our classmate Astrid Lund was murdered."

The murmuring came back in, mixed with high tones of alarm.

She raised a palm, as if directing traffic. "The crime was a brutal one, and the situation—for us and for you—is obviously serious."

From about halfway down the room, Jessy Webster—sitting with husband Josh and the Wunders, Frank and Brittany—called out, "Krista, does this have anything to do with Sue Logan?"

She could have done without the prompt, but she said calmly, "It may well have. As many of you know, late last summer, in Clearwater, Florida, our classmate Susan Logan was also a homicide victim. Some elements of Sue's death mirror Astrid's."

Hands went up, here and there, as if this were a big classroom. And, in a way, wasn't it? She ignored them.

"The only other thing I am at liberty to tell you about Astrid's death," she said, "is that very preliminary findings indicate the crime occurred around midnight."

Whispering, muttering. Some tears and sobs from the women.

Krista's hand again came up. "Because of the reunion that brought us all together," she said, in that same loud but calm tone, "I must ask you to cooperate as my officers and I talk to you this afternoon, doing our best to determine who among you might add something of value to our investigation. If you have photos on your phone from last night that include Astrid, we'll want to see them. Any posting about the reunion you need to share with us."

A male toward the back yelled, "How long are we going to be here?"

"We will move as quickly as we can," Krista assured them. "You are required to answer a few brief questions, provide identification, contact information, and so on. We will ask you to cooperate further by way of a more thorough interview. If you refuse, you will be free to go . . . but we will wonder why."

Silence blanketed the big room.

"Wonder why," she continued, "you wouldn't want to help us determine who murdered your classmate."

The murmur threatened to become a clamor.

She spoke over it: "Though you may decide only to provide minimal cooperation, remember—I have a limited number of officers and this is a large group, and many here will cooperate in full. We will likely be here, some of us at least, well into the evening. And, possibly, into tomorrow."

She let them chew that over. It got loud. Nobody was happy. That included Krista, but she seemed to be the only one keeping it to herself.

As the din decreased to an undertone, she said, "In that event, those of you from out of town may have to stay the night . . ."

Some other male blurted an expletive, loud enough to get some spontaneous nervous laughter.

". . . but in that event, your generous host, our classmate David Landry, is going to comp you on your rooms."

The hum of conversation that followed seemed almost positive.

"For those of you who do cooperate fully, we request that you stay until we say go. This is a murder investigation. We would like the opportunity to clear you."

Suddenly the faces wore surprise, some even seeming stunned, as everyone here realized what they were.

Suspects.

"For example," Krista said, "we will be checking security footage that may demonstrate that your car was in the lot all night."

Whispering between significant others made it sound like the entire hall was shushing her.

Again she spoke over it: "What I pledge to you as your friend, classmate, and chief of police is that we will move this as quickly and efficiently as we can."

"What about meals?" another male cried out.

The women, she noted, seemed more accepting of the inevitable.

"Your lodging is being taken care of," she reminded them. "Paying for any meals and beverages, in particular alcoholic ones, seems a nice way to say thank you to your already generous host."

David's voice came from her right—she hadn't seen him step in. He said, almost yelling, "You will dine as the lodge's guests this evening! We're preparing a limited but complimentary menu."

Sudden applause and even a few whistles and "Yay, Dave!" came up.

Krista said, giving the group a small smile, "Better not bring up tomorrow."

That got both laughs and moans, the latter louder.

"Again, we mean to get you out of here quickly, back into your homes and your lives. You can help us in the meantime by writing down your license plate numbers—to help us check security footage for your cars. That will help us rule you out."

Or identify you, she thought.

"Also," Krista said, "if anyone has contact information for the Lunds in Florida, I need that ASAP. And please, please, stay off social media. I don't want Astrid's parents hearing this news the wrong way."

As if there were a right one.

"In addition," she went on, "gather your thoughts about last night. Were you in the bar? How late were you there? Who did you see? Did you gather in rooms or in the lobby sitting areas with friends?"

She didn't use the dreaded word "alibi," but it hung in the air.

"Try to have any relevant information ready for the officers," she said. "We'll begin soon."

The assemblage went back to its murmuring, and the waitstaff began doing a land-office business.

David came up to her and said, "I have some information that might be helpful."

"Good. Share it with my investigators, would you?"

She walked the resort manager over to the table where her father and Booker sat.

They looked up at David as he said, "One guest checked out already—very early this morning. Around five a.m. Alex Cannon. From Chicago?"

Her father got to his feet.

Krista blurted, "Where are you off to?"

"Not the buffet," he said.

FOURTEEN

Keith got to his destination by late afternoon. He'd made only one stop, outside Rockford, for gas and a restroom break, and finding the Naperville address on Gatesfield Drive had been easy, thanks to the Toyota's GPS.

The lawn was vaguely green, like cloth after a few washes too many, with one small bony tree but many house-hugging evergreens, a tall central pine nearly reaching the three-peaked roof of the two-story redbrick Georgian, one peak over a three-car garage. This was less than a mansion but had surely cost its owner more than half a mil.

Two cars were in the wide drive, side by side: a pearl Lexus and a dark gray BMW. Keith pulled in front of the house and got out, wishing he'd brought a topcoat—February was turning cold again. He'd had the chance to grab something, when he stopped back at the house to pack a small bag, just in case this turned into an overnight. But he hadn't.

He crossed some brittle grass to get to the sidewalk and up to the one-step porch and rang the bell by the inset front door.

A second ring wasn't necessary—the door behind the glassed-in screen opened halfway, and a pretty brunette looked out, lip gloss her only makeup, her longish hair beautifully styled. She was maybe twenty-three, slender but curvy in a camel turtleneck sweater and dark skinny jeans. Her eyes were big and brown, and a plastic surgeon had given her a nice if overly carved nose. She looked vaguely familiar.

Her rather neutral expression blossomed into a smile of recognition and she opened the door wider. "You're that police chief's father!" she said, her voice on the soprano side.

He smiled tentatively. "Yes, my daughter Krista is Galena's chief. Do you know her? Have we met?"

"Oh, I'm sorry. I don't, we haven't. But Alex pointed her out, and you, as well. Said you were a police officer, too, or used to be."

Now he realized he'd seen her at the reunion last night, with her hair up and more makeup, but hadn't realized she was married to Alex Cannon, who he was here to see. Lodge manager Landry hadn't mentioned a Mrs. Cannon checking out with her husband, perhaps thinking it unimportant, since this lovely young woman was not a classmate.

Keith got out his wallet, flipped to the badge, held it up casually, not wanting to alarm her. "I'm working with my daughter as a police consultant. Something unfortunate occurred last night, after the reunion, and I'm hoping to chat with your husband."

A crimson-nailed hand gripped the edge of the front door. "Oh. What unfortunate something?"

"Death of a classmate. I need to inform Alex."

That should be vague enough to make it sound important but not overly troubling. And mentioning her husband as "Alex" should help.

Her frown wore worry not irritation. "I'm sorry, but a client of his dropped by and I think they're—"

"Excuse me!"

The voice was male but not Alex Cannon's, whose wife disappeared behind the open door, like a mouse scurrying to its hole. In her place was a big guy in his thirties in a navy orange-trimmed BEARS sweat suit, looking like maybe he'd once played tackle for them, judging by his Cro-Magnon forehead, oft-busted nose, and thick scarred lips. His hair was blond and short and his eyes blue, like some ancient Viking ancestor of the Larson family.

Only Keith was not getting greeted like a member of the family.

"You need not to be here," the BEARS sweat suit guy said, his voice breathy, the words almost ridiculous—but not quite, considering the belligerent face they were emanating from.

Keith silently blessed his daughter for giving him that badge, which he held up to show the guy, who squinted at it with a scowl.

Badge still aloft, Keith said, "I need to see Alex Cannon. This shouldn't take long."

"That says Galena."

"Right. Galena, Illinois. This is Naperville, Illinois. Would you like to see some badges that say Chicago on them? Like Barney Davis's maybe?"

Davis had busted an LCN (La Cosa Nostra) client of Cannon's and, though the mobster had gotten off, put him through a world of trouble. Of course, Barney knew nothing of the Astrid Lund murder, but the BEARS sweat suit guy didn't know that, and—after some painful-looking thought transpired—backed away and disappeared.

Mrs. Cannon reappeared and offered up a nervous, embarrassed smile as she held the door all the way open and gestured Keith in.

"I'm sorry," she said. "Alex doesn't usually do business here, but a few of his clients find it more convenient to, uh . . . anyway, I'm Ashley Cannon."

"Mrs. Cannon," he said with a nod.

Keith kept his billfold with badge in hand as he stood in the foyer from which open stairs rose. To his left was a formal living room with gleaming hardwood floors and expensive but bland maple furniture, somewhat countrified to go with views onto the forest preserve. Down a hall to the right of the stairs, the BEARS sweat suit guy was talking to someone Keith had never met, but recognized.

He was Sonny Salerno, grandson of Salvatore Salerno, who had been a Sam Giancana crony back in the bad old days. Sonny's father was widely thought to be the current Chicago mob chief. This later edition Salerno was small, dark, and almost handsome, also wearing a sweat suit, but a blue-and-red CUBS one. Keith had been similarly dressed earlier and now for some reason was glad he wasn't.

"It may be a few minutes," Mrs. Cannon said, leading him into the living room. "Something to drink? Beer, pop, coffee?"

"Diet anything would be great, thanks."

He slipped his billfold with badge in his back pocket, happy not to linger in that foyer. He had noticed that the guy's BEARS outfit had a lump where the sweatshirt covered his pants waistband and might be a revolver tucked away.

They moved through the living room, which had the staged look of a Realtor's open house, and into the kitchen with its shining silver stove and refrigerator and a wealth of maple cabinetry. She sat him at an island on a tall maple chair and served him a Coke Zero in a can.

"Big place," he said. "Lovely," he added, not exactly meaning it. He knew he would never live in a house worth half this kind of money, but had no desire to, either.

She leaned over the other side of the island, as if she were working the counter at a diner. "We haven't been here long. Alex and I were only married last year."

"Place this size," he said, "would be perfect for a family."

"That's the plan," she said.

An awkward silence fell as she found herself a chair down from him, leaving one between. She was having coffee.

Between sips, she said, "Do you mind my asking who died? I met quite a few of Alex's classmates last night."

"You may have met her then, or possibly already had, right here in the Chicago area. Or know of her, certainly. Astrid Lund."

Her eyes got even bigger. "Astrid? . . . not? Oh, no! I did know her. Everybody in Chicago did, from TV! She's a celebrity in this part of the world. But I knew her as, you know . . . a *person*."

"I'm sorry. Were you close?"

She shook her head, sending her brunette hair flying, but losing none of its shape settling back down. "I only knew her from Alex's work."

"How so?"

"Well, WLG-TV, that's one of Alex's clients. Or his firm's, but Alex is the partner who represents them."

"How does someone as young as Alex become a partner at a major Chicago law firm?"

Her shrug, accompanied by an open hand, was casual. "He was top of his class at Loyola. And, well, his best friend there was the son of one of the partners. Alex admits that helped."

"He's a lucky man." Then with a little smile that conveyed his meaning, "In a lot of ways."

She smiled back. "You've known Alex a long time? Through your daughter?"

He nodded. "They were in the Young Democrats together. I knew him when he had more hair than Jennifer Aniston."

She laughed a little, and from behind them came a male voice—not the BEARS sweat suit guy this time.

"Now, that's unkind," Alex Cannon said, his courtroom baritone delivering the words in a good-natured way.

Keith slid off the chair as the two men met each other halfway across the big kitchen and shook hands. Alex betrayed neither surprise nor annoyance with this unscheduled visitor; he wore a dark gray polo and stonewashed jeans. His running shoes were gray, too, like his gray-framed glasses.

"I don't have the evidence with me," Keith said, "but I can produce my daughter's high school yearbook, if a judge demands it."

They both laughed a little, politely. Ashley was looking from her husband to Keith and back again, wondering what was really going on.

"Ash," Alex said, "I'm going to take our guest back to my study." He said to Keith, "We usually order pizza Sunday night, if you'd care to join us."

That may have been a veiled dig at the time of day Keith had chosen to drop by.

"No, that's generous, Alex," he said. "But I'm probably heading back to Galena after we talk a bit."

"Understood. Bring your Coke along. I already have a beer going."

As Alex led him out of the kitchen, Keith smiled at Ashley, said it was nice meeting her, and she, still seated, said the same.

Soon, Keith and his host were in a modest study with a bookcase filled not with law books but with legal thrillers, from vintage Erle Stanley Gardner to current John Grisham. The desk, like the bookcase, was again countrified maple, though its swivel chair was black leather and pricey-looking. No filing cabinets were on hand to make it more a work space, or TV/sound system to make it a den.

This was strictly where a client could confer with his attorney out of the Chicago Loop and, in the case of a Sonny Salerno, away from prying eyes, whether human or video.

Alex closed the door as Keith settled into a less expensive but comfortable black leather chair across from his host. The desktop was uncluttered, really nothing but a phone, a pack of Parliament Lights, an ashtray, and a nearly empty bottle of Blue Moon on a coaster.

"I apologize," Alex said, "for the less than warm welcome."

"I came unannounced," Keith said with a shrug. "But I have had warmer ones."

Alex twitched a smile. "Well, Bruno has his merits. I was meeting with a client who has specific needs, including heavy security. And discretion. Did you notice who it was?"

"I did. Never met the man, but for all his discretion, his face is well known among law enforcement professionals."

Alex reached for the Parliaments. "Mind if I smoke?"

"No." The smell of tobacco already hung in the air.

"I wasn't aware," his host said, "that you were still a law enforcement professional. I heard you retired."

He'd probably heard it last night, asking about Keith at the reunion.

"I retired from the Dubuque department, yes."

"Was that after your wife's passing? I was sad to hear about Mrs. Larson. She was a wonderful teacher. I had her in third grade. And when Krista and I were in the Young Demos, her mom was always so gracious, so friendly."

Yes, he'd been asking about Keith at the reunion.

The attorney was lighting up with a silver horsehead lighter. "So what brings you to Naperville?"

"Astrid Lund was murdered last night."

The cigarette suddenly hung slack in his mouth. "What? Jesus. No . . ." He shook his head. Set the cigarette in the ashtray. "Oh, that's awful. I know her well. *Knew her* well. I represent the station where she works, as you may know."

"I didn't, but your wife mentioned it."

Alex took a moment to retrieve his cigarette, a pause that told Keith the attorney was wondering just what Mrs. Cannon had said to their guest.

"This is terrible," the attorney said, sighing smoke. "What are the circumstances, anyway?"

"She was stabbed in her sleep, repeatedly, presumably with a butcher knife. If she slept through her death, that would be a blessing. But I think it's doubtful. She likely suffered, though not for long."

Alex swallowed. His surprise seemed genuine enough, if slightly guarded. "When was this?"

"Too early to know precisely. Likely around midnight."

"Do you have any idea who . . . ?"

"No. You asked about law enforcement—I'm helping my daughter out on this. As a pro bono consultant. This is the first homicide she's had since taking over."

"I grew up in Galena," he said, the gray-blue eyes tightening. "I don't remember there ever being a murder . . ."

"Twenty years ago, I'm told, was the last previous." He sipped the Coke Zero. "You left first thing this morning, I understand. Very early."

Alex's eyebrows flicked up and down. "Yes. I wanted to get back."

"For the meeting with Mr. Salerno?"

"No," he said too quickly. "That was something that just came up. I wanted a quiet Sunday with my wife, is all. I have a busy week ahead."

"Seems a little funny."

"What does?"

"Leaving first thing, like you did. Beautiful weekend for this time of year. So much to do in Galena on a Sunday. Bet your wife would have loved the shopping, so many fun little boutiques."

He let some smoke out. "All right, I did have a meeting scheduled, here at the house. Informal, but a meeting. Not with Mr. Salerno."

"Do you mind my asking with whom?"

His first frown. "What do you think? A client."

"What client?"

He sat up. "Really, I don't think that's pertinent. Anyway, you people may have heard of client confidentiality back in Iowa, and Galena, too, for that matter."

Keith smiled. "We have. We know that it applies to communications between an attorney and his client, not the identity of his client." He sat forward. "I didn't drive three hours to have a nice conversation with your lovely wife, though it was pleasant. And the Coke Zero is appreciated. I'm here representing the Galena Police Department. There was a murder last night of someone attending the same class reunion you and your wife came to Galena for. A lot of other classmates from out of town were also staying at the Lake View Lodge. You and Mrs. Cannon were the only guests to check out before the final event of the festivities, a free buffet breakfast. You have a work connection to the victim. So I will ask you again, and perhaps spare you a trip back to your old stomping grounds, where you would be held as a material witness."

The attorney's face was blank now. "Not for long."

"No. And if your wife comes, maybe you can take in those boutiques before you head back to Naperville. But I want to know right now who your client is."

"Daniel Rule," he said.

"The construction contractor."

Alex nodded.

"How many schools and hospitals has his company built, in the greater Chicago area, do you suppose?"

"Many."

"Isn't he contemplating a run for mayor this year?"

"He is."

"How do you think that will go?"

"Very well, I hope."

"Still interested in politics, Alex?"

"Yes. And still a Democrat."

"So is Krista. I haven't voted for a while. Call me an independent, because next time it's going to be for the man."

A nasty little smile. "Or the woman, Mr. Larson. Stay with the times."

"Good advice. But some old-fashioned things never change."

"Such as?"

"Such as people in the construction business in Chicago sometimes being known to have disreputable ties. Would you mind answering a few questions about the reunion? There's also another date I need to clarify."

"All right."

Keith reached into his pocket for his phone. "Do you mind if I record this?"

"Yes."

"Yes I may record this . . . ?"

"Yes I mind, and no you can't. But I'll answer your questions as I did the earlier ones—informally."

The attorney did. He and his wife had gone right to their room after the Saturday event, knowing they'd be leaving early. And in the second week of August, they were vacationing in Cancún.

Then Alex stood. Smiled that same barely polite smile he'd given Keith before disappearing into the banquet hall last night. "Thank you for dropping by, Mr. Larson. I'm sure my wife enjoyed meeting you. Safe journey home."

Keith stood. "Thank you."

On his way out there was no sign of Mrs. Cannon. And the pearl-colored Lexus was gone. As he got into his daughter's Toyota, he was glad he'd taken the time to stop by the house to pack that small bag.

Because he was definitely not heading back to Galena.

Not just yet.

FIFTEEN

By nightfall, the reunion attendees—whether viewed as witnesses or suspects—had been considerably narrowed.

Krista had brought in her two lieutenants and two patrol officers to help out. No one was needed at the Lund house now, so Officers Cortez and Clemson, after an unproductive canvass of the North High Street neighborhood, took over for two officers who had been at Lake View Lodge all afternoon, dealing with the out-of-town attendees.

The other two officers from the now processed crime scene, Reynolds and Deitch, relieved two others who had been doggedly going through the security-cam footage in the resort's modest security center, matching license plate numbers and models or makes of vehicles belonging to the attendees. Those officers now had the unenviable duty of going on patrol. Yet another was scouring Facebook and Instagram.

But with only twelve on her staff, including herself, Krista knew her people were getting stretched to the limit. Maybe overtime would take out the sting.

The nonlocals were sent back to their rooms and interviewed there. In every instance, these were couples, though not every significant other was a classmate. For efficiency's sake, and because this was after all preliminary, Krista had the couples interviewed jointly, instructing the officers to watch for inconsistencies as well as any stumbling or undue coaching from one to the other.

Krista and all of her officers were using their cell phones with a mobile field interview app. She instructed her officers to inform the subjects they were being recorded. But as these were informal interviews, they did not need to read Miranda rights prior to questioning.

She had her own notions about who were the best potential suspects among the sixty-two attendees, all of whom—excluding Alex Cannon, who Pop was off to track down in Chicagoland—were local. As a classmate and friend of Astrid's, the chief of the Galena PD knew at once who she wanted to personally interview.

The Galena attendees—forty-one of the fifty-six present (last night's teacher's table being truant)—were corralled in the banquet hall, but toward the back, down at the end where the band and portable dance floor had been. The out-of-towners were now in their rooms, which left a number of empty tables. Three of these were commandeered for Sergeant Jackson and her lieutenants, Lauren Cole and Dylan Mitchell. Krista took the table where she, Booker, and her father had eaten breakfast.

Lauren, Dylan, and Booker had then gone around with clipboards gathering names, so they could summon interviewees. When they'd completed the task, Krista took their clipboards and circled the names of the handful she wanted to make sure she interviewed personally.

She was just settling in when Jerry Ward came up. But for a white dress shirt, he was all in black—jacket, jeans, and running shoes. Not a good ensemble for somebody who hoped not to be singled out as the villain.

He leaned in. "Do you mind taking me first?"

"Well," she said, pleasantly, "since we're old friends, why not?"

She had intended to start with him, anyway. She set the phone on the table and said she'd be recording.

He sat next to her, handing her a slip of paper. "That's the info about my car. Actually, it's my folks' car. I don't have one right now. But then you know that."

"I do. But thanks for this." One of the two officers working the security center would be in to collect more of these slips when needed.

"I could use a favor," he said, his smile uneasy.

"I thought I just gave you one," she said, hating that she still found him attractive.

He scratched his fashionably scruffy chin. "I want to talk to you about, you know . . . media coverage."

"Hasn't been any yet."

"I didn't think so. How about cutting me a break so I can get a story over to the *Telegraph Herald*? And after that, keeping me in the loop?"

Did he know when he tilted his head forward like that and looked up with those big brown eyes, it made her want to reach over and fiddle with his curly dark hair? And then slap him? The trendy beard would cushion it.

She said, "Let's start with a few questions."

"Sure. No problem."

Why should it be a problem?

"I obviously don't need your name and address and phone number."

"No. Obviously."

"State them anyway."

"Oh." He did.

"Now I need to know about last night, Jerry—what time you left here. And what's the name of that young girl you were with?"

"Okay. The young *woman's* name is Jasmine Peterson."

"You were here at the resort, in the lounge, after the reunion?"

"Yes."

"For how long?"

He shrugged. "Till last call. Two. Talking old times."

Not with Jasmine, surely.

"Can you tell me exactly who you talked old times with?"

"Sure." He rattled off half a dozen names, then thought awhile, and rattled off four more. "She drove us home, by the way. Jasmine.

Designated driver. Do you want her contact information? She works at Vinny Vanucchi's."

"If you know her phone number and address that would be helpful."

"You're going to talk to her?"

"Yes."

He gave Krista the info.

She asked, "Did you talk to Astrid at all?"

He frowned, shook his head. "Awful. So awful. Such a talented young woman."

Was he trying too hard?

"Did you talk to her last night?"

"Just said hello."

"Really, that's all? You were something of an item back at GHS, as I recall."

"Are you going to bust my . . . chops over that?"

"No. I'd just like to know if you stayed in touch with Astrid."

"Not really."

"That doesn't sound like 'no.'"

He sighed. Thought for a bit. "You really probably do need to know this, though I doubt it has anything to do with anything."

"Why don't you tell me and I'll decide?"

"She called me about a week ago. From Chicago. She wondered if I was interested in helping her out on a story."

"What story?"

"She wasn't super specific. It was about men taking advantage of women. In a sexual way, I think."

"You think?"

"We were going to get together . . . today, actually. This afternoon. She was going to tell me what it was about, and could I do some interviews for her, and so on. She said there was a local angle . . . not local Chicago, local Galena . . . but she wouldn't be able to spend enough time here, and needed some 'help on the ground.'"

"So is this workplace-related?"

"You now know what I know. Are we cool?"

She laughed faintly. "Sure. We're cool. Go write your story. And file it."

"You make that sound like an insult."

"You writers. Always looking for subtext. Thank you, Mr. Ward. Would you mind sending Frank Wunder and his wife up?"

Frank and Brittany came unenthusiastically over. He was in a brown jacket, tan slacks, and yellow shirt; she was in a black lacy thing that cried out for tattoos. Her husband's expression couldn't make up its mind whether it was a smile or not, and Brittany's blonde boredom was coming off her in waves.

He sat opposite Krista, and couldn't have looked more uncomfortable if he'd been duct-taped to the chair. His short brown hair looked like he'd slept on it funny and the normally attractive green eyes, crowding his football-badge-of-honor broken nose, were bloodshot.

Brittany tossed Krista a slip of paper with their license plate number and car make/model. Frank was staring at the cell phone on the table like he'd never seen one before.

He asked Krista, "Are you expecting a call?"

"No. I'm recording us. Is that all right?"

Brittany asked, "Do you need our permission?"

"Not for the basic information, names, address."

Frank said, "You know our names. Where we live."

"I do know your names, but state them for me, would you? And I don't know your phone number or numbers, or your street address, off the top of my head."

Brittany rattled all that off. She had the expression of someone who would feel contempt for you if she only had enough interest.

Krista asked them about the evening before. Like Jerry, they had after-partied in the Lake View Lounge. Krista asked Frank who he'd seen there and specifically who he'd talked to. He told her. The list was similar to Jerry's, though not exactly.

"Brittany," Krista asked, "is there anyone Frank has left out?"

Brittany shrugged. "They're not in my class."

Which sounded a little ambiguous.

"Frank," Krista said, "you and Astrid were something of an item at one time."

Interceding, Brittany said, "Is that a question?"

"No, but—"

"I started going with Frank not long after he broke it off with her. They were only together a couple of weeks."

That could be an eternity in high school time.

"Of course," Brittany said, "she dated a lot of guys for a couple of weeks. Popular ones like Frank."

"Did either of you talk to Astrid last night?"

Frank shook his head.

"You didn't even say hello?"

"No. Astrid and me, we didn't . . . you know, part on good terms."

"How not good were those terms?"

Frank shrugged. "Oh, you know that was years ago. But some time passing doesn't make me somebody she wanted to talk to now, and me her either."

"What about you, Brittany?"

"I never talked to her at GHS and she never lowered herself to talking to a sophomore. If you're looking for somebody to shed tears over that skank, find somebody with less mascara at risk." She leaned forward and spoke to the cell. "This is Brittany Wunder speaking, in case there's any doubt."

Krista asked, "Were you in town in August, you two? Did you go anywhere? Vacation maybe? Either of you?"

Frank looked at Brittany and Brittany looked at Frank.

Then Brittany shook her head, saying, "No. We were both right here in glorious Galena. Why?"

Krista didn't tell her.

After a few more questions, Krista thanked them and said they were free to go. That there might be follow-up.

Frank, already on his feet, looked startled. "Why would there be?"

Krista smiled and said, "I don't know. Should something come up."

"Why should it?"

His wife took him by the arm, a little thing hauling the big lug away, saying, "Come on, Frankie baby. Don't question a hall pass."

Krista mulled for a few moments. Frank seemed really thrown by Astrid's murder—the Buick dealer for once hadn't ragged her about not driving American.

She glanced over at the other officers and Booker, at their respective tables, talking to other classmates of hers. She doubted they'd get anywhere—none of the subjects were from Astrid's crowd.

Then she glanced over at Jessica and Josh's table, among the closer ones, and quickly caught Jessy's eye. Smiled and nodded at her, and Jessy gathered her purse and her husband and joined Krista at the table.

Jessy, petite and curvy in a navy pantsuit and cream-colored silk blouse, sat across from Krista. Josh took the seat beside his wife; he unbuttoned his brown sport coat over his cranberry polo, both a little small for him. He was one of those slightly overweight guys who couldn't face up to reality. Still, he was handsome enough, his dark blond hair combed, his dark blue eyes not at all bloodshot, and for once she detected no scent of caramel corn.

Jessy leaned over, batting her big brown eyes, and touched Krista's hand. "You are doing so well, sweetie! I'm proud of you. And you always said you were shy! Going out for that musical really paid off. Standing up there, you were . . . honey, you were commanding."

"Right," she said. "Thanks. Do you have your vehicle info written down?"

Josh handed the slip to her.

"I'm recording this," Krista told them. "Would you each state your name and would one of you give your address and any phone numbers?"

They did that.

Jessy sat forward, smiling tightly, her purse on her lap. "Honey, we were here last night, like a lot of people, till well after two. First, in the bar. Then we sat by that fireplace, the sitting area in the lobby? You want to know who we saw, who we talked to?"

"Yes," Krista said.

Jessy told her.

"You know," Jessy volunteered, "Josh went with Astrid for a while. But I mean, what guy on the Pirates didn't? The backfield, anyway. Backfield in motion, like they say."

Behind all that chatty chatter, she knew, Jessy was a nervous wreck. Why?

Again, with no prompting, Jessy started in. "I said hello to Astrid, talked to her for about two seconds. Told her how cool it was she was doing so well. That was it. That was early, before the band started. I don't think she stayed very late. Josh? Did you talk to her?"

He shrugged. "Said hi. I was standing right next to you, sweetheart."

Krista said, "You were gone in August, I remember. Something to do with your sister?"

"Right, yeah, we visited her and Gary. Right, Josh?"

"Yeah," Josh said. "They got a cabin. On Timber Lake. Real nice."

Krista asked, "Would either of you know anything about Astrid that might be helpful?"

Jessy shook her head. "We haven't stayed in touch, honey."

"What about something dating back to high school?"

"Well, just the rumor mill. There's always that!"

"Any specific rumor?"

Her eyes fell to the phone. "If you turn that off, maybe."

Krista paused the recording. "Off the record."

". . . Well, I'm probably not telling you anything you don't already know."

"Try me."

"I don't even know if it's true."

"That's what makes it a rumor."

Jessy leaned very close. "You know, the girls, some of them, always said Mrs. Bragg, the coach's wife? Well, she's a coach, too, girls' basketball. They always said Mrs. Bragg took a real interest in her girls. The girls on her teams and all. A real interest. Follow?"

"I follow."

Jessy shrugged. "It's probably just high school b.s. Some girl, maybe, got a bad grade in gym and made up some wild dumb thing to get back at teacher."

"Such as what?"

She sighed. Drew even closer. Whispered. "Such as somebody saw Mrs. Bragg in the shower, soaping Astrid's back. And they were naked."

"Wouldn't they be?"

"It was way after hours. And Mrs. Bragg was . . . well, Astrid was soapy all over. I didn't see it! I don't believe it. She's married. She and Coach Bragg, they're such a cute couple. I don't buy it."

Maybe Jessy didn't buy it, but she sold it pretty good.

"Okay," Krista said. "Thank you. I'm turning this back on."

She un-paused the phone, asked them both a few more questions, then told them they could go. They might hear from her later, and if either of them had to go out of town, please let her know. They scooted out the nearest door.

David Landry came over. "Things going all right? Any way I can help?"

"You can sit down here. I have to question you like everybody else, no matter how generous a host you are. Is your wife here?"

He sat in the chair Jessy vacated. "No, I'm sorry. She'll make herself available to you, obviously. But this was a workday for me, and Dawn had plans to see her mother over in Dubuque. We'll set something up for you two to talk."

"Fine. You're aware we're recording this."

"Certainly."

"Tell me about your post-reunion doings."

"Surely. I was circulating some, mostly in the Lake View Lounge, but also at several small parties in suites. So I made the rounds. You want the names? Approximate times?"

"That would be helpful."

He gave her all that.

Krista said, "Astrid apparently left fairly early. But did you see her at the event? Speak to her?"

"I did. We . . . I guess you know Astrid and I dated for, oh, several months senior year. For her, and for me, admittedly, that was a long run. When we broke up it was emotional and pretty rough. It was . . . my idea. I was jealous. She was getting friendly with . . . Josh Webster, I believe."

"You're not sure? I think you'd remember."

He grinned, busted. "Yeah, it was Josh. But they didn't last as long as Astrid and I did!" He shook his head, his eyelids at half-mast. "This is just so . . . it's unspeakably sad. I wish . . . nothing."

"What?"

"I wish I had spoken to her last night, more than just to say hello and welcome home and so on. To let her know how much I admired her, and all she's accomplished."

"Would you happen to know where you were the second week in August?"

He frowned, blindsided. "Well, that's a very busy time for us. I was right here. Will I need to prove that?"

"Possibly. Not right now. And you have no trips planned in the coming weeks?"

"No. We have several conventions coming in. I *have* to be here. Getaways come rarely when you run a vacation wonderland."

She asked him a few more questions and he remained unfailingly helpful and even charming.

"Okay, David. Thank you. For everything you've done for us here today."

"Happy to help."

That took care of everyone she wanted to zero in on, so Krista pitched in and interviewed other attendees until, by midevening, all of the locals had been released. The out-of-towners were a different matter, because some checking up would need to be done, particularly on their alibis for the Sue Logan homicide.

Dog tired, she took a break in the Lake View Lounge herself. She was slumped in a booth, sipping ginger ale, when Booker lumbered in. That sharp suit of his looked a little bedraggled.

He plopped down next to her. "Can I be officially off damn duty?"

"Sure. Get yourself a beer."

"I was thinking more a Jack on the rocks."

". . . Who's stopping you?"

He went over and got that and returned. They compared notes. Neither felt they had learned much, and she wasn't ready to share the rumor about Kelly Bragg.

"David Landry," she said, "has been very helpful."

"Suspiciously helpful?"

"Maybe. But his alibis for both crimes are likely to hold up."

"So what?"

She frowned. "So what?"

Booker chuckled. "David Landry has spilled more money than you and me will ever see. You don't think he could afford to hire somebody killed? Some fancy way that makes it look like some psycho did it? Or somebody with a hell of a grudge, so it doesn't look like a hit job?"

She was too tired to have an opinion. But she filed that away for when she was rested.

SIXTEEN

If he'd thought to bring a topcoat, Keith would have hoofed it. From the Drake Hotel to WLG-TV on West Washington was only a half-hour walk, and he might have enjoyed it, if February hadn't decided to turn cold on him, that lake wind earning its reputation. After all, this was a part of the Loop he knew well.

He and Karen had often spent getaway weekends here, the Drake their lodging of choice. They'd leave Friday, after she got home from teaching, or earlier during her summer vacation, if his work schedule allowed. They would check into the Drake, dine right there at the hotel, then have what married people sometimes refer to as "a romantic evening." On Saturday she would shop the Miracle Mile while he and his cop pal Barney would take in a ball game at Wrigley Field or at the Cubby Bear bar, after which he and Karen would go to Second City on North Wells and eat somewhere in the neighborhood. On Sunday they would take in a matinee of a play or musical, and have deep dish pizza at Gino's East before heading home.

They had done that so many times, it was now a sweet, pleasant blur.

But the Drake had not been a good idea. Oh, it was still a lovely old hotel, fairly recently restored. Only this was his first time there without Karen. Warm memories only went so far. Getting to sleep in a hotel room so like those the two of them had often shared, well, that hadn't been easy.

Last night—this was Monday morning—he had checked in with Krista, calling her cell (no landline anymore at the old homestead), and found her just getting in.

"We've talked to everybody," she said, "except the teachers. And I'll be doing that tomorrow. They have an in-service day, I've been told, so I won't have to pull anybody out of class, or look them up at home."

"Small breaks," he told her, "are still breaks."

He was in his T-shirt and boxers, propped up on the bed with pillows behind him and a John Wayne western (one of the old Warner's "B" ones, pre-*Stagecoach*) on the TV, muted. He listened to her fill him in on what she'd learned, which chiefly came from those who were already her favorite suspects.

"Everybody has the same alibi for Astrid," she said, "and they all have something for Sue Logan, too, but I'll be looking into those. Vacations and such."

"What 'same alibi'?"

"They were mostly in the bar, the lounge. Some were sitting around a lobby area, a few in suites where people were gathering to drink and talk, take selfies, and compare kid pics and travel photos."

"What do you think of that as an alibi?"

"I'm thinking somebody could slip away for half an hour or even a little more and not raise suspicion. And leave the impression they never left."

"Your mother and I raised a smart girl. And you figure a wife or husband who noticed that absence might cover for a husband or wife, in such a case."

"Or be an accomplice."

"Wouldn't rule it out. Any special insights?"

He could hear her in the kitchen, getting in the fridge.

She said, "People were hiding things. The guys particularly."

"What kind of things?"

"Not sure. Yet."

Talking to his daughter, even about a murder investigation, was somehow comforting.

She asked, "Where are you staying?"

"The Drake."

Long silence.

Then: "Was that a good idea, Pop?"

"No. Seemed like it, but no."

"Do me a favor."

"Sure."

"Think good thoughts."

"I'm on it."

"And come back soon as possible. I could use you here."

"See what I can do."

They had said goodbye and he got off the bed, leaving John Wayne silently shooting at bad guys, and went to his laptop, which he had set on the little table apparently provided for that purpose. He looked up the television station's address and more, and wrote some information down.

Twelve hours later, Monday morning, a cab dropped him off at WLG-TV's private entrance on West Washington. His breath was visible as he identified himself on an intercom as an investigator with the Galena, Illinois, PD; he got buzzed in. The lobby was small, warm, and cold-looking, all light gray faux marble. A dark-haired young woman in a business suit behind a slab desk looked up at him with red eyes behind brown-rimmed glasses. She had been crying. Word about Astrid had beaten him here, not surprisingly.

He held up the badge pinned in his wallet.

"This is about Ms. Lund?" she asked, confirming his assumption.

"Yes."

"I'll let Mr. Carlson know you're here."

William R. Carlson was president and general manager of the station, or so Google had informed Keith last night. Also the husband of Rebecca Carlson, the longtime anchor of the morning news and a local celebrity. No Chicago channels were available in Galena, but Keith nonetheless knew who she was, just from his occasional visits here with Karen.

A small bank of elevators was to the receptionist's left, which—after he signed in—she gestured to.

"Twentieth floor," she said.

He nodded and was moving toward the pair of elevators when behind him her voice, less businesslike than before, said, "Do you know who did it?"

He turned his head and gave her a tight smile. "No. But we will."

She smiled a little and nodded. "Good."

On the twentieth floor, he was met by a young female production assistant in a headset with mic, in jeans and a long-sleeve white T-shirt rolled to the elbows. She ushered him past a sprawling silver-and-blue news set in a studio setting. It looked like a million bucks. Then the PA led him down a narrow hallway—lined with small open-door offices, makeup areas, and dressing rooms—that looked like a buck-ninety-eight.

Scurrying PAs seemed to have split off like amoebas and appeared to be in a perpetual state of hurried distress. Some, he could tell, had been crying. But that didn't stop them in their tasks.

Finally, rather than walk into a wall, the PA took a left and the world transformed into a standard modern business building, the narrow hall given over to a wide corridor. Light gray walls were all but blotted out by huge framed posters of newscasters with big smiles and bigger station logos, between glassed-in offices with receptionists and expensive furniture worthy of a top legal outfit or a plastic surgeon.

With a "wait right here" nod, the PA deposited Keith in a window-less conference room, where an endless narrow table could seat twenty but didn't. Looming flat-screens were at either end of the room. The walls were cream, the tabletop maple, the leather chairs tan. All very high-end, and with no more personality than an empty glass.

What the hell. Keith sat at the head of the table. For five minutes, he checked his email on his phone, and then through a nearby door, a man came in who went very well with the room, though he was neither cream nor maple nor tan.

He shut the door behind him. Tall, maybe six three, in a charcoal suit with a light gray shirt and black-and-white tie, so well tailored that by comparison Keith might have shopped at Walmart, not Men's Wearhouse. Lincolnesque, if Lincoln had been better looking, the black frames of his glasses so heavy they intimidated. So did the quietly judgmental eyes, which were a disturbingly light gray, like the corridor walls.

"Mr. Carlson," Keith said, rising, recognizing the station's president and general manager from the photo at the WLG-TV website. "My daughter is chief of Galena Police. I'm a retired police detective from Dubuque, helping her out on this."

"Officially?"

"Yes."

Accepting that, Carlson offered his hand to shake, and Keith took him up on it. The grip was bony and strong but didn't show off. About what he might have expected from Lincoln.

"We're devastated to hear about Astrid," Carlson said, in a voice resonant enough for him to have been on-air talent. He took a seat next to Keith, allowing his guest to resume head-of-the-table positioning. "The AP had it this morning."

So Krista's former roommate had made the big time, a little.

Keith said, "I haven't seen the coverage, but I imagine you know at least the basics, probably more. It was a brutal thing and we are committing all of our resources to the investigation."

Smiles didn't come fainter. "All of the resources of a twelve-person department, I understand."

The station manager had access to Google, too.

"Yes," Keith said, "but for a small town, Galena has an exceptional PD."

"With all due respect," Carlson said, with a smile that twitched at one corner of his mouth, "I would think calling in the state police would be advisable. And there are several other options for major crime support."

"Yes, and we're aware of that. I understand your concern, and your vested interest. Astrid Lund was something of a star at this station."

Carlson's head went back; he seemed to bristle at that. "She was a valuable contributor to our news team. We didn't think of her as a 'star,' but as a journalist, and a very fine one."

"My understanding," Keith said pleasantly, "is that she was your top investigative reporter."

"That's true."

"And, also with respect, sir, I am not here to seek your advice on how to conduct our investigation. I will assure you, if it puts your mind at ease, that if we feel we're in over our heads, we will certainly call for help."

"Good to hear." Carlson adjusted his glasses on the bridge of his nose. "But what are you here for? Is there information about this crime that's been withheld, that you might share with us?"

"No. I'm here because Ms. Lund was an obvious target of certain people, and certain elements in Chicago—because of the investigative journalism that's made her a star."

His chin came up, his gaze came down. "From what I understand, from the wire service story, this was a crime of extreme violence. With none of the earmarks of . . . a professional assassination."

"Some assassinations pose as something else. A killing that appears to be the work of a psychopath might be that of a cold-blooded hired killer disguising what he's up to."

He nodded. "So what is it you want from me, Detective Larson?"

"I need to ask you a few questions that I'll record on my phone, if you have no objection."

"None."

Keith got out the phone and placed it between them on the table. "Ms. Lund was working on a story about sexual misconduct, presumably in the workplace. Were you aware of that?"

An eyebrow rose above the black frames. With light sarcasm, he said, "Of sexual misconduct in the workplace? Certainly. But this station has a very clean record in that regard. We've had a zero tolerance policy for that kind of thing, long before doing so became fashionable."

Keith raised a palm. "It may not be in this workplace. I don't think she was necessarily looking into, say, sexual harassment at one workplace, rather that subject, that problem, in general. Possibly as involving various Chicago-area businesses."

He nodded. "I can look into that. I didn't work directly with Astrid, of course, but she did intersect with any number of others on our staff. She was, however, something of a self-contained . . . shall we say, force of nature. Tended to do her own research, pick her own subject matter, clear it with me only when she'd done some preliminary homework, at least."

"Did you know about this story?"

He shook his head. "No. I'm not surprised, in the wake of the #MeToo phenomenon, however, to find Astrid looking into that area. And we haven't done a major investigative piece on it, so it makes sense."

"Anything else she was working on?"

"Not that I know of."

"Something political maybe? Possibly involving the current-day Outfit?"

Carlson seemed amused. "Gangsters, Detective? You are an old-school type. Galena may be frozen in time, but this city isn't."

"Understood. I do have to ask you where you were Saturday evening."

"At a play with the woman I'm seeing now," he said, adding, "my wife and I are separated." He provided the specific information, then Keith asked about the second week in August.

"Out of the country. A vacation in the UK with the same individual." He provided that information, too.

The station manager stood. Keith—knowing he was being dismissed—collected his phone and rose as well.

"I'll make sure any calls to me from you go right through, Detective Larson. Any way I can support you in this endeavor, I will. I would hope you folks in so small a town will soon come to realize that this is bigger than you can handle. If you need me to pave the way for you, say the word."

Carlson opened the door and revealed the PA waiting in the corridor to show Keith out. A huge framed poster of a beaming Astrid Lund was looking over her shoulder.

Soon Keith was following the PA down the narrow hall again, where from a dressing room—larger than most, but its door open just the same—a woman with her back to them called out, "Detective! Could we talk?"

The woman had seen him in the mirror, which was where he saw her now, framed by the traditional backstage lights as if this were Broadway and not a news station.

Rebecca Carlson.

The wife of the handsome Lincoln with whom he'd just spent an unproductive fifteen minutes—the real star of the station, whether her husband liked the word "star" or not.

She wore a dark blue satin robe, her light brown hair pinned up out of the way as she cleaned her face with cold cream. She was forty-something and at her worst, yet astonishingly beautiful.

Looking back at him in the mirror, as he stood in the hall frozen next to the PA who was also in pause mode, she said, "Come in, would you? And close the door."

The PA shrugged at him, and he shrugged at her, then went in, closed the door, and pulled up a chair—not too close to his hostess, just a little to the left of her back to him.

"If you'll excuse me," she said. "I always take the war paint off, after the noon broadcast. I do the morning show and leave it on for noon, and then it's off for the day and so am I. Not a bad way to make a bundle, huh?"

"Not bad at all," he said to her back. He couldn't see much of her face.

"You've been talking to my ex?" she said.

He nodded. "I hadn't been aware he *was* your ex."

"Not final yet, but trust me. It'll take. That's not a divorce either one of us is questioning. No-fault divorce in Illinois kicks in after a two-year separation—'irretrievable breakdown.'"

He said, "Sorry to hear it."

"I'm not. He's a charmer, isn't he? Funny how he knows more than anybody he meets, particularly about whatever it is they do."

"I noticed that."

"Told you how to run your investigation, right?"

"He started to."

"Ah! And you cut him off! Good for you. I hate the son of a bitch. I don't remember why I married him. Job security maybe? Thank God we have no kids. Thank God I'm past that. This is your investigation, isn't it? You just have that look."

"Actually I'm retired. Just consulting. My daughter is chief of police in Galena. I was a cop for a long time, detective in Dubuque."

"Galena is charming. I love Galena. I didn't do it, by the way."

"Didn't do what?"

"Kill the bitch. Sorry. She wasn't a bitch, not really. Just ambitious, which makes me a bitch and a half. It's just . . . well, you'll find out anyway."

"Find out what?"

"That she broke me up with that bastard. Her and my cold-fish husband, although she warmed him up, I'll bet. They had an office affair, didn't you know that? You'd find out soon enough."

"Would he have any reason to kill her?"

"I wish he did. And you'd get him for it. Be nice not to have him around. The minute my ratings slip, my pretty bottom . . . and it's still very pretty, I assure you . . . will be bounced out of here. I'll be looking for work at a small station somewhere. Is there a station in Galena?"

"No. There's a couple in Dubuque."

"Good to know." She was unpinning her hair. "You know, I had a lot to do with her success, Astrid's. It was an *All About Eve* thing. I'm Margo, she's Eve Harrington. You know that movie?"

"I know all Marilyn Monroe movies."

"Ha! Anyway, I helped her climb, then she climbed on me, on her way over. I keep my eye on her, believe me."

"Not anymore."

She was applying some cosmetics now, from her purse. Leaning into the mirror. "I'm sorry. I sound cold."

He said, "Astrid may have been a bitch or Eve Harringbone or whatever. But she didn't deserve to get hacked up by some lunatic, or somebody pretending to be one."

She turned to him. Her personal makeup was perfectly applied, very subtle, just right for a woman her age. Of course, to him forty-something was a kid. And oh you kid . . . big blue eyes, lovely carved features, just the face you want to deliver you the news, good or bad.

"I'm the bitch," she said, "talking about her like that. She was very good at what she did, and she was going places. I don't resent her that—certainly now I don't. And it was my ever-loving ex who made the moves on her, I'm sure."

"He has a motive."

One eyebrow hiked. "Does he? Well, I know she dropped him. She has the ratings to get away with it. What motive? Getting dumped? Even my ex wouldn't carve a woman up over that."

"She was doing an investigative piece on sexual misconduct, presumably in the workplace."

Both eyebrows hiked. "Was she? I heard she was looking into something more dangerous than that."

"What?"

She stood. One nice leg peeked out from the dark blue silk dressing gown. "I'm going to put the rest of my clothes on now. This conversation is over, and I have things to do this afternoon. If you'd like me to answer that question, and really answer it, maybe we could . . . how long are you in town?"

"Probably just tonight."

"Staying where?"

"The Drake."

"Ever eaten at that little old-fashioned bar on the lower level—the Coq D'or?"

"Many times."

"Good. It'll be my treat."

"What?"

"I'll meet you there at seven. Can you wait that long to eat? You have that Midwestern meal-at-five kind of look, but I like you anyway. Now shoo."

She got up and literally shooed him out and the door closed on him.

He looked at it.

Did he have a date?

SEVENTEEN

Krista had returned to Galena High School a number of times as a patrol officer, but this was her first visit in the uniform of chief. Like many former students walking the halls of a school they'd attended long ago, she felt like a ghost haunting the place, particularly since these halls were largely empty. This was an in-service day and teachers were holed up in committee meetings and training sessions, temporary prisoners of their own classrooms.

GHS hadn't changed much. The building dated back to the mid-1950s, but the interior had been updated and renovated over the years. On the fringes of Galena's west side, an educational oasis in a fast-food and Walmart wilderness, GHS was well maintained, with a small, handsome campus serving 260-some students. The local sports teams were well supported by the community, and the school itself was highly rated nationally.

She felt lucky to have gone there.

At a table at one end of the otherwise deserted library, Krista interviewed one by one the teachers who'd attended the reunion Saturday night. All were cooperative and happy to get out of training sessions they seemed to find redundant and committee meetings they appeared merely to endure.

First up was Chris Hope, the drama teacher, handsome as ever in a crisp white shirt and dark jeans, his short blond hair perfectly parted above his dark brown eyes. He sat back casually with an elbow on the arm of the hardwood chair.

Krista indicated her cell phone on the table. "I'll be recording this."

"Fine. Anything I can do to help."

"You're aware this is an inquiry into Astrid Lund's murder."

"I am."

"Are you up for answering a few questions about Saturday night and early morning?"

"Certainly."

"This is an informal interview." Which was her way of saying he would not be read Miranda rights.

His grin was a little uneasy. "I'm starting to feel like a suspect."

"We just need to establish a few things so we can eliminate you in that way, and also to see what you may know or may have seen."

"All right." He shifted in the chair, leaned forward, resting his forearms on the wooden table. "Astrid Lund was a gifted young woman, who in my small way I helped to get off to a start. I was fond of her. You can bet I'll do anything I can to help you here."

"That's appreciated, Mr. Hope."

His grin, a charming thing, lost its uneasiness. "I'm not your teacher now, Krista. You can call me Chris."

"All right, Chris. Before we get into the specifics of Saturday evening, why is it you say you gave Astrid her start? I understand she almost certainly considered you an influential teacher of hers. But she was president of student council before she got into drama, outgoing and very popular already."

He frowned just a little, as if she'd struck him a glancing blow. "She was, but . . . you knew her pretty well, didn't you, Krista? I got the impression you'd been friends since forever."

"That's right," Krista said, a little thrown that the questioning was turning back on her. "Since childhood."

"She was a tubby little thing then, wasn't she? Didn't she blossom fairly late?"

"Yes. But she made up for lost time."

Chris laughed. "Yes, she ran through her share of boys. I don't think she was very popular with some of the other girls. You two had a falling out, didn't you, over that Jerry Ward, boy reporter?"

"Yes." How had the grill-er become the grill-ee?

"Well, you may recall I always went out of my way to talk to students, one-on-one, and see what had drawn them to drama, or music, if they were going out for the musical that the two departments mount together annually. To see what a student hoped to accomplish. To derive from the experience."

"I remember," she said. "I was not outgoing."

"No, you weren't. Not shy exactly, and I would say fairly self-composed. But drama allowed you to express yourself, come out of your shell."

"Astrid wasn't in a shell," Krista said.

"She was as a girl, though, wasn't she? In grade school? In early middle school?"

"That's right. I guess I hadn't really thought of that."

Chris gestured with an open hand. "Well, inside the lovely young woman, who seemed so self-confident, was the unhappy overweight child who often overcompensated for a lack of self-worth. She could speak in public, but it was contrived, artificial, wooden. In drama, we worked toward a naturalness, a composure that, frankly, Krista, you already had. And where did it lead Astrid? To great success as a performer, which is what a newscaster is. That's where it led."

And to her murder, Krista thought.

"Which is why," Chris went on, "her role in *Into the Woods* was a perfect sort of coming-out party for the realized woman she would become—Cinderella."

Krista smiled at the drama teacher. "We'll save why I made a good Little Red Riding Hood for later."

"Why wait? Someone among us may be pretending to be Grandma when she or he is actually a monster."

They both got quiet. Glib conversation had turned into something troubling . . . and accurate.

Krista asked, "Did you have a chance to speak with Astrid at the reunion?"

"Yes, briefly," he said. "A lot of people wanted to talk to her, and I would have liked to've had some quiet, quality time. We did talk about getting together soon—not reunion weekend, but soon."

"Soon meaning . . . ?"

"She said she was working on a story, an investigative piece that would be bringing her back to Galena. She'd give me a call ahead of time so we could arrange a lunch or drink or something."

"What story?"

"She didn't say. Not a hint."

"Astrid left the event rather early."

He nodded. "Yes, I noticed her going. The band was still playing. I don't know exactly when that was."

"When did you leave?"

"Tyler and I stayed around till last call and beyond—mostly in that lounge, but also there's a little area by a fireplace where a lot of the 'kids' sat and chatted. I don't imagine we headed out till well after two a.m."

"Did you see anything at the reunion that caught your attention where Astrid was concerned? An argument maybe? Anything at all?"

"No. In fact, I was struck by how classmates of yours would, frankly, suck up to her. She's kind of famous and was obviously even more beautiful now than then."

"Would you happen to know where you were the second week of August?"

"I do. I don't have to check a calendar or anything. I attended the National Teacher's Council of Language Arts in Atlanta. That covers the language arts as well as journalism, debate, and drama. Anything to do with the written or spoken word. Big affair."

"Did Tyler Dale go along? He's not a teacher, I know, but—"

"He did, yes. Turned his shop over to his assistant manager and went along. During the days, when I was in various meetings and seminars, he went shopping and to museums and films. In the evenings we had . . . I almost said a gay old time."

His grin was a dazzler, and infectious.

"We took in some plays," he continued, "and hit some music venues. Grabbed some great barbecue."

"Was anyone else from GHS at the conference?"

"Yes. Ken—you remember Mr. Stock, teaches English, advisor on *The Spyglass*." That was the school paper. "His wife Mary didn't go along, probably because art isn't one of the disciplines the NTCLA includes."

Ken Stock, who'd been among Krista's favorite teachers, confirmed that.

Sitting where Chris had been, the dark-haired, dark-eyed head of the English department seemed far more somber. He wore a black polo with a red alligator logo, good-looking if not as overtly handsome as the drama teacher.

"Astrid was my editor, you know," he said. "A lot of people, the kids, her other teachers, could see how well she presented herself. That made her a natural for drama, you know, and to shine on the student council. But I was the one who saw her writing ability. Now, she didn't have your artistic flair, Krista."

Krista, flattered, also noticed that when it came to being interviewed, these teachers seemed prone to turn the tables.

"What Astrid had," he was saying, "was a concise clarity of style. And an eye for detail, too. Plus . . ." He smiled, though still quite serious. ". . . she had a real built-in bullshit detector. She could see through people. Knew just what probing question to ask."

"Had you kept in touch?"

"No." Another sad smile. "That's one of the realities of the teaching profession. You cast these kids like seeds into the water. They seldom come back to thank you or catch up, but trust me, Krista . . . it's not expected. That's not why we do this. For praise. For thanks. It's for the satisfaction of getting kids ready to go out into the world."

"Did you talk to Astrid at the reunion Saturday night?"

"I said hello, and mentioned how proud I was of her. She smiled and said something like, 'Wonderful to see you again,' and that was all. She had a lot of kids swarming her. That's natural. Who has gone farther? Next stop would've been national TV, don't you think?"

"I do. What time did you head home?"

"Not till the band stopped playing. Bitter end, I guess. Bittersweet end. Mary and I visited with a few kids, and then headed home."

"Didn't stop in at the bar?"

"No. We're not big drinkers, Mary and I. And we were both pretty tired. It was a long, fun evening."

His wife, Mary, the art teacher, agreed. She looked even sadder than her husband. Attractive, just a tad overweight, she wore a tan pantsuit that went well with her short golden-brown hair and expressive brown eyes.

"I didn't know Astrid well," Mary said. "She had talent, though. A nice eye for color. But she only took the one class, her sophomore year. GHS limits the amount of classes in the arts a student can take—you may recall that. She went into drama and was in journalism, too, but you probably know that. Ken is still the advisor on *The Spyglass*."

"Did you speak with Astrid at the reunion?"

"No. We exchanged smiles from a distance. I'm afraid that's about it."

"Did you witness any awkward encounters or arguments involving Astrid and one of her classmates, or with anyone?"

"No. Quite the opposite. I would say . . . and I don't mean to sound unkind . . . but there was quite some fawning over her. You asked about awkward encounters or exchanges, and while I didn't see any of that, I could tell the young woman was embarrassed by the attention. It's as if . . . nothing."

"What?"

"Well, as if she resented, and that's a harsh word, but she didn't seem to like having people who hadn't been friends coming up to her and acting like friends. Because she was somebody special. Of course, she was. Somebody special."

"I understand your husband attended a teacher's conference in Atlanta. The second week of August."

"Yes, he loves that kind of thing. I'm not as social as Ken, I'm afraid."

"What did you do while Ken was away?"

"Nothing. Well, painted. Watercolor is my passion." She sat forward and gave Krista the saddest smile in the world. "Do you mind my saying . . . how proud I am of you? Did your mother know you'd made chief?"

Mary and her mother had been such good friends.

"Yes. She was gone soon after, but yes."

"That makes me so happy," she said, terribly not.

Next up was Coach Bragg. He was a big, blue-cheeked man who almost overwhelmed the hardwood chair opposite Krista. Inducted several years ago into the Illinois Football Coaches Hall of Fame, Bill Bragg was a legend in this part of the world—his Pirates had won three state 1A championships.

"This is a terrible thing," Bragg said.

The fifty-something coach—his salt-and-pepper butch almost bristling, his thick, wild eyebrows threatening to fly off his face—wore a white sport shirt with a royal-blue-and-white Pirates logo, a little bow-legged buccaneer with an eye patch, a cutlass, a skull-and-crossbones hat, but no parrot.

"I mean," he went on, "that's obvious, but my God, is it sad. And frightening! The things people do to each other."

"How well did you know Astrid? Was she ever a student of yours?"

"Yes, in Driver's Ed. She was quiet. Pretty girl. Guess that's obvious, too. Learned quick. Smart. Didn't panic easy. Lots of kids panic behind the wheel, at first."

"Never took her under your wing?"

"No. Now, Kelly did, Kelly knew her well. You should talk to her about that."

His wife, Kelly, the girls' gym teacher and basketball coach.

"Coach, did you interact with Astrid at the reunion?"

"I never 'interacted' with her in my life. I didn't speak to her at the shindig, or nod at her or anything. We barely knew each other. I noticed people making a fuss. That's it. Still, a fine-looking young woman. What a damn waste!"

Krista knew some man would say that sooner or later. That it was somebody from Bragg's age group was no surprise.

"What time did you and Mrs. Bragg head home?"

"Ummm, I would say around one in the morning. We hung out awhile with your classmates in the lounge there, threw a few back, had some laughs, shared some old times. A lot of those grown men were my boys on the Pirates. Senior year they were state runners-up."

"Would you happen to know where you were the second week of August?"

"I do know. But I'd have to think to be exact about the this-and-that of where we went and what we did. Kelly and I have a cabin on the Mississippi, up in Wisconsin, near Prairie du Chien. Spend our summers there. Beautiful country. Go biking, some nice trails."

She tried to imagine this big man on a bike. "You didn't go on a trip, a vacation?"

"That is our vacation. We just kick back. Talk to Kelly about it. She'll fill you in."

Kelly Bragg, in her vague fifties like her husband, said much the same thing about Prairie du Chien and their cabin on the river. They rarely went anywhere else during the summer. And during the school year, they stole weekends up there, when football and basketball season allowed.

"Do you remember what you did, specifically, the second week of August?"

"Well, I believe that was the weekend we had company. A friend of Bill's, another coach, stayed with us at the cabin, I think. I'd have to check my calendar, but it was in August. Why do you ask?"

This was the first any of the interviewees had inquired about the significance of the second week in August. And the Logan murder had not yet been connected to Astrid Lund's in the media.

"Another classmate," Krista said, seeing no reason to keep a lid on it, "who you may recall . . . Sue Logan?"

"Yes, I remember Sue. She was on the basketball team when you were, Krista. Don't you remember?"

"Yes. Well, she was murdered, too. On the Thursday of the second week of last August. Very similar circumstances."

The hazel eyes grew large and began welling with tears. "How terrible. How perfectly . . . is the same person responsible?"

"We don't know. We think it likely, but we don't know."

"So . . . where we were, what we did, in August . . . you were asking for an alibi?"

Krista thought about how to answer that, then finally just said, "Yes."

The gym teacher sat and stared for a few moments.

Then Krista asked, "Did you speak to Astrid at the reunion?"

She nodded. "Yes. Just briefly."

"What did you say exactly?"

"Just . . . that I was proud of her."

The woman began to cry.

Krista handed her a tissue and waited for a while. Then: "You and Astrid were close, I believe."

"We . . . we were. I guess you could say I was a kind of . . . mentor."

Krista took air in and let it out. Sat forward.

"Mrs. Bragg, I'm going to ask you about something, and if it makes you uncomfortable, I understand. I won't ask you about it again, unless it becomes a necessary element in the investigation."

The gym teacher swallowed. Her eyes were red. "That sounds rather . . . ominous."

"There's a rumor, and it is just a rumor . . . for now . . . that you and Astrid were seen in the shower together, in the gym dressing room."

The woman's face turned white as a blister. But she did not deny it, instead saying, "The girls shower together frequently. On occasion I'm among them. If I've . . . worked up a sweat."

"This wasn't a group of girls. Reportedly, it was just you and Astrid. You were soaping her back. Though nothing overtly sexual was seen, there was a shared intimacy."

Her chin came up, but trembling. "You were one of my girls. Did I ever . . . touch you or say anything to you, inappropriate?"

"No."

"Every girls' gym teacher has these kind of mean things said about her. It's a cruel cliché. I'm a married woman!"

"You would characterize your relationship with Astrid as . . ."

"It was not a relationship! She was a girl who needed support after a . . . after a troubling incident. I joined her in the shower and washed her back and comforted her. This was after an evening practice where she hadn't shown up. Astrid came in late, after all the girls were gone and I was just getting ready to take a shower myself. She came in, crying, and I helped her. Helped her undress. Took her into the shower and, yes, I washed her and I comforted her."

"What troubling incident?"

"It was what you would probably call . . . date rape."

EIGHTEEN

The Coq D'or, midafternoon, was not hopping, which was okay with Keith. Drinks and casual meals shared here with Karen over the years were enough to keep him company, the kind of memories that could warm a cold, windy February day. The narrow, low-ceilinged bar, snugged away on the ground level of the Drake as if to utilize a spare hallway, claimed to have been the second such establishment to open for business the day Prohibition ended. He believed it.

He had two dates here tonight. One was later, with a beautiful woman. The other wasn't.

Keith walked past the low-riding tables with their white tablecloths and red leather chairs and selected a high-backed stool at the long, half-a-wall's worth of bar. An ancient bartender in a black vest, white shirt, and black tie nodded in recognition, though it had been a year since Keith and Karen had last visited.

"Heineken?" the white-haired relic asked.

"No Carlsberg?"

"Still no Carlsberg, sir."

"Heineken."

The bartender went to get that and Keith glanced around. The familiar place comforted him—the wainscoting, the French murals, the red leather banquettes.

The Heineken arrived and the bartender poured it. "Alone today?"

"A friend is joining me."

"Not the lovely lady?"

"Passed away last September."

". . . Life is sweet, life is cruel."

"Who said that?"

"Me."

The two men exchanged weary smiles. They didn't make bartenders like this anymore. Of course, the old boy could be both sweet and cruel himself, as Keith had seen him treat many a customer down the bar with surly resignation.

The man in a trench coat–style topcoat came in looking like a detective, a well-dressed one, which is what he was, and how he intended to look. Lt. Barney Davis of the Chicago Homicide Bureau—some years ago a detective with Keith in Dubuque—might have been Sam Spade in pursuit of a dame or maybe Eliot Ness after a keg to empty, one way or another.

As if that weren't enough, Barney looked a little like Jack Webb, in the fading days of *Dragnet*—a sixtyish, slightly puffy-faced guy who'd seen every awful thing men could do to each other and had traveled from the moral indignation of the young to the contemptuous boredom of the middle-aged.

The homicide detective settled onto the stool. "You know what they charge for beers in this rarefied dive?"

"I'm paying."

"That helps." Then a smile blossomed on the lumpy face and Barney slipped an arm around Keith for half a hug. "You look skinny."

"You don't."

"You're a ways from Galena."

"Astrid Lund was a ways from Chicago. But maybe you can help me see if her murder started here."

Barney sighed. "About five hundred humans got murdered in this town last year. We have about four hundred less detectives on the CPD than we did ten years ago—less than a thousand now—and you think I need a Galena murder to give me something to do? . . . You're supposed to be retired."

"We went over that on the phone."

"I'll say again, you should let your daughter handle this. Be a proud papa. You delivered a bouncing baby police chief. Go about your business, which is no business. And certainly no business of mine."

"Finished?"

"Yeah."

The bartender, waiting for a lull in the conversation, came over and Barney also ordered a beer—a Budweiser. No accounting for taste.

Keith said, "Alex Cannon was a classmate of Astrid's."

The seen-it-all eyes studied him. "Okay, now that's interesting."

"He met yesterday, at his Naperville home, two clients—first, Daniel Rule, contractor of buildings. Second, Sonny Salerno, contractor of . . . contracts."

"Not together, I trust."

"Not together. Well, separate meetings anyway. My question is, are they together, in any way? Or was that just an attorney meeting at home with two separate clients who didn't care to be seen at his office?"

The Budweiser arrived. Barney made a motion to the bartender that meant he'd pour it himself.

"Is Daniel Rule connected?"

Barney asked, as he poured, "You do know this is Chicago we're sitting in, don't you? Not that the Outfit is what it was. You know what the Organized Crime Bureau mostly handles these days? Black and brown gang activity, as it pertains to drug trafficking and local gunrunning.

These Outfit guys, drugs were never their thing, and gambling is all but over—who needs it illegal when the state is in the business? Some bookmaking goes on, sure, and of course loansharking."

Keith knew it was hard to do anything about the latter-day mob, because they had, over the years, wormed their way into unions and legit businesses, restaurants, pizzerias and bars, where they could hide money.

"They still back crews pulling scores," Barney was saying. "Home invasions and robberies and such. So the Outfit isn't dead. But hardly thriving—only when their front businesses start accidentally being profitable. It's like that movie, *The Producers*—where did we go right?"

"So is that the case with Rule?"

"I know the guy a little. From what I see, he's just a very successful construction guy, who not surprisingly's had to swim in some dirty waters now and then, to get the job done. Garbage collecting, real estate, and, yeah, construction are more than fronts—they're going concerns."

"Maybe you see why I think it's suggestive that Rule and Salerno both met with their attorney yesterday."

"Why is that suggestive? Why would those two want the Lund woman dead?"

"You tell me."

Barney drank some beer. "Think maybe the Lund woman was investigating Rule and any mob ties he might have?"

"Or her old classmate, Alex, and his mob ties."

Barney smiled and sipped. "Cannon's a defense attorney. That's not just legal, it's the American way. Everybody gets their day in court, and hired guns like Alex Cannon give it to 'em, if they can afford it. Now, if Lund was getting too close to something . . ."

"The story she was working on was about sexual misconduct."

"What flavor?"

"Well, I don't know . . . I assume sexual harassment in the work-place, on up to actual sexual assault, though I have no idea in what context. But it's not exactly Family Secrets."

That was a notorious case, ten years ago or so, hurting the Outfit, tying major LCN figures to numerous professional killings.

Barney was shaking his head. "This thing doesn't sound like a contract killing. You have these two homicides . . ."

Keith had filled Barney in on the phone.

". . . half a country apart. The tie-in, besides a near identical MO, is both young women bein' in the Class of '09 at Galena High. Both are literally hacked to death. That looks like a psychopath, not a hit."

"Maybe that's what it was supposed to look like."

Barney sipped beer, mulled that. "Maybe. Maybe. What do you want me to do?"

"I'm not somebody who knows this city, not well anyway, and I'm not authorized to work here. Oh, I can flash my Galena badge around, and if it's not laughed off, somebody might want to know what my official status is."

Barney smirked at him. "Which is consultant. To your daughter, who's a small town police chief? Yeah. You got a problem."

"Solve it for me."

"How?"

"We have a banquet hall full of potential suspects to sort out back in that small town. Astrid made a lot of enemies in high school, ten years ago—maybe not worth getting killed over, but tell that to who killed her. This Chicago lead could be important. But I'm not the ideal one to chase it down."

Barney nodded slowly. "So I talk to Rule. Talk to Sonny. Rattle cages some."

"Yes. You'll know, just talking to them, if there's anything to this."

"You mean if my Spidey sense starts to tingle?"

"Something like that. Will you do it?"

"On one condition."

"Name it."

"Go back to Galena. Give me a couple days."

"Fair enough. I'll even pick up another round."

"Yes, you will."

They talked some more, mostly about Barney and his family—wife and two grown kids and half a dozen grandkids—and promised each other to go to some Cubs games together this summer. The third round was on Barney.

Before Keith left the Coq D'or, he made a reservation for tonight with the bartender.

Back in his room, Keith called down to see if he could have his coat and pants dry-cleaned, and get them within a couple of hours. That proved possible. With three beers in him, he decided to have a nap while his clothes were tended to. At his age, he was entitled.

At a little after six o'clock, a knock awoke him, obviously his pressed clothes, and he went to answer it wearing the shorts, T-shirt, and socks he'd been sleeping in.

He didn't open the door wide, of course, but wide enough for Rebecca Carlson to get a good look and have a good laugh. She slipped in past him.

"That's a charming greeting," she said, shutting the door behind her. "I'd hoped to catch you, so I asked the desk for your room number."

He just looked at her. She was tall, particularly in the heels, and still curvy but maybe working too hard at staying slender for the camera. A black wool coat over one arm, she wore skinny blue jeans and a white long-sleeved blouse with lacy touches. Her golden-brown hair bounced at her shoulders; her model-like loveliness would have been breathtaking even if he'd been wearing clothes.

"I got to shopping, then met a girlfriend for a drink," she said in a rush, "and didn't have time to go back to my apartment and dress properly . . . although if we're going to be this casual, I guess I'm overdressed."

She handed him her coat to hang up and went over and sat on the bottom edge of the double bed. "How do you feel about room service?"

"In general?"

A knock at the door proved to be a bellman with the dry-cleaned clothes. Keith traded him a five for them, and signed the bill.

Now that they were alone again, he took a few steps deeper into the room, carrying the plastic-bagged clothes by their hanger. "You mind if I put these on?"

"Up to you, Detective Larson."

"Why don't you call me Keith? I'm starting to feel like we're getting to know each other."

"Before you do that," she said, meaning put on his clothes, "find me the room service menu, would you?"

He did, then got a fresh sport shirt from his bag on the luggage rack, before slipping into the bathroom with the dry cleaning. He ran some water, brushed his teeth, washed under his arms, used deodorant, gargled, spit, turned off the water, and got into the clothes. He looked at himself in the mirror. He brushed the remains of his hair. No time to shave, but . . .

Good to go, he thought.

He emerged a new man, with the sudden realization he was in a hotel at the Drake with a new woman. Her purse was on the made bed—he'd slept on top—and she was on her feet, reading the menu.

"You can't go wrong with the Bookbinder soup," she commented.

"You really can't," he said. The stuff was delicious—tomato soup with sherry and bits of red snapper. Karen had loved it.

"Would you share a salad with me?" she asked. "I like the chopped but I could be talked into the Caesar."

"Chopped is fine. So we're eating here in the room?"

"I think that's best. I think talking murder in public, particularly if you're a journalist, which is what I claim to be, is in bad taste. And some of what we might discuss about the late Ms. Lund . . . well, let's just make it the two of us, okay?"

"Okay."

"How do you feel about a burger?"

"Sure."

"Anything to drink?"

He shrugged. "Does wine go with burgers?"

"If we say so. Merlot?"

"Sure."

"Shall I make the call?"

"Please."

She did.

An area opposite the bed had a coffee table and two modern but fairly comfy chairs. She took one and he took the other.

"It'll be a while," she said of the food. Then, as if little or no time had passed since their earlier meeting, she said, "So. Astrid Lund. You think this story she was working on, about sexual harassment, may have gotten her killed."

"It's a possibility."

"I doubt it. Not at WLG. Where my ex is concerned, at least, she was the aggressor."

"You said Astrid was working on another story? Something . . . 'dangerous'?"

She crossed her legs, which seemed to go on forever. "We're not exactly close, Astrid and myself. Sorry. I keep thinking present tense. The thing is, we were polite and professional at work, but icy anywhere else. I did have my spies out."

"Why spies?"

"She had those washed-out pretty blue eyes on my anchor desk. By TV standards, I'm an old woman, you know. I've held on to my job because the ratings are good and I've gained some local celebrity. On the other hand, I've climbed as high as I'm ever going. You don't get picked up by a network, not even cable, at my age."

He frowned at her. "How old are you?"

"Forty-three. I don't lie to police. But I do to reporters—thirty-seven, I've been giving them lately. Which is old enough."

"Barbara Walters lasted a long time."

Her smile dimpled one cheek. "You date yourself with that reference, Keith. Where were we?"

"A dangerous story."

She shrugged. "I don't know much. It was something to do with what we call the Mafia here in the Windy City, the Outfit, although nobody who lives here calls Chicago the Windy City."

"Pretty windy today, though. What about the Outfit?"

"Astrid was looking into a construction guy out in Oak Brook named Daniel Rule and his supposed connections to the Salerno crime family. Rule wants to run for mayor. That's pretty much all I know."

That wasn't much, but still was confirmation of what he'd suspected. He'd pass that on to Barney.

"Why hasn't this connection been exposed before?"

She shrugged. "Well, a lot of that kind of thing happens in this town. If everybody in the business community who had dealings with those kind of people couldn't run for office, then who'd be left?"

"Honest people?"

"Interesting. I hadn't thought of that."

That was when he realized she was already a little drunk. Not much. A bit.

"Problem, though," she said. "My ex . . . I've mentioned my ex before, haven't I? He's a big booster of Rule, who I understand is a decent sort with some good ideas and good intentions and . . . well, I have a theory."

"Let's hear it."

"That our late lamented diva wanted to work that story up and use it to get my anchor chair. Agree to drop it, if . . . sorta kinda blackmail. But president-slash-station-manager Carlson doesn't want to alienate me, because I'm cooperating on the no-fault divorce. But I'm morning and noon. The five o'clock and six o'clock female anchor is almost as old as I am—Astrid might've been able to maneuver into that."

"What do you know about the sexual misconduct story?"

She shrugged. "Nothing. I heard that's what she's unofficially working on. I also heard . . . well, this is vague."

"Go on."

"I heard that it's the opposite of the Rule thing."

"How so?"

"It's not her angling for anything. She really cared about that story. I think maybe . . . I'm reaching here."

"Reach away."

"I think something bad happened to her once. And she wants to get even by taking on the topic. You know, the #MeToo thing." Her own pretty blue eyes got bigger. "The stories I could tell!"

"Maybe Astrid had stories to tell about her high school days. Maybe that's why she went to the reunion dressed to kill."

"Dressed to be killed, you mean." She frowned. Yes, a little drunk. "Sorry. Not the best of taste, that . . ."

"My daughter says Astrid's ensemble was worth thousands. What kind of money was she making, anyway?"

She laughed. "Sweetie, Cinderella only has to *look* like a princess at the ball! That ensemble would've been rented or most likely loaned to her—she was celebrity enough around here to rate that."

"She pulled up in a Jag."

"Cinderella's coachmen were mice, remember. A rental. One of Ms. Lund's agendas was a pitifully obvious, very sad one—impress her old classmates."

A knock at the door announced dinner, rolled in by a waiter in a white jacket and black bow tie. Keith and Karen had room service here a couple of times. He hadn't known what to tip then and he didn't know now. The smiling youngish man held out the bill for Keith to sign to the room, and Rebecca got up and said, "Let me see that."

The waiter handed it to her, and she said, "Ah. Gratuity's included, I see . . . But let me give you a little extra." She went to her purse, and before Keith knew what was happening, she handed the waiter a hundred dollar bill and a twenty.

The waiter left, smiling even more, and Keith shut the door. Frowning a little, he said to her, "You didn't have to do that."

"Oh, it's such a thankless job. Maybe he's working his way through college."

"He's thirty if he's a day. I was going to sign it to my room."

"I'm sure you were, but I said I'd treat, and I don't go back on my word. Now be a good boy and sit down and shut up and eat."

They didn't shut up as they ate, though. She told him about growing up in Michigan and he did the same about Iowa. The experiences were not dissimilar. After Keith rolled the table of dirty dishes out into the hall, they sat in the comfy chairs and worked on finishing the bottle of wine.

She asked about his daughter, wondering how Krista wound up a police chief of all things. A few mentions of Karen were of course included, but he didn't dwell on it.

She said, "I don't mean to sound maudlin, but I would've liked to have a daughter. Or a son. Too late now. I put my career first, and I have no real regrets . . . at least not till I hear a proud papa like you brag."

"You are having a hell of a fine life, lady. Don't knock it, or yourself."

They finished the wine, and then somehow, later he would try to remember and fail, she was in his arms. They kissed. They kissed quite a few times. Then they lay on the bed, on top of the covers, fully dressed but for their shoes, and they necked and petted. Like those classmates of Krista's once had, not so long ago, really.

He started unbuttoning her blouse, but he was clumsy and she did it for him. She unzipped her jeans. Then she unzipped him. Clothes got kicked to the floor.

She stayed the night, sort of—she was up before five, having to get to the station by six. He heard her in the shower, and he heard her running the water in the sink. Her purse was in there with her. He sat on the edge of the bed, as she had, when he'd been standing in his shorts and T-shirt and socks. He was crying when she emerged and he couldn't hide it.

She sat next to him. She smelled good. Fresh. He glanced at her and she wore no makeup, probably in anticipation of applying it for the cameras.

"Don't you worry," she said. "You're my first."

Now he was laughing with tears on his face. "What?"

"Since the separation. So you didn't catch anything. Just like an early menopausal babe like me can't get pregnant. No harm, no foul."

She gave him a kiss on the cheek.

He said, "My . . . first, too."

". . . How long has she been gone?"

"Six months."

She held him. He allowed his arms to go around her.

"The pressure's off now," she said, smiling at him, close enough to kiss but not doing it. "Think of the fun we'll have next time."

And she slipped out of the room.

NINETEEN

Krista was at her computer in her office when she heard her father's voice as he came in the front way, through the reception area. He paused to chat with dispatcher Maggie Edwards, whose good friend Krista's mother had been. He made Maggie laugh, which was no surprise.

She watched through the window onto the bullpen as her dad paused to say hello to the officers at their desks in their collective U joined by Plexiglas. Pop was in his tan sport coat, brown slacks, and yellow-and-brown tie, all of which looked surprisingly fresh, considering that was what he'd been wearing Sunday, when he took off unexpectedly for Chicago.

As he approached, he waved at her through the window and she smiled and gestured for him to come on in.

He opened the door and shut it, came over and gave her a smile—a kiss, even between father and daughter, seemed inappropriate here—and pulled up a chair to the near side of her desk.

"You either made good time," she said, "or you left pretty early."

It was about eleven thirty.

"Little of both. I only grabbed juice and a Danish, though, so maybe I could treat you to lunch."

"That's a deal. But I fill in for Maggie, as dispatcher, while she takes lunch, at noon. We couldn't do that till she gets back at one. You too hungry to wait?"

"I'll survive. Maybe we can quickly bring each other up to speed."

"Good idea."

They did.

"So," she said, "you had dinner with Rebecca Carlson. Sounds like a date!"

"No, just a regular interview."

"Where did you eat?"

"At the hotel. I, uh, didn't record any of that interview. It was just some off-the-record info about what Astrid was working on."

Krista frowned, just a little. "Well, from what you said, this Carlson woman had her own grudge against Astrid. What was her alibi?"

"I, uh, didn't exactly ask her."

She just looked at him. "For either Saturday or the second week of August?"

He shrugged. "No, I don't consider her a suspect."

"Well, maybe you should. You mind following up with her?"

"Not at all."

"Otherwise, that app I got you for your phone? To record field interviews? You used that?"

He nodded, sat forward. "Yes. Why don't we trade phones, and I'll duck into the conference room and listen to your interviews from Sunday night, and Monday at the school."

They swapped.

He said, "Chris Hope's partner, Tyler—we haven't talked to him yet, have we?"

"No."

"Want me to take that?"

"Please." She gestured to the landline phone on her desk. "I spent the morning making calls, confirming various alibis of my favorite persons of interest. That teacher's conference in Atlanta that Chris, Tyler, and Ken Stock attended? It's legit, and all three were there, all right. And I have two officers checking alibis of less likely suspects."

Her father nodded, leaned back in his chair, folded his arms. "Have you looked into that cabin of the Braggs'? All summer and occasional weekends, huh?"

"I'm sending Officer Cortez to Prairie du Chien to scope that out. And I have the name and contact info of a coach pal of Bragg's who they say was staying with them the second week of August. He lives in Fargo. Probably just call him to confirm. Maybe talk to the Fargo police, too."

Pop nodded. "You called Astrid's parents with the death notification?"

"No. I considered it, since Astrid was a friend, and a classmate, and they know me. But procedure is to inform the family in person. Which in this case would be Naples, Florida. And obviously I couldn't do that."

He nodded again. "So you called the police down there to have them do it. That was the right thing."

She sighed. "Glad you agree. I did speak to Astrid's mom yesterday. Had a nice visit, considering, but of course they are devastated. She was their only child, you know."

"And so much promise. So accomplished. Heartbreaking. When's the service?"

"Saturday. Furlong Funeral Home. They'll be coming up for it, her folks, of course. She'll be buried here. It all seems so . . . I just don't quite believe it."

Her father was gazing past her. "Wouldn't it be sweet to find the son of a bitch before then, and give those poor people some closure?"

"Yes. But I don't have to tell you . . . closure doesn't come so easy."

"No," he admitted, looking at her now. "It doesn't."

He summoned a smile and went off to listen to the interviews.

Just after one, her father returned and gave her back the phone, saying, "Interesting stuff. Didn't get through it all—I'll come back for more this afternoon. Has anybody talked to Jasmine Peterson?"

That was the young woman who'd accompanied Jerry Ward to the reunion.

"No," Krista said. "But I called over to Vinny Vanucchi's and she's working today. How does Italian sound for lunch?"

"Molto bene," her father said.

Soon the Larsons were walking down Main. The day was cold and Pop could have used a topcoat. She was in her thermal jacket with its chief of police patch. A Tuesday this time of year could be awfully dead, but a few hearty tourists were afoot. Most stores were open for the season now, a handful waiting for March.

Main Street in Galena was a crafty combination of old and new, the nearly one hundred storefronts of the redbrick buildings, often dating to the Civil War, housing modern boutiques, art galleries, antique shops, and restaurants. One of their favorites of the latter category was Vinny Vanucchi's.

Up several outdoor flights of aged concrete stairs hugging the building, past a closed-off cobblestone street, then winding through a brick patio of tables with their umbrellas closed, Krista and her father went into the cozy restaurant, where music by Sinatra, Dino, Darin, and the like met you at a deli counter. This floor was mostly kitchen, with a second deli counter around the corner at right, a friendly greeter at his post to lead you through the racks of wines and shelves of salad dressings for sale.

The uppermost floor of Vinny's was expansive, the lowest a sunken nook, past which a short flight of stairs took the Larsons to their preference, an intimate dining room of ten tables with traditional red-and-white tablecloths. All around were winery posters and framed pictures of old-time Italianos, the air nicely heavy with the tangy aroma of marinara.

As luck would have it, Jasmine waited on them, the pretty, slender brunette wearing the white blouse and black trousers of all the waitstaff—"all" being around three, as business wasn't brisk on an off-season weekday.

Pop asked for Auntie Gracie's Sausage Ragu, and Krista, Joey Z's Shells—what they always had—with two iced teas.

Jasmine was smiling throughout, very efficient, but once the order had been made, she dropped the smile and said, "That was so terrible, Saturday night."

It might have been a review of the reunion as entertainment, from a nonclassmate's point of view; but she obviously meant Astrid's murder.

"If there's anything I can do to help," the waitress said, "do let me know."

Krista smiled pleasantly if not warmly. "Actually, there is. You're one of the few attendees of the reunion who hasn't been questioned."

"Oh, I'm not a classmate. I was . . ." She obviously knew Jerry and Krista had a history, and had to work for the right words. ". . . you know, I was just along."

That was suitably vague and even tactful.

Pop said, "We'll be kind of lingering over the lunch, Ms. Peterson. When things get slow, perhaps you could join us. You might tell your manager so he won't think you're slacking."

He had done that in a low-key, nonthreatening way; but she was clearly a little thrown anyway, like most people who offer to help and are then, unexpectedly, asked to actually do so.

"Of course," she said. "Anything."

When Jasmine had gone off to put their order in, Krista said, "When she said 'anything,' I thought she might mean she'd do anything not to have to talk to us."

"She's understandably on edge," her father said with a shrug. "Probably never had a police chief who used to go with her boyfriend want to question her in a murder case."

She smirked at him.

Within a minute, Jasmine was back, delivering a basket of garlic bread. Both of the Larsons dug in, as they were equally convinced the butter-soaked, Parmesan cheese–topped stuff was the best garlic bread on the planet. Then a communal bowl of salad came, full of onions and peppers and cherry tomatoes and tart Italian dressing. It got similar treatment from father and daughter.

And once Jasmine had brought their dishes of pasta, neither detective bothered interrogating the other, all of their focus on the delicious food.

Fifteen minutes or so later, Pop—after making judicious use of a napkin, and pushing away an empty dish—said, "There are things to be said for a small town with a big list of restaurants."

"Yes," she said, "but nobody tops the chef I have at home. I mean, really—sixty-some restaurants and not a single Danish one?"

He grinned, pleased by her compliment, and said, "It is criminal."

They were basking in the glow of a feast that had stopped just short of unpleasantly stuffing them when Jasmine reappeared, not with more food—just the bill. And of course herself.

The cozy dining room had almost emptied out—just one other couple over by the window, with its view of South Main. They were having coffee and tiramisu.

Jasmine stood by the table. "I'm free to talk for a while," she said.

Krista hesitated, thrown a bit herself at dealing with Jerry's latest, uh . . . Jerry's latest.

But her father filled the gap.

With that friendly low-key way of his, Pop said, "Ms. Peterson . . . may I call you Jasmine?"

"Jasmine is fine."

"I should introduce myself. I'm Keith Larson, Krista's father."

"I know," she said, smiling but clearly nervous. "You've been in a few times, and people told me who you are. I know you had a loss not too terribly long ago. I'm very sorry."

"Thank you. Are you a local girl, Jasmine?"

"No. Well, yes."

Krista asked, "Which is it?"

"I'm from Menominee."

That was a village on the nearby Little Menominee River here in Jo Daviess County. Population around 250.

Pop said, "Are you living here in Galena now?"

"Yes. I share an apartment with some girls over Honest John's. I'm saving to go to college. Over in Dubuque. You used to be a police detective there, didn't you, sir?"

"Yes. Call me Keith, or if that doesn't feel right to you, Mr. Larson is fine. I'm sure you're aware that my daughter here is chief of police."

"Yeah. Uh . . . I see the uniform."

If that was a smart-ass remark, nothing in the young woman's tone said so.

"Do you mind," Krista said, "if I record this interview on my phone?"

Pretty eyes tightened. "Is that what this is? An interview?"

"Yes."

"I thought it was called an interrogation."

Pop said, "First of all, we don't use that term at all. Second, you're not a suspect. You just attended the reunion with one of Astrid Lund's classmates."

Krista said, "Who used to date Astrid Lund. They have a history."

"Jerry mentioned that," she said, nodding. She shrugged. "You can record me. Don't you have to inform me of my rights, though?"

Pop said, "No. This is just a short, informal interview."

"Go ahead. I said you could record me."

Krista got out her phone and engaged the app. "Could you give me your name and your contact information—address and cell number."

The waitress did.

Krista went on: "You were at the Class of '09 reunion on Saturday night." She put the date on the record. "Jerry Ward was your date. Is that right, Jasmine?"

She nodded.

Krista said, "Out loud, please. This is just audio."

"That's right," she said. "I went with Jerry. It was his class reunion."

"Did he point Astrid Lund out to you?"

"He did. Said she used to be his girlfriend."

"Did he say anything else about Astrid?"

"Yes, he said he decided she was too stuck-up and dumped her. Back then, I mean."

A lie. Astrid had dumped him. Jerry had always been a would-be fiction writer.

"Did Jerry talk to Astrid at the reunion?"

"I think they said hello."

"Didn't talk otherwise?"

"No, not that I saw."

"Were you separated from him at some point in the evening?"

"Well . . . I went to the restroom."

"When did you leave the event?"

"I think it was pretty late. Two? It was last call, and I was glad."

"Glad?"

"Yeah. It gets really boring hearing people talk about 'old times,' you know, when they aren't your old times. Especially when you're sober."

Krista glanced at Pop, then said, "You were the designated driver?"

"Right. It was Jerry's parents' car."

"So how did that work? He dropped you off at your apartment, and then drove himself home, risking a DUI?"

"He wasn't very drunk." Jasmine looked at Pop, frustrated. "Could I talk to *him*? Alone?"

Krista's father said, "You don't have to talk at all, Jasmine . . . but you're going to have to at some point. Might as well get it out of the way. And you said you wanted to help."

"I do."

"Well, this is my daughter's job. It isn't personal."

"Good. 'Cause he came up with me."

Krista asked, "Up to your apartment?"

"Yes. My two roommates, they were out on their own dates. Their guys don't . . ."

"Don't what?"

Jasmine made a face. "Live at home with their parents, okay? Like Jerry does. Well, anyway, we had the apartment to ourselves."

"So he stayed awhile."

She nodded.

"How long?"

"Till dawn." She shrugged. "In time for his parents to go to church."

Her head lowered. She was embarrassed. Whether this was from making her admissions in front of an older man like Pop, or doing so in front of her boyfriend's former girlfriend, Krista couldn't guess. Maybe both.

Pop said, "Thank you for your help, and your frankness. Jasmine, do you know where you were the second week of August?"

"Sure."

"Where?"

She gestured around her. "Here. Working at Vinny's. Living downtown in Galena. That's a busy time. Lots of tourists. I wouldn't miss that. Really nice tips."

"What about Jerry?"

She shrugged. "I wasn't dating Jerry then."

Pop nodded. "Okay. I think that's all I have. Chief Larson?"

Krista said, "That's all. Thank you very much, Ms. Peterson."

"No problem," she said, and was about to go when Pop said, "Just a moment."

Jasmine looked at him, at least mildly alarmed.

But all Pop wanted to do was give her thirty dollars to take care of the bill and her tip. Then she scurried off.

"So," Pop said, "we better check up on Jerry."

"Not necessary."

"Oh? He has an alibi for Thursday of the second week of August?"

"Yeah," she said.

"What's his alibi?"

"Who's his alibi, you mean."

"Okay. Who's his alibi?"

"Me."

TWENTY

Keith spent the afternoon at the station, at a laptop computer in the conference room, listening to the interviews taken by Krista, Booker, and the other officers on Sunday and Monday. He took notes, and had a few thoughts and questions to share with his daughter, but nothing really new and/or substantial emerged.

Krista, off at four, stuck her head in and asked if he was ready to head home.

"I want to stick with this till around five," he said.

The station locked up to the public at four-thirty, but activity in the building continued. "I'm going to drop in on Tyler Dale around his gallery's closing time. Catch him for a quick interview, unless you already have."

"No, do that, would you?"

"Glad to."

He asked if he could hold on to her Toyota, but she preferred to take it and got him the keys for the unmarked car.

"Use the Impala," she said, "as long as you're working this case with us. Fill it up when need be, keep track of your mileage, and we'll reimburse."

"Decent of you, considering I'm pro bono."

"Anything for you, Pop. You want me to heat up the rest of that sailor's stew?"

"Please. See you at home around six."

They exchanged smiles and nods, and Keith got back to it. He took a few more notes but still didn't feel he had much of anything new. Maybe talking to Chris Hope's partner, Tyler, would be more productive.

The walk from the station to Galena's Own Artworks on South Main took only five minutes, but the temperature had dropped even more and Keith was still without a topcoat. He walked quickly, chasing his own smoking breath, and got to the gallery just as Tyler was hanging the CLOSED sign in the door's window.

Keith raised a forefinger and caught the shop owner's attention. Tyler in his signature black—the usual Tom Waits porkpie hat and vintage music T-shirt (Elvis Costello and the Attractions this time)—frowned for a moment, then recognized Keith, worked up a smile, and unlocked the door.

"You're our police chief's daddy, right?" he said, waving Keith in. Tyler's voice was deep and with a little gravel. Maybe the Tom Waits hat was catching.

"I am," Keith said, as the shop owner locked them back in. "I've stopped in a few times, just to browse. But we haven't met—you're Tyler Dale, right?"

"Right. Christopher said somebody would be around to talk to me. You're it, huh?"

"I'm it."

"More *I'm* it, as in tag. Come along, would you, Mr. Larson? While I lock up in back?"

Like many of the stores on the west side of Main, where the buildings fell to North and South Commerce below, Galena's Own Artworks took up a narrow space that seemed to go on forever. The bright, cheery gallery sported beautiful hardwood flooring, brick walls, and a vintage tin ceiling painted silver-gray. The central space was given over to spin-ner racks of hip greeting cards, the walls home to high-riding framed paintings and prints and low-riding white shelving of craft items. Near the front register was a long display case of funky jewelry, and here and there were bins of unframed, plastic-covered art. The overall effect was fun and eclectic, the wall art a mix of landscapes and more free-spirited styles.

Locking up the rear entrance, Tyler said, "Shall we talk in my office? Or I could treat you to a beer at the Log Cabin, if you don't consider that a bribe. I don't have much help working with me, this time of year, and I could use it . . . a beer, I mean."

"Beer sounds fine," Keith said. "But I'm buying."

They walked back through the colorful shop, pausing at half a dozen paintings of various '80s rock stars depicted with heavy black outlines and bright, unrealistic colors.

"What do you think of my latest mini-exhibit?" Tyler asked.

"Very good," Keith said, not giving away that he'd noticed the art-ist's signature was that of his host.

"They're mine," the flattered artist said. "The Galena landscapes sell better, though. We did sell quite a few of Bowie and Prince, right after they died. Then things slowed down."

"For them especially," Keith said.

Tyler smiled at the darkly comic remark. His mouth was somewhat Jagger-ish and he had pockmarked cheeks that lent him a rough-hewn charm.

They strolled one block south on Main to the Log Cabin, a steak-house with the faux-rustic trappings its name implied and a Rat Pack feel like walking into 1960, including signed celebrity photos up front. The horseshoe bar, beyond which was a dining room, was a favorite of locals. About a third of the stools were taken as a dark-haired waiter of maybe thirty-five, clean-cut in a crisp white shirt with black-and-white-striped tie, was over tending to regulars with cheerful familiarity.

Keith and Tyler found a spot with no one immediately nearby, ordered their beers; this was a Greek steakhouse, so they both had the Hillas. The bartender poured for them as Keith set his phone on the counter.

"I'll be recording the interview," he said.

Tyler seemed to find that off-putting. "What am I, a suspect? I didn't even know that Astrid what's-her-face."

"You're not a suspect. You're not even a person of interest."

Tyler shrugged a shoulder. "Some people find me interesting."

"I'm not surprised. But you were at the reunion Saturday night, and while Chris isn't a suspect either, he did know Astrid. He took her under his wing, encouraged her, when she was a student of his."

"From what I saw of her," Tyler said with a smirk, "she didn't look like she needed much encouragement. Not with those looks, and that poise."

"Agreed. But it sounds like you did notice her well enough to make that observation."

Tyler's voice lowered to a whisper, barely audible above Dean Martin singing "An Evening in Roma" on the Greek restaurant's sound system.

"Well . . . I'll tell you something," he said, nodding to the phone on the counter, "if you turn that thing off."

Keith said, "All right," and paused the app.

Tyler sipped beer, then looked sideways at Keith. "I don't have any reason to think that Christopher ever did anything inappropriate with a student, okay? I want that understood."

"All right."

Now he looked right at Keith, still barely audible. "But what you almost certainly do not know . . . because it's personal, and private . . . is that Christopher, before we got together, over a dozen years ago now . . . had a few relationships, sexual ones, with women."

"He's bisexual."

Firmness came into Tyler's voice, though not volume. "No. He's gay. But when he was younger, he hadn't come to terms with that. So when he'd talk fondly about this Astrid person, I never really read anything sexual into it. He was proud that someone he'd seen potential in had gone so far. He thought she'd make it as an actress, and wasn't he right? Isn't the news just another venue for pretty people who don't stutter to perform in?"

Keith sipped beer. "No offense meant, but you almost sound jealous."

Tyler laughed silently. Had his own sip of the Hillas. "I think anybody in a relationship is always at least a little jealous when their lover talks with dewy eyes about . . . look. All I'm saying is, I'd heard all about how special Astrid Lund was, so I scoped her out. Watched her when we first got to that reunion. That's all."

"Did you notice Astrid talking to anyone in particular? Maybe arguing with someone?" Keith had seen one such instance himself that night, when Astrid and David Landry seemed to be exchanging heated words down the lodge corridor.

But Tyler only shook his head. "No. She didn't mind being the center of attention at the affair, only I don't think she enjoyed being crowded. She wasn't courting that, certainly. I didn't make her for stuck-up, either—just somebody who, once she got there, wished she could duck under the radar and maybe enjoy herself a little."

"Really? Dressed to the nines like that?"

Another single shoulder shrug. "She wanted people to know she was successful. Nothing wrong with that. Human nature, right?"

"How closely did you observe her?"

He batted the air. "Oh, not really all that close. Well, a little, but just when she first came in and got rushed on by the huddled masses. Christopher had a good number of these aging kiddies come up and fawn over him, too—he is a teacher who really likes his students, and they like him back, boys and girls. I think he realized I was getting bored or maybe had my nose out of joint, and he grabbed me and yanked me out on the dance floor. We danced and danced, and I suddenly didn't give a damn about his precious former students, and I don't think he did, either. All in all it was a pleasant evening."

But not for Astrid Lund, as it worked out.

"Okay," Keith said. "That's all I have about that." He indicated the phone. "Mind if we start recording again?"

"No. Go right ahead."

Keith un-paused it. "Do you remember what you did and where you were the second week of August last year?"

Another Jagger-esque smile. "Christopher said you'd ask about that. I hear another classmate of your daughter's got killed much the same way as La Lund. Is that right?"

"Yes. In Clearwater, Florida."

He shuddered. "What a terrible place to die. Well, we were in Atlanta, at a teacher's conference. *There's* a town."

"How long were you down there?"

"At the conference? Oh, four days."

"Could you tell me what airline you took? The particulars of the travel?"

"Well, we took Christopher Hope Airlines! That is, we went by car. We have an Audi. Left the kids with Christopher's folks."

"You drove all that way?"

"Yes."

"Why?"

"Because we like to. We had friends we dropped in on and stayed with, and fun cities along the way. Clubs, music, and so on."

Keith frowned a little. "Isn't August your gallery's busy time?"

"From spring through early fall it's busy. But I have plenty of summer staff and it's not unusual for me to take a couple of weeks' vacation around then. Gotta take advantage of Christopher being on summer vacation. Didn't he tell you we'd taken two weeks?"

"No," Keith said, and he wasn't happy with himself or Krista. This showed how superficial their first round of interviews had been.

Keith said, "Chris's colleague, Ken Stock, was also at the conference. Did he travel with you?"

"No. I assume he flew."

"Did you see him there?"

"Yes, any number of times. We didn't socialize particularly . . . oh, I guess we had lunch once. We're certainly friendly—he's no homophobe. It was a big conference, probably a thousand in attendance from all over the country." Tyler had one last sip of the Hillas. "Is there anything else, Mr. Larson?"

"No." He had finished his beer, too, and the interview.

Keith thanked the gallery owner for his cooperation, and frankness, though much of it had been off-the-record and unrecorded. That teacher's conference needed some looking into. Atlanta to Clearwater and back was not exactly a round trip to the moon.

Just before six they exited the Log Cabin, the world already all but dark, Main Street a ghost town; the two men paused in the reddish blush of the old-fashioned hanging neon (the place had been around since the '40s).

Tyler said, "Let me know what else you might need."

"How about a Blondie painting?"

The gallery owner grinned. "I'll give you my special discount, reserved for police chiefs and their old men."

"Take you up on that."

Snugging on his porkpie hat, Tyler headed left with a big nod and a little wave, turning the corner, likely hiking down to Commerce, where many shopkeepers and employees parked.

Keith started up the sidewalk of the slope that was Hill Street, past the Kandy Kitchen, heading to Bench Street. Behind him came the throaty purr of a car with a good-size engine, making him turn his head and frown—Hill Street was a one-way and this vehicle, bright headlights bearing down on him, was going the wrong way.

The car swung over, just missing a mailbox, and a man quickly emerged from the front rider's side, the engine still going, a vague dark form staying behind the wheel. The lights were so bright as to be almost blinding, but Keith made the car as a familiar pearl Lexus, and recognized too the shape and the BEARS sweat suit even before the Cro-Magnon shelf of the guy's forehead, his blob of a nose and thick scarred lips identified him as Sonny Salerno's guy, Bruno, from Alex Cannon's house on Sunday.

Like the former football player he likely was, Bruno rushed at Keith and slammed him against the brick side of the Kandy Kitchen. They were on an angle and Keith's back was literally to the wall.

Big hands took hold of his sport coat and bunched the cloth—so much for dry cleaning and pressing—and a face unleashed garlic breath on Keith in a cloud of human exhaust, thanks to the cold.

"You're on the wrong track, asshole," the sandpapery voice advised.

"Let go," Keith said calmly.

Bruno didn't let go. Instead he shook Keith like a naughty child, then pushed him back hard against the brick. "Mr. Rule and Mr. Salerno and Mr. Cannon, they got nothing to do with anything. Got it?"

Keith reached down with his open hand in a cupping motion and, gripping between his assailant's legs, squeezed hard and twisted. The assailant's head went back, his eyes going wide and skyward, and he howled like a werewolf hit by a silver bullet, reflexively letting go of Keith, who slipped to the right and grabbed at the brute's back, taking two handfuls of sweat suit and shoving him hard into the brick wall, face-first.

The guy didn't go down but just staggered back a step and stood there, his face bleeding, his nose mashed even more than before, and Keith did what any brave man would do in such a situation.

He ran.

Ran up the sidewalk, with Bench Street beckoning. But footsteps on the pavement echoed from behind him, and somebody tackled him. Facedown on the sidewalk, Keith felt strong hands grip him, then flip him over. A new cast member glowered down, younger, with long dark hair and wide-set eyes in a round face that didn't go with a trimly muscular fat-free build, in jeans and a CUBS sweatshirt. Just in case he hadn't figured out from whence these two came.

Bruno, bloody but unbowed, came lumbering up toward them, footsteps slow and heavy on cement, telling Keith things had taken a very bad turn.

"I'm a cop, damnit!" he sputtered at them.

"Yeah, we know," the new guy said.

And started kicking him.

Where Keith had fallen left room for the guy whose family jewels he'd briefly confiscated to start in kicking on the other side, getting it in the ribs from both men on both sides. For a guy still in pain, Bruno made a pretty good showing. His kicks damn near kept pace with the new guy's.

In between kicks, they offered advice: "Stay out of Chicago, ya bastard!" was the general theme.

Keith was just wishing he could pass out when headlights washed over him again, this time from the top of Hill Street, coming around from Bench. A siren started and the kicking stopped. He heard but didn't see his attackers scramble for their waiting Lexus, their heavy quick footsteps like scattered gunfire.

Then more footsteps and voices: "Police! Hold it right there! Get those hands up!"

Keith wondered if gunfire would follow, but it didn't. He closed his eyes. He was almost asleep when Booker's voice said, "We have your friends. This should be a pretty story. Meantime, an ambulance is comin' for you. You need a checkup, son."

"What . . . what are you doing in uniform?"

"My turn to ride patrol. We all got to take a turn, except for your child. She's special."

"I . . . I always thought so," Keith said.

Another siren was screaming.

So were his sides.

Then everything went blessedly black.

TWENTY-ONE

You are not anxious to do this.

Well, that's not exactly right. You are anxious, in the sense that anxiety is a low fluctuating hum beneath your surface calm. You are prepared to do this only to protect yourself. You really have no wish to hurt her. The memories with this one are too fresh. Too sweet. Too vivid.

But you will probably have to do it.

And, you tell yourself, several other important functions may well be served. Confusing the issue is one. Throwing suspicion elsewhere is another. Sentiment cannot be allowed to defeat self-preservation.

First, you must check on the person to whom you hope attention will be drawn. Is he at home tonight? That could prove a deciding factor. If he is with her, or is planning to meet her when she gets off work, you would have two people with which to deal, simultaneously . . . and that would not do.

Your hope is that he will be at home, that is, the home of his parents, in the basement apartment they have provided him. The house is at the end of a cul-de-sac on Bluffwood Drive, barn-shaped but with modern touches against a wooded backdrop. You park down the street, walk to where two houses have no lights on and then cut between them, to work your way through the trees and around to the barnlike structure's nicely landscaped backyard.

Staying low, you are able to peek in a window into the finished basement. There's a massive wall-screen TV, and a big open area with comfy chairs and a couch arranged for viewing. But against the far wall is a single bed and a dresser; also a desk with a computer on it. Seems to have been a family room until it was turned into this studio apartment.

Its inhabitant is sitting on the couch with his feet on an ottoman. He has a can of beer in hand, wears a T-shirt and jeans, no socks. Next to him is an open bag of Sterzing's potato chips. He would appear to be in for the evening.

Good.

Even better is that the rest of the lights are off in the house and there's no car in the drive or the garage. The parents and their Chrysler are nowhere to be seen.

Perfect.

You drive back to downtown Galena, park on Commerce, and walk up the slope of Washington Street to South Main. It's after eight and, with the stores closed and few restaurants or bars at this end of Main, things are very quiet. Not many cars parked on the street; traffic's light.

And it's only going to get quieter.

You take the old concrete stairs by the narrow closed-off cobblestone street, to the right of which is a modest park-like area, and go up to the patio of Vinny Vanucchi's. No one around, but lights are on in the restaurant. They don't close till nine.

You go in. Take a left to go down the short hall to the restrooms. You duck into yours, relieve yourself, wash your hands. You look at yourself in the mirror. It's you. Normal. Nothing shows. You check your hair, brush it back in place, and smile at your reflection. Not pushing it. Just friendly.

Walking past the little unattended deli counter, you find the greeter, the thirtyish assistant manager who you know a little, leaning at the station where he seats guests. Another deli counter, also unattended, is at right, its low electrical hum a manifestation of your anxiety.

The restaurant is fairly empty. Dean Martin is singing "Sway." Somebody in white is working in the kitchen. The sunken wine-cellar nook at left that you pass has both its tables empty. Up the stairs your host pauses at the bottom of the stairs to the main dining room, from which there is no noise at all. You are taken into the cozy dining area that you like best and are seated by the faux fireplace in the corner. By the window onto Main, a middle-aged couple are having a late dinner. They are the only other diners.

Jasmine appears to be the entire waitstaff at this hour, late in a slow day. She comes over, looking surprised to see you, her expression falling, but then picking itself up into something pleasant that could be called a smile.

"Alone tonight?" she asks.

She is pretty as ever, her medium-length brown hair framing her face beautifully. You feel a pang and it's not hunger. Well, really, it kind of is. There are hungers and there are hungers.

"Everybody at home but me has the flu," you say.

A real smile. "I sure hope you're not contagious."

"No, I've already had it. You're perfectly safe."

She has a menu for you, but you say you don't need it.

"Rocky's Ravioli," you say.

"Your favorite."

"No."

"No?"

"You're my favorite."

Her smile is gone but a frown hasn't replaced it. "Don't say that. It's cruel."

Sammy Davis is singing "Something's Gotta Give."

"I don't mean to be cruel," you say. "It's just that . . . I've missed you. I am not coming on to you! Just telling you. I've missed you."

"Yes," she said, cheerfully, "it's nice seeing you, too. I'll bring your bread and salad."

She goes off to do that. The middle-aged couple are finishing up. After Jasmine returns with the bowl of salad and basket of bread, she goes over and gives them their check, then disappears.

In a few minutes, when you are still just getting started on your bread and salad, she returns and takes the middle-aged couple's money. A little while later she brings them their change, and you are done with the salad and bread.

You only eat half of what she brought. That low hum inside you means your stomach might not like any more.

You sit and think. Ponder. Consider. You may not have to do it, after all. She seems friendly. She seems not at all scared, though you would imagine by now she has reason to be. Your belly seems to be handling the rich buttery garlic bread and the tangy Italian salad. You even eat a yellow pepper.

You are doing fine.

Bobby Darin sings "Call Me Irresponsible."

She brings your order of ravioli—a half dozen good-size pasta puffs filled with ricotta cheese; the marinara they luxuriate in is excellent. You ordered this because it's your favorite all right, but also to take it easy on your stomach, which is not made of cast iron. Neither are you. You are human. You once felt something for this girl. You still do maybe.

Maybe you won't have to go through with it.

While you are eating, Jasmine comes in and clears the middle-aged couple's table. No busboy is working this evening. When she bends over, her slender shapely figure reminds you of the needs that drive you, needs you can't help, needs you must respond to or you might just go mad.

When you are finished, eating only half of the serving, Jasmine returns, brings the check, and asks if there's anything else.

"I would like a glass of white wine," you say. "Chardonnay. The Main Street."

"From California. Good choice."

"Why, is that your favorite?"

She smiles a little. "One of them."

"Why not sit and talk? You'll be closing, in what . . . twenty minutes. I don't see any other customers."

"No. I'd imagine you're my last."

"If Tony spots you," you say, referring to the assistant manager who seated you, "you can scurry off like a good girl."

"I . . . I have to clear the table first."

You say fine, and then give her two twenties. "Settle up for me later, and keep the rest."

She nods, or you think she does—it's barely perceptible. She clears the table.

So you sit awhile and wonder if she'll disappear with your money. Maybe Tony will show up with your glass of wine.

But it's Jasmine who comes, bringing a bottle and a glass. She sets it before you, and takes the seat beside you. Then she fills the glass all the way, which is what Frank Sinatra is singing. You sip. Then she looks around surreptitiously and does the same—an under-drinking-age girl, stealing sips. How much sweeter the wine tastes because of that.

You speak very softly. It's barely audible above "Ol' Blue Eyes." You tell her how much you miss her. How often you think of her.

"I think of you, too," she admits.

"That makes me happy."

"But I think we both know it was wrong. You told me so yourself. You told me how wonderful it had been, how much you'd cherish the memories. But that we would have to go our separate ways. You were kind about it. Sweet, even. But it hurt. Do you know how much it hurt?"

You put sadness in your smile. "Wasn't it Roy Orbison who said, 'Love Hurts'?"

". . . I think it was Nazareth."

She steals a sip. Yours takes its time.

Then she says, "We haven't spoken since then. Except when you and your family were here and I took your order. Do you know how hard it was for me to see you living a life like that without me? But at the same time . . . how could I deny you that? No. I was in the wrong. I made the first move."

They always did. They always thought they did. You were really good at maneuvering that. Which always paid off, when it came time to talk about blame.

"I'm not here," you say, after a sip of wine, "to start things up again . . . as hard a reality as that is to face. You have a new love in your life. I saw you at the reunion."

She shrugs. "We're not real serious yet. Getting there, maybe, but . . . not like *we* were. Maybe that'll happen. I know I haven't really been in love since . . ."

Her lovely brown eyes are swimming with tears. That's good! That's perfect.

You consider touching her hand, but think better of it. If Tony should peek in, and saw that, you would have to call it off. They trade sips.

"Sweetheart," you say, "I just had to talk to you because . . . well, you've been much on my mind."

"I have?"

"You have. After what happened to that reporter from Chicago, Astrid Lund—"

"She was from here, you know. One of the girls I room with had a sister who went to school with her. She was on TV in Chicago, I guess, really kind of a big deal."

"Yes, I know. I wanted to make sure you weren't too upset about it."

"Why would I be?"

"Well, that boy you're seeing, I don't know if you know this, but he used to date her. The dead girl."

When she was living.

"I knew that," Jasmine says. "But that's old news."

You almost smile at that—Astrid the big-time broadcast journalist . . . old news.

"I think," you say, "that everyone at the reunion has been questioned by the police. I know I was."

"Me, too!"

"Oh?"

"Earlier today. Right here. Police chief and her father."

"I hope you weren't too alarmed."

"No. It was just a matter of giving them . . . I guess you'd say an alibi for Jerry."

"He was with you after the reunion?"

She seemed embarrassed now. "Yes, I, uh . . . we spent the night."

"You're not just saying that to make me jealous."

"No! No. You didn't have anything to do with it. Uh . . . that sounded wrong. I didn't mean anything by it. But you must know I've gone on with my life. I had to. And I've never told a soul about us. Not a soul."

You sip wine. "The age difference, I'm afraid, would have people judging us."

She sips wine. "That's what I think. It's not fair. So what if I was sixteen? Some places people marry younger than that!"

Yes, but seventeen is the age of consent in Illinois. You'd been all too aware of that, but not enough for it to matter.

She asks, "Is your . . . situation at home better now?"

"Not really," you say. "But I have to think of the bigger picture."

"Oh, I know. I don't blame you. I really don't."

"Good." You put concern in your expression. "Really, I just wanted to make sure this horrible event hadn't upset you terribly."

"I don't consider what we had to be horrible at all!"

"I'm not talking about us. I'm talking about what happened to the Lund girl."

"Oh. Well, yes."

Again you trade sips, hers cautious, yours not.

"By the way," you say, "did anyone see you and Jerry together after the reunion? I mean, if you'll forgive me for snooping, where did you . . . wind up?"

"My apartment. Over Honest John's Trading Post? But my roommates weren't around."

"Not even the next morning?"

"No. I know how to be discreet. You know that."

She has her last sip of wine and says, "Well, better say good night. There are a few things I need to take care of before closing."

Dino is singing "Arrivederci Roma."

You gesture to the sound. "What he said."

That makes her smile.

She is talking to Tony at the register by his station when you pass, nodding to the host, but not acknowledging Jasmine, who does not even glance at you. She was right—she always was good at discretion.

You slip outside.

The night is cold. Colder. You have a coat on, but not the coat you need. You move the car, parking it on Bench Street. You go around to the trunk. You glance about—nothing around but the rear of stores and the front of churches, neither doing business right now. No traffic at all.

You pop the trunk. Exchange your coat for the black hooded raincoat. Climb into it. Again, it's a new one, the previous one discarded in a dumpster in Dubuque. You take out the fresh pair of kitchen gloves and snug them on. You're getting used to the feel. The butcher knife you had not needed with Astrid is here for you now.

You shut the trunk and head down the concrete stairs. The world is not just cold but empty and almost silent, just some distant bar noise. You are at Main now. You tuck into the trees of the park-like area adjacent and wait as a couple of cars glide by. Through the trees you have a view on Vinny Vanucchi's. You hear a door open and a good-night exchange between Jasmine to Tony, clear yet distant in the chill.

You rush across the street.

Along the side wall of Honest John's Trading Post a wrought-iron stairway with wooden steps rises to the door to the apartment where Jasmine and two other girls live. You know that already. You do your homework.

You rush up the steps, your running shoes making a little noise but not loud, not echoing. At the landing where her apartment door awaits, you tuck yourself into the recession. You wait. Not long.

Because she comes up just as quickly as you had but with no worry about being heard. Her feet are gunshots—she's in shoes not sneakers—and you count her steps, because you know how many there are. Homework.

And when she reaches the landing, you raise the knife and jump out and bring the blade down.

But without her in front of you, to judge, you only slash the sleeve of her red thermal jacket. There's enough street light conspiring with a nearly full moon to show you her face as her eyes go so wide they might have fallen from her face, dark brown centers and stark white in an almost as white face, her mouth open in a silent scream.

She reacts quickly and well, you have to hand her that, turning and running down those stairs and by the time she reaches the sidewalk she *is* screaming. It resonates through the canyon of the facing buildings. You are close behind her but not close enough to strike, though as she runs across the street, she pauses, whether to duck any car that might be coming or to flag one down, only there isn't any car, and when she starts running again, she stumbles a little.

Then you are right behind her and you bring the knife down once, hard, and it plunges deep, and when you withdraw it, red spurts from the red jacket, as if the jacket itself were bleeding. She goes down, half in the street, half on the sidewalk, and she isn't dead yet, her motions like a swimmer trying not to drown, her back to you and you are in a way glad, because you loved this girl, and part of you still does as you plunge the blade in another five times, and she stops swimming.

TWENTY-TWO

The sprawling ultramodern Midwest Medical Center on the outskirts of Galena on Highway 20 West had, a dozen years ago, replaced the much smaller Galena-Stauss Hospital.

For a police chief like Krista, the Medical Center was unquestionably a real boon to the community. But she also found it a little over-the-top, from the lobby's high vaulted ceiling and indirect lighting to the self-noodling mahogany baby grand and sweeping ceramic-tiled staircase leading to a "family meditation" room. The modern design and mission-style trappings of the overthought facility might have been comforting to her if her mother hadn't died here.

Not that Mom hadn't received the best care—Krista herself had recommended the Medical Center to her father and mother over the Dubuque options, in part to be closer to her mom but also because it was so highly regarded.

But she was worried about Pop. Booker Jackson had called and said "no worries, everything's fine"—her father had been assaulted by two "Chicago goons" (now in custody and jailed) and taken to the ER at the Medical Center. Her first reaction, past the initial alarm, was relief—she knew he'd receive top treatment there.

When she was on her way to the hospital, however, Booker called again to say her father had been treated and admitted to a room for an overnight stay and observation. Which on the face of it was fine. The patient "suites," as they were called, were the most attractive, spacious hospital rooms Krista had ever seen.

Her mother had died in one.

Krista worried about the psychological impact that might have on Pop. She told herself she was being silly, but then she thought about him sitting in his comfy recliner in the ranch-style on Marion Street with a gun barrel in his mouth.

As she slipped into his room, closing the door behind her, Pop appeared to be sleeping. She was relieved to see he was not on an IV. The "suite" was exactly like the one Mom had been in—all shades of yellow and green with hardwood flooring, a wood-paneled wall behind the sizable hospital bed with its country-style quilt; above the bed a framed Galena landscape, a hot air balloon floating over the town. A lime-colored recliner sat in a corner, a green-and-yellow couch stretched beneath a big window, blinds shut.

She pulled up a hardwood visitor's chair as quietly as she could and sat beside the bed, her father on his back but his face angled toward her, eyes closed.

"It's quiet out there," he said. "Too quiet."

She laughed softly. "You're such a cornball."

He opened his eyes and smiled at her. "You should see the other guys."

"You don't look so bad." She was on her feet now, at his bedside.

"You haven't seen my ribs."

She leaned in. "How bad, Pop?"

"Broke one and I was lucky at that. Both those SOBs were kicking me in the sides."

"I'm so sorry . . ."

"Don't apologize for them. Anyway—maybe I deserved getting kicked."

"Why is that?"

"Going around Chicago, poking into politics and dirty dealings."

She gestured behind her, toward Galena. "Booker has both of them locked up. He says he's going to look into this himself."

"Tell him I have a Chicago police contact for him."

"Will do. Your friend Barney?"

"My friend Barney."

"So does this mean you're on to something?"

His eyebrows went up; even so, his eyes looked barely awake. "You mean, are one or any combination of Alex Cannon, Daniel Rule, and Sonny Salerno involved in these killings? Unlikely. I just got warned not to poke into their business. I doubt your classmate Alex knows anything about it."

"Might be able to embarrass all of them, though. And those two strong-arms will do some time. Assault charges. Beating up on a Galena cop who came asking questions."

"Beating up on me? Sounds kind of schoolyard."

"Well, 'schoolyard' is closer to our case. Something ten or more years ago, involving my classmates, sparked these murders, don't you think?"

"No argument."

"Even with you getting leaned on, hard, the idea of a professional killer being responsible for the Sue Logan and Astrid Lund homicides, playing psycho as a sort of cover-up? . . . It's just too far-fetched."

"Smart daughter I got."

"They're keeping you overnight?"

"Yeah. They took some X-rays. Gonna keep an eye on me. Should be out of here in the morning."

"Good."

"Something we haven't talked about."

"Oh?"

"Crank this thing up."

"You sure?"

"Yeah. Not all the way, just enough."

She did as she was told. He winced and smiled at her at the same time.

Then he said, "In Chicago, I looked over the complete case file that cop Hastings in Clearwater sent. About the Logan homicide. I've been mulling it ever since."

"And?"

"In both instances, the killer had been known to the woman."

"You sound sure of that."

"Two cups of coffee at Logan's, two cups of tea at Lund's. He or she was invited in. Takes the time to wash the cups out in the sink, after each crime. Logan answered the door and was stabbed where she stood. Lund allowed the killer in and on leaving, he or she placed duct tape on the latch to reenter."

She was slowly nodding. "Both had a friendly conversation with the victim, left . . . and returned."

"That seems to be the case."

"Why would it go down this way, do you think?"

"If both women knew the person, and opened the door for him or her, the killing could have taken place right there and then. But the washed-out cups, and bloody footsteps leading to and away from the sink, revealed by luminol, indicate a pre-kill visit that required some cleanup."

"Why the pre-visit, though?"

Pop's eyes narrowed. "If something in the past—something bad—is at the root of these homicides, perhaps the killer wanted to determine whether the victim needed killing."

She was nodding again, quicker now. "People reminisce at class reunions. Who they talk to, and what memories they're inclined to share, could matter."

"Could really matter here. And two . . . two women are dead. So whatever . . . whatever that bad thing is they . . . they share it."

She could see he was fading. Shouldn't have allowed him to talk so much. This visit had gone on long enough.

She asked him, "How much are you hurting?"

"Right now not much. I'm on really good drugs. But I'm . . . I'm taped up like half a mummy."

"Well, get some sleep . . . Daddy."

He smiled at her. "That I can manage."

She glanced around. "Does it . . . bother you? Being here?"

He knew what she meant. "No. When I think of your mom, in this setting? She's smiling."

Krista nodded. "Know what you mean."

"Now, if they wheel me into the ICU, I just might get depressed."

She laughed gently, gave him a kiss on the forehead. "Goofball."

When she was at the door, he called out to her. "Honey?"

"Yes?"

"Don't go over to the sheriff's office."

That was where the holding cells were. Across the street from the PD, in the massive, mostly old Courthouse and Public Safety complex.

"Let Booker handle it," he said. "You've had a long day. Go home and get some sleep. We have things to do tomorrow."

"Now you're ordering the chief of police around?"

"I'm telling little Krista Larson. Do as your daddy says."

She saluted and, in her best Charlie Chan's number one daughter–style, said, "Okay, Pop."

Ten minutes later she was pulling her Toyota into the brick drive at home. She got out, locked the car with the fob, then walked over to the back door, the kitchen entrance, which both she and her dad almost always used.

The front porch—with its view of the downtown, broken by church steeples, and the river beyond that—was for sitting and taking it all in . . . at a different time of year. But soon enough it would warm up and she and Pop would be sitting in rockers with iced tea or lemonade or more likely Carlsbergs.

She was unlocking the door when the male voice startled her.

"Krista!"

He came walking up from the street, first in shadow from a tree, then distinct in the combined glow of moon and street light. His car was parked across the way.

Josh Webster.

Jessy's Josh. Ambling toward her in a blue sweatshirt with red letters (ALL AMERICAN) over white ones (POPCORN STORE), tan khakis, and white sneakers. He came up to her and she knew at once he and his crew had made a batch of cheese corn today.

"You got a few minutes?" he asked shyly.

He had a nice half smile and even now, smelling of his business, borderline pudgy, this remained the handsome guy with dark blue eyes and blond hair who had made many a GHS girl's heart flutter. Including a cheerleader named Jessica Dolan.

"Sure," Krista said. "What's up?"

He nodded toward the house, frowned just a little. "Is, uh . . . Mr. Larson home?"

"Not right now," she said, and for some reason didn't go any further.

"Good," he said.

"Good?"

"This is private. Personal. I mean, you can tell him, if you like. That's up to you. But I think it'd just about kill me to have to sit and tell you with him listening in."

"Starting to sound serious, Josh."

"It kind of is," he said, and shrugged. He seemed embarrassed. Or was he . . . ashamed?

Suddenly she was glad the Glock 21 was on her hip. Maybe that was stupid—this was Josh, for Pete's sake!—but what her father had told her was fresh in her mind. That the killer probably visited his victims in a friendly way before calling back later with a butcher knife.

She went to the door and unlocked it.

"Go on in," she said, gesturing for him to lead the way.

Soon they were sitting at the same end of the table where she and her father took their meals.

"Can I get you something to drink?" she asked. "I have some Coors Light I'm trying to get rid of. And Carlsberg is the house favorite."

He smiled a little, her friendliness seeming to put him at ease some. "I'd take a Coors Light off your hands."

She got it for him, nothing for herself. Then she sat, resting her left hand on the table and keeping her right hand in her lap. Near the holstered Glock.

He gulped a couple of swallows. He was looking straight ahead, not to his left where she sat. He rarely blinked. His mouth moved around, like he was trying to say something but his lips were glued shut. In the silly sweatshirt, he looked like a big kid.

Finally he said, "There are some things you should know."

"I could stand to know a lot of things," she said with a smile. It was a remark that would work if this were about nothing. But she already thought it was about something . . .

He said, "Some of what you need to know? . . . I don't want you to talk to Jessy about. If you can manage it. I mean, if you have to . . . if for some reason you think it's necessary . . . okay. I understand. You got my go-ahead. But only then. Only then."

What the hell was he talking about?

"I follow," she said, as if she did.

He sighed. Then blurted: "I went out with Astrid, end of junior year, and over the summer. Maybe you remember."

"I think so." Keeping track of Astrid's romantic activities was tough at the time, let alone reconstructing them ten years later.

He swigged Coors Light. "Well, I, uh . . . it got serious."

"All right."

His eyes swung to hers. "I mean . . . real serious."

"Okay."

He looked away again. "Luckily I'd been saving up. I worked summers at a gas station. I wanted a car. I had a car, an old one, my dad bought me, but . . . I wanted something really cool. I mean, I was kind of riding high back then. Football team, basketball, too."

She was starting to understand, or anyway she thought she might. "Go on."

Another swig. "So, uh . . . hell. Damnit. This is harder than I thought. And I *thought* it was going to be hard!"

"You got Astrid pregnant."

He looked right at her. His mouth dropped like a trapdoor. "How . . . how did you know?"

"You two were real serious. Luckily you had money saved up. You gave her money to take care of it."

He gazed at her, astonished. "That's right. Are you psychic?"

She almost said, I'm a detective, but instead said, "No. It just makes sense."

"And do you know what it means?" He didn't wait for her to answer that, though she could have. "I paid for an abortion. I took a child's life! A child of mine!"

"Let's not go there," she said. "Let's go to the real problem."

He said nothing.

She said it for him: "Jessy. She doesn't know, does she?"

He shook his head. "No." He kept shaking it for a while. His eyes were downcast. When they came up, and swung to her, they were haunted. Not red from crying. Not tearing up. Haunted.

"Senior year I started dating Jessy," he said quietly. "We'd known each other for a long time. Since youth group at Saint Mary's. We were friends who got to be more than friends, but it was based on that. Knowing each other forever, I mean."

"You got married right out of high school."

He nodded. "Jessy was pregnant. I think you knew that. I think everybody knew that. But there was no question that I wouldn't marry her. I loved her then and I love her now. We have wonderful kids. I put my family first. Don't I?"

She knew two things about Josh: he put his business first; and he was apparently a fertile sucker.

But she said, "Of course you do."

"Even now," he said, "it would break her heart to know what I did. That I paid for Astrid's abortion."

If her right hand wasn't below the table near her Glock, she'd have patted his hand. "Jessy would stand by you. You must know that, Josh. Anyway, it was a long time ago. She'd forgive you."

He was shaking his head again. "She is such a devout Catholic. I was always more just a half-ass of a one. She would say she forgives me. But she wouldn't. She wouldn't leave me. Because she can't. God wouldn't let her."

Now he was tearing up.

Krista said, "I won't pretend to tell you I know exactly how she would react. I know her, she's my best friend, but I don't know her like you do. But I think she'd be an adult about it. And I promise you, Josh . . . this won't come out unless it's absolutely necessary."

"Thank you. Thank you, Krista. Bless you."

At least he didn't add, "My child."

"You okay, Josh?"

"There's, uh . . ."

"Yes?"

"There's more."

What was this, an infomercial?

His shame gave way to embarrassment again. "We told you we were visiting Jessy's sister and her husband. And we were."

"Okay."

"What we, uh, didn't tell you . . . and should have, because you wouldn't have to look very hard to find out . . . is Jessy's sister and her husband have a time-share in Florida. And that's where we were. With them. Not at the Timber Lake cabin, like I made it sound."

". . . Where in Florida is the time-share?"

"Saint Petersburg. That's close to Clearwater, isn't it?"

"Yeah. Very."

He sat forward. "But my in-laws, they can vouch for us. We were with them every day, every evening that week. Just ask them."

"I will," she said.

Her phone vibrated in her pants pocket. She answered it: "Yeah."

Booker again. "We have another one."

"Another beating?"

"No. Another one. A murder. That waitress. Jasmine Peterson."

Her stomach fell. ". . . Same MO?"

"Pretty much. You know that little park off Main? She was killed and dragged there. She got off at nine and that's close to her work. So it must've been around then. It's, what . . . ten-something now."

"On my way." She clicked off.

Josh was just sitting there, apparently oblivious.

She asked, "Were you waiting long for me, Josh? Out front?"

He shrugged. "Maybe half an hour. That's okay. I was collecting my thoughts."

So even if Josh was the killer, she didn't figure she was in immediate danger—his presence here might mean he was establishing an alibi.

"I have to go," she said.

Josh chugged the rest of his beer and went to the door, opened it for her.

"After you," she said.

TWENTY-THREE

Keith was riding in the front seat—which was a good thing, since the back was caged in—of a Dodge Ram four-door pickup, white with GALENA POLICE markings. He was in clothes his daughter had sent over, a CUBS sweatshirt, jeans, running shoes, and lined jacket. Behind the wheel was Patrol Officer Cortez, a short, sturdily built attractive young woman in her midtwenties.

This was Wednesday morning, cold and clear, and Keith had been picked up by Cortez (sent by Krista) at Midwest Medical Center, after a long wait for a doctor to look him over and a nurse to have him sign all the necessary release documents.

He'd been required to be taken by wheelchair to the front door and out to the waiting vehicle. He thought about bitching, then decided to enjoy the ride. He was a little high from the pain meds and didn't mind at all.

"Officer Cortez," Keith asked the pretty police officer, "what is your first name?"

"Maria, Mr. Larson."

"Make it Keith. Maria is a nice name. Did you ever see *West Side Story?*"

She nodded, her eyes on the road. They were in fast-food alley now. "Yes. It's a little racist, don't you think?"

Keith winced inwardly. Political correctness would be the death of them all.

He said, "It's of its time. But 'Maria' is a lovely song."

She shrugged. "Your daughter . . . Chief Larson . . . wanted me to fill you in on some things."

He was glad she had identified Krista as both his daughter and the chief, otherwise he might have been really confused.

"Please do," he said.

"I was in Prairie du Chien yesterday," she said. "Checking out the Braggs. Their alibi?"

"Yes?"

"Something funny there. Not ha ha funny. Strange. Odd."

"Which is?"

"Mr. Bragg has a cabin, all right. Or at least there's a cabin at that address. A gentleman is living there, a Mr. Clauson, who is also a teacher, but not a coach. He teaches art at Prairie du Chien High. I spoke to him, after school. At the cabin. He was evasive at first."

Keith smiled. "But you persisted."

"I did. He invited me in after an unproductive session on the porch. He gave me coffee and, I think, the truth. The cabin belongs to Coach Bragg and Mr. Clauson. Coach Bragg lives with Mr. Clauson during the summer months, school vacation. Did I mention the cabin is not in town, but a few miles outside?"

"No."

"Well, it is. A few miles outside of town."

They were driving through a residential area now, nicely wooded, with bed and breakfasts popping up like friendly rustic mushrooms.

"The coach joins Mr. Clauson," she said, "on occasional weekends during the school year and during various vacations and breaks."

"I see. Where does Mrs. Bragg fit in?"

"She lives elsewhere. With a woman in Dodgeville, which is nearby. The woman's name is Melissa Adams. She's a gym teacher, too. Girls' gym, like Mrs. Bragg. When I say they live together, Mrs. Bragg and Ms. Adams, I mean in the summer months and weekends and such, like Coach Bragg and Mr. Clauson? I believe what's going on is clear."

He raised a hand. "So do I. Officer, please keep this information to yourself."

"I will, Mr. Larson."

"Keith."

"I will, Keith. The chief, who I informed of this, has already instructed me likewise. Your daughter?"

"Right. I know."

With the bridge over the Galena River up ahead, Cortez took the left onto Main Street.

"Also," the officer said, "I should mention I've attempted to interview Dawn Landry, David Landry's wife?"

"'Attempted' sounds like you haven't got it done."

"No I haven't. I just was unable to connect with her on Monday and was in Prairie du Chien on Tuesday. I'll be following up today. She's the last of the first round of interviews."

Keith thought for a moment. "Hold off on that. I'll handle that interview."

"I'll have to get that okayed by the chief."

"Do that. She's my daughter, you know."

When they rolled past the Jasmine Peterson crime scene, the area nearest the minipark (already bordered with a red "no parking" curb) was closed off and crime scene tape was posted from there to the edge of the grass. Several yellow evidence markers were in place. A chalk outline indicated where the young woman had fallen, and died. Three CSIs in blue jumpsuits were packing up their toolbox-like kits. Several of Krista's officers were still on the scene.

At the station, Cortez dropped Keith off and he went in the front way, through the reception area, buzzed through by clerk-dispatcher Maggie Edwards.

From her chair at the reception window, Maggie looked over and pointed past him. "Your daughter's in interview room A. She said to tell you to duck into the observation booth."

"Who is she interviewing?"

The redheaded dispatcher smiled. "That ex-beau of hers—Jerry. He's such a nice boy." The smile vanished. "He hasn't done anything wrong, has he?"

"Hmmm. If they're in there patching things up . . ."

"Yes?"

"I don't think she'd want me watching."

Maggie looked startled for just a moment, then smiled big. "You are a bad man, Keith Larson."

"Not the first woman to make that observation, Maggie."

In the shallow, unlighted nook behind the one-way mirror, Keith stood and watched. The eight-foot-by-ten interview room was home to a rectangular pine-topped table with chairs for four, light green walls, a window with its blinds shut, a big-screen TV over some low-slung cabinets, a clock, and a wall locker for officers to stow weapons during the interview.

Only two chairs were in use. Jerry—his unbrushed dark curly hair and extra-scruffy beard as if he'd been hauled out of bed and dragged here—wore a pale blue shirt and pale white expression. His hands were folded and he was leaning forward, his body posture suggesting he was begging police chief Krista for his life.

He kind of was.

"I was home last night," he said, sounding pitiful. "I was watching a movie! My folks went out for dinner. They took the car! I don't have a car right now—you know that."

Keith had apparently missed the part where Jerry was upset that his latest girlfriend had been murdered.

Krista, businesslike, asked, "You were home all evening? By yourself?"

He shook his head more than was necessary. "No. Mom and Dad came home shortly after eight. You can check with them."

"Your parents are your alibi."

Keith smiled to himself. Using the word "alibi" would rattle Jerry's cage. Innocent or guilty, Jerry squirming a little was fine with him.

"Yes," Jerry said, exasperated. "My parents. Do I have to tell you they're honest, upstanding people? A banker? A librarian?"

"No. But you have an apartment downstairs at their house. An entrance of your own. After they got home, you could have borrowed their car without asking. Slipped out. Slipped back."

Jerry's expression was so pained Keith almost felt sorry for him. "You can't think this of me! That I would . . . Jasmine's a sweet girl . . . I would never . . . she doesn't deserve . . ."

He covered his face. He was crying.

This Keith didn't enjoy at all.

Krista pushed a box of tissues across the table to Jerry. He used several, to wipe his eyes and blow his nose. His embarrassment embarrassed Keith.

His voice came back softer. Less shrill. "My folks came home around eight, eight fifteen. I was just finishing up a movie—*Red Sparrow*. Jennifer Lawrence? They yelled down and said they were home. I answered. I yelled up that if they wanted to watch something with me, all it would cost was Mom making some popcorn."

"Did they take you up on that?"

He nodded. Swallowed. "Yes. They'll tell you as much. You won't have to prompt them in any way. It's the truth and that's how they'll tell it."

"What did you watch together?"

"*Game Night*. It's . . . really funny."

"Netflix?"

"Blu-ray. I can't prove that last night's when we watched it, or even that we watched it together. But that's the truth, too."

Keith exited and asked Maggie to get him the numbers of Jerry's parents at their various places of work. She provided that, Keith made the calls, and when Krista emerged from the interview room, leaving Jerry behind, Keith told her he'd verified Jerry's alibi.

She shrugged. "I believe him. Let him sit awhile. He was crying again."

"For himself or Jasmine?"

"I'd like to think for Jasmine."

"But you don't really."

"No."

Maggie, at her window, called over to Krista, "The Illinois crime scene investigator is waiting in your office, dear! Hope it was all right to just send him in like that."

"Thank you, Maggie," Krista said. "That was fine." Then she motioned to Keith to join her.

He did, saying, "You let Maggie call you 'dear'? Aren't you the chief?"

"Yes. And at least I've broken her of calling me 'honeybunch,' if you're wondering about my ability to maintain discipline."

Deitch was the only officer in the bullpen. Keith nodded to him and he nodded back, looking frazzled.

Keith asked her, "Everybody else at the crime scene?"

"Or home grabbing a couple hours' sleep," she said. "I worked everybody all night, canvassing South Main. Needed to catch the apartment dwellers before they went to work, and see if anybody heard or saw anything."

"And?"

"Nothing."

"Nice to know you can scream on Main Street and nobody notices." Or maybe cares, he thought.

In the office, just inside, Eli Wallace was seated at the mini conference table at right, his arms folded, his body leaned back, eyes closed. The African American CSI in the blue jumpsuit was snoring softly, his thick mustache riffling in the self-created breeze.

Keith said, "Kind of a shame to wake the little darling."

Eli's eyes popped open and he shook his head, clearing it, and said something rude to Keith that should never be spoken in front of a man's daughter, especially if she is chief of police. Keith and Krista laughed and sat at the table, her opposite the CSI, Keith next to him.

"Put in a long night, did you?" Keith said.

"Might say that," Eli said. "Anyway I wasn't relaxing in a hospital bed being waited on, like some people I know. How you feeling?"

"Not bad. Excellent drugs. Wrapped up like this, I look twenty years slimmer. Your team about done?"

He nodded. "Rest of the work'll be at the lab back in Rockford. We've recovered some items that might be useful."

"Oh?"

Eli nodded. "We checked the trash bins. Plenty of those to go through." He gave Krista half a smile. "You guys keep your little town nice and clean for the tourists."

"Part of why they keep coming back," she said. "Find something interesting?"

"Two somethings. A hooded raincoat, black, with plenty of blood spatter. Not much doubt the source of the latter. Also a butcher knife. Blood-smeared. Almost certainly the murder weapon." Eli shifted in his seat. "You've got a problem, Chief."

Krista said, "You think?"

"I think. This appears, strongly—as if I have to say it—to be the same perpetrator. The stab wounds this time are mostly on the back.

The previous homicide, of course, the blows came from the front. Same is true of the Clearwater homicide."

Keith said, "A shift in MO?"

"Not really. Blood trail on the stairs—wrought iron and wood, alongside the corner building—indicate the incident began at the landing. The killer was waiting outside the victim's apartment, tucked in the recession of the doorway. The first blow caught her in the left arm."

Krista said, "She saw him and reacted."

The CSI nodded. "And fled, running down the steps. The killer pursued and caught up with her and the attack came from behind. Knife plunged deep, half a dozen times. A savage assault, like the Lund woman."

"Right there on Main Street," Keith said. "With a high risk of potential witnesses."

Eli tapped his nose—the "on the nose" gesture. "That's the other obvious aspect here."

Krista frowned. "What is?"

Keith sighed and said, "The killer is devolving. Accelerating. Six months between the first and second kill. Three days between the second and third kill. Precision planning for the first two kills, more on the fly for this one."

The CSI was nodding. "There's a real danger to the community. You need to call in the state police investigators. And Major Case Assistance. ASAP."

Krista said nothing.

Keith said, "We'll give that serious consideration, Eli. Thanks. You heading back to Rockford now?"

Eli frowned a little. "You changing the subject on me, Keith?"

"Maybe. Where we go from here is the chief's call, and I'll consult, of course, which is my job. You've done yours and we appreciate it."

Keith stood, smiled, extended his hand and Eli, his expression wary, shook Keith's hand, then stood himself.

"Oh-kay," Eli said. "And, yes. I'll be in Rockford. I hope you don't need me . . . I'll let you know our results."

Eli closed the door behind him.

Keith said to Krista, "You should eat. I'll take you to lunch."

She was studying him. "You want to talk, don't you?"

"I want to talk."

But they didn't talk on the way to Otto's Place, which would still be open for lunch for another twenty minutes. He was thinking and so was she. In the few days since Astrid's murder, the number of things they had to consider had accumulated into a dizzying spire of suspects, suspect alibis, and an increasingly out of control madman.

Otto's wasn't busy. They hung their coats up, found a corner table, then ordered bowls of turkey-and-black-bean chili and glasses of iced tea. Now they talked.

Keith asked, "What does Jasmine's murder mean to this investigation?"

Krista thought for a moment, then said, "She's not from the Class of '09."

He shrugged. "She was at the reunion."

"But we think the motive of the killings lies in the past. And the first murder was six months ago. Was Jasmine a cold-blooded, coldhearted attempt to throw us off the track? To muddy the waters with . . ."

"Blood," he finished. "Maybe. And to provide us with a good suspect in Jerry Ward. My suspicion? This is a premeditated killer. He or she will have established that Jerry would be home without an alibi. That the parents would be away, stranding Jerry without a car. The lack of a car, however, was something we might well dismiss—a killer can always find a way to get to a killing."

"But Jerry's mom and dad double-crossed our killer," she said. "They came home early. They in fact spent the evening with their son, and are not likely types to cover for him in a situation like this."

Keith frowned, shook his head. "Was trying to frame Jerry enough of a motivating reason? Certainly confusing the issue alone, to maybe throw us off some, wouldn't inspire it."

She leaned toward him. "What made the killer, so careful, so controlled in the planning of these acts, suddenly take a risk like striking in public? On Main Street of all places?"

"That's the only silver lining in this very dark cloud," he said, with a tight smile. "It means we're getting close. It means the investigation has lit a fire under our quarry."

Krista's eyebrows went up. "So who was Jasmine in all of this? What marked her a victim?"

"When we answer that," he said, "we'll know who we're looking for."

Their tea came.

Krista smirked humorlessly and said, "Don't you think we can rule Chicago out? And even if we're wrong to do so, we're covered—your friend Barney is networking with Booker. With luck those two creeps who jumped you will sell out who hired them."

"Don't count on that," he said. "Even today, the Outfit is scarier than anybody in law enforcement."

He sipped the tea. His phone vibrated in his pocket.

"Speaking of Chicago," he said, looking at the caller ID.

REBECCA CARLSON.

He excused himself and went outside.

"Hi," he said. His breath was visible in the cold; he didn't care.

"Hi yourself. Are you okay? Are you in the hospital? Did you break anything important?"

"Yes. No. And nothing important except your heart."

She laughed at him. "Heal up and come see me."

"How did you know about this?"

"You're in the news and I *am* the news. Listen, my news is that I've connected with a researcher of Astrid's."

"On the sexual predator story?"

"No, the Daniel Rule Meets the Mob exposé. My pretty nemesis had some good stuff. I'm picking up where she left off, and my ex has agreed to let me, and to air it when I'm done. Of course, I'll need to talk to you, since the two Salerno guys sitting in the Galena jail are your handiwork."

"Maybe, but my bruises and broken rib is theirs. Don't get yourself killed like Astrid."

"You don't really think the Chicago end of this is what caused that, do you?"

"No, I don't. Neither does my daughter, and she's smarter than both of us. But people have been known to die in Chicago under sketchy circumstances."

"Really? I try not to cover unhappy news like that. Ciao."

"Did you really just say 'ciao'?"

She laughed. "I did. Aren't I just the worst?"

Rebecca clicked off. He smiled at the phone and clicked off, too.

When he got back to their corner, the chili had come. He broke some crackers up and dropped them in. Had several spoonfuls of the stuff. Great. The simple act of eating something that tasted good seemed like such a privilege, suddenly.

Krista, between spoonfuls, asked, "So I need to call the big boys in, huh? Like Eli says?"

"No, and not the big girls either. Not today. This is a key time for you, honey. This is the first big thing that's come along since you made chief."

Obviously surprised and pleased by this, she said, "Right, and I don't want to screw it up. Many more dead bodies on Main Street and they'll take me down on littering."

He dropped his spoon and took her hand. "You need to step up. We're close. Very close. If we haven't wrapped this up by tomorrow this time, yes. By all means. Call Major Case Assistance. Call whatever cavalry you want. But right now, we have another shot at this."

"We do?"

He nodded. "Have your people assemble all the suspects. Do it at the Lake View Lodge, in the banquet hall again, if it's not in use—Landry will cooperate. And I want his wife there—she's been slippery. We need Frank and Brittany Wunder. Your friends Josh and Jessy. The Braggs. Everybody else has alibis that seem to hold. But if we don't shake the killer out of this bunch, we can try again with the others—Jerry, Chris and Tyler, Ken Stock and his wife, Alex Cannon and the entire Chicago Outfit. Can you make that happen, honey? Can the chief of police gather the suspects?"

"Like Charlie Chan?" she asked.

"Just like Charlie Chan."

She shrugged. "Okay, Pop," she said, and started in on the rest of her soup.

TWENTY-FOUR

Krista found David Landry not only cooperative but eager to please, again maybe trying too hard. At any rate, the Lake View Lodge manager had the banquet hall set up as she'd instructed—at the far end where the band had played, four round tables were arranged with as much space left between them as possible. At the other end were two more tables, one at far left, the other far right.

Each table had plastic water glasses and a pitcher of ice water. No alcoholic beverages would be served this time around.

As Krista and her father stood facing their guests, Frank and Brittany Wunder were seated at the far left table; the Braggs at the next; then Landry and his wife, Dawn; and, at far right, Josh and Jessica Webster.

With dusk approaching, the tall windows onto the lake were letting in not streaming sunshine but the gloom of a dying overcast day, the skeletal vastness of trees blotting out the horizon.

Their guests wore the apparel of business or home—Frank in his Buick salesman mode, a sport coat and tie, Brittany in an oversize pink sweater and black leggings; the Braggs still in their coaching togs; David in a gray suit with darker gray tie, Dawn almost matching in a gray skirt with white blouse; Josh in his blue sweatshirt hawking his popcorn shop and Jessy in a navy suit and light blue silk blouse.

Krista and her father made a slightly off-key pair, she in her standard police chief uniform, Glock 21 on her hip, he in sweatshirt and jeans.

No need for many preliminaries. Krista had decided to call them personally, since these were all friends or friendly acquaintances. She'd again said they'd be recorded, but that this was voluntary, and informal. She would stop recording anytime they wished to go off-the-record. They could refuse now, or accept the invitation and leave at their own discretion.

Now, as she faced the group—each couple at their own table to discourage conversation—Krista felt she should repeat something she'd already made clear on the phone.

"You are not suspects," she said, technically true. "You are not even what we would call persons of interest. Everyone here is aware of just how many people were in this room on reunion night, who will all have to be talked to several times, in increasing depth."

Her father, looking from table to table, said, "We are only in day four of the Astrid Lund investigation. Consider this exercise part of our process of elimination."

Jessy, not surprisingly, spoke up. "There was a second murder last night, wasn't there?"

"Yes," Krista said. "A young woman named Jasmine Peterson."

No surprised reaction followed. The word had clearly gotten around.

Jessy asked, "Is the same person responsible?"

"It would appear so, but we are in very early stages of that inquiry." Her eyes roved from face to face. "We are a small department—a dozen of us including myself and a civilian employee and our consultant here. That's why your help and cooperation are so vital."

Pop said, "We're going to talk to you individually." He gestured to the corner tables behind him. "We should be able to move quickly. We encourage you to be frank. And I'll be frank with you—we have reason to believe several of you have withheld useful information, or have been self-serving in what you've told us so far."

A murmur rose from the small group.

"Keep in mind," Krista said above it, "that only the person responsible for Astrid Lund's murder . . . and presumably Jasmine Peterson's . . . has any reason to fabricate."

Jessy, not hiding her irritation, said, "Isn't that a nice way to say 'lie'?"

"If you have secrets," Pop said, "that pertain to Astrid, revealing them would be helpful . . . and do know that unless giving those secrets a public airing bears upon putting a killer away, we will protect your privacy."

Everyone looked quietly alarmed. Krista didn't mind—she wanted them to understand what was at stake, though they might feel they'd come here under slightly false pretenses. Things were ramping up, and the phone call summoning them with words like "voluntary" and "informal" might seem now to smack of bait-and-switch. Too bad.

Pop said, "Frank, would you join me?" He gestured behind him to the table at the other end, by the tall windows.

Krista said, "Brittany?"

And gestured to the other table at that end.

"In the meantime," Pop added, as Frank Wunder rose and lumbered forward, "we'd like you all to reflect on anything involving Astrid that you may have seen at the reunion—any conversations you witnessed her having that may have looked at all . . . confrontational. Thank you."

Keith said, "Frank, I believe you said you didn't speak to Astrid reunion night."

The roughly handsome onetime jock sat back hanging his head some. Those close-set, hooded green eyes and the several-times-broken nose gave him a rugged handsomeness but also made him look slightly stupid.

"I think I told you," Frank said, "there were some hard feelings between her and me. Astrid."

"Even after all these years?"

He was looking at the tabletop. "Some things hurt a long time."

"Like what, Frank?"

Now the eyes came up, still hooded. "I will tell you something if you turn that damn thing off."

The car salesman was indicating Keith's phone on the table, where the field interview app had been utilized.

"Okay," Keith said, and paused the recording.

"I went with her awhile. You know that. We used to make out. We were . . . it was prom. We, uh, wound up in the back seat. I'd had some beers. She hadn't. We were parked out in the boonies. I got out and peed, and then we got in the back, like I said, and it was getting hot and heavy."

"Okay."

The eyes lowered again. "I had trouble."

"What kind of trouble?"

The eyes came up. Not hooded. "Trouble."

Oh.

"Couldn't get it up, Frank?" Keith asked, deliberately needling him.

Frank sighed, looked away again. "Too much beer. Astrid, she . . . at first she, it was odd, but she took offense. I mean, let's face it, she was a real nice-looking girl and I guess the idea somebody couldn't . . . perform, she found insulting . . . Anyway, then she laughed at me. Made fun of me."

"That must have hurt."

"It did. I . . . I had some beers, remember? I lashed out at her."

"Lashed out how?"

"I . . . I slapped her." He was reddening with shame. "Keith, I swear I never hit a girl before, and never have since. That night when I went home? I went in the can and I threw up."

"Well," Keith said. "That's understandable."

"Yeah, right?"

"You'd had a lot of beer."

Brittany, her arms folded, her brown eyes hard, her long blonde hair surrounding her face like a hundred angry spiders had spun it, had just told Krista much the same story. With the interview app again in pause.

"Frank was in college," she said, "I was still at GHS. We started going together—to me, it was a big deal. He was one of the most popular seniors when I was a sophomore. Now I was a junior and . . . look, if I was to tell you Frank and I did it when I was just sixteen, could he get in trouble for statutory whatever? After all this time?"

"No," Krista said.

"Anyway, I really loved him. To me he was everything. Understand, I still love him." She leaned forward, whispered. "Maybe now he's not so big a deal, but I love him."

Krista nodded.

"Frank has an emotional side I didn't know about till I really started going with him. One night, after he had a lot of beer, he really opened up and told me about how, prom night, he couldn't satisfy Astrid . . . couldn't get going, you know? And how he slapped her. It was like, over a year later, but he cried about it."

"Has he ever been rough with you like that?"

"Not hardly. Next day, when he wasn't drunk? I told him if he ever struck me, I'd be gone so fast he wouldn't know I'd ever been around."

"What about the other thing?"

"If you mean . . . as far as . . . you know, sexual performance? That was always fine till a couple of years ago. But that's what little blue pills are for."

Krista nodded to the phone between them. "I'm going to turn this back on, okay? Something I'd like on the record."

"You mean, unless I don't want to answer and tell you talk to my lawyer."

"Right."

Brittany nodded. "Go for it."

"You said you and Frank were in town, the second week of August."

"Yes."

"Do you keep a calendar or appointment book of any kind? So you can demonstrate that you were in town? What you were doing and so forth? Specifically on Thursday and Friday of that week?"

She shrugged. "Well, I know exactly what we were doing the second Thursday of August."

"You do?" That seemed unlikely, unless after Krista's previous inquiry, Brittany and Frank had looked (or cooked) it up.

"Sure," she said. "We were at Fried Green Tomatoes."

A popular restaurant on Main.

"You remember that off the top of your head?"

"Sure. It was our wedding anniversary."

Bill Bragg sat across from Keith, looking like the beefy man's man you might expect from one of the state's most respected and successful high school football coaches. He was smiling in a good-natured but serious way.

"Before you start," Bragg said to Keith, "I should tell you that I heard from my friend Ed Clauson in Prairie du Chien. I know he talked to that Officer Cortez, so I figure you and your daughter have a pretty good picture of things."

Keith nodded. "I would like to hear it directly from you. I can stop recording for now. If it needs to be official, that can happen later."

Bragg said, "Please."

Keith paused the recording.

The coach said, "You and I are about the same age."

"I'm a little older."

"Not much. But you understand that when I started teaching, almost thirty years ago, things were very different. 'Coming out' just wasn't on the table."

"I remember."

"And I'm not sure that, even now, times have changed enough for a guy with my interests and skills to be openly gay and coach young men. To do that, I can envision riding out protests and having to go through lawsuits and . . . if I were younger, that might be an option. Mrs. Bragg is in the same boat where young girls are concerned."

"You and Kelly met at GHS and discovered you shared a secret."

Bragg nodded. "We did. And we hit it off. We became great friends. Still are. We travel together and, in some very real respects, we are husband and wife. I was very lucky finding her."

"You live with Ed, and she lives with a woman from Dodgeville, I understand—in the summers."

He nodded. "And there are weekend visits and school breaks and such."

"Have you ever been involved with a student?"

The coach's frown stopped just short of threatening. "Never. Do you consider yourself a professional, Keith?"

"I did. I'm retired now."

"Funny kind of retirement. Tell me—did you ever compromise yourself with a woman in your custody? A runaway teen who was tricking perhaps? A woman of age who wanted a pass on some thing *she* did, shoplifting maybe?"

"Of course not."

"That's my answer to you. Of course I never compromised a teacher-student relationship for sexual gratification." He shifted in the chair and his frown softened. "There is . . . I will mention something."

"Do."

"I briefly . . . briefly . . . had a moment with Chris Hope. A teacher not a student, of course. I was married to Kelly but had hit a rough patch with Ed. Chris and I were friendly and when it was about to get a little more than friendly, someone came in on us after school."

"Who?"

Bragg sighed. "Astrid Lund."

"Would you repeat that for the recording?"

"No. If it's necessary to be more . . . forthcoming about all this, I will. But Astrid just smiled and laughed and ducked out. She never said a word about it. Not then. And not at the reunion."

Krista and Kelly Bragg had been covering much the same ground.

"Call it living a lie, if you like," the slender, attractive woman said, her chin up, "but Bill and I have had, and still do have, a lovely existence together. We are great friends and companions who enjoy each other's company and interests."

"I would never call it 'living a lie,'" Krista said evenly. "I do wonder why you might not choose to go public at this stage? Things are very different now."

She nodded. "Strides have been made, but hatred and prejudice die hard, if they ever die at all. But this is still a country where gay people wanting to order a wedding cake causes a court case. Do you really think a high school football coach coming out would be warmly received in this conservative town?"

"No," Krista admitted.

"And Bill is one of the most admired and celebrated coaches of high school football in the state . . . in the nation! To risk his reputation? . . . No."

Krista smiled. "You haven't done so shabbily with the girls, either. Playing for GHS, with you as coach, is one of my fondest memories."

Kelly swallowed. Her eyes were tearing up. "Thank you, Krista. Thank you very much for that."

Krista leaned in. "But we do have to return to what we spoke about the other day . . . only in this new context."

The gym teacher nodded. "Astrid and me in the shower."

"Did you have a sexual relationship with her?"

The chin came up again. "Not with her or any of my girls. It was exactly as I told you. She'd had a terrible experience, something at least verging on date rape. She did not provide any details, not the boy's name or . . . really anything more. But she needed comforting. Support. I see providing that as part of my role."

"You have no idea who the boy was?"

She frowned in thought. "Well . . . she dated a lot of boys. Would go with them, steady, for a while, then move on. We were close. I was a mentor to her. So I remember who she was going with at the time."

"Who would that be?"

"David Landry."

"Thank you, Coach."

The two women shook hands, and Krista got up and went over to her father, where Bill Bragg was getting up. She leaned in and whispered the new information.

The manager of Lake View Lodge sat across from Keith and offered up a businesslike smile.

"I hope the way we've set everything up for you," David Landry said, "is satisfactory."

"We appreciate the cooperation," Keith said, with his own business-like smile. "There's something I've been wanting to ask you about—something I witnessed the night of the reunion."

"Please."

"I saw you and Astrid Lund having words. Seemed fairly heated. Considering she was butchered a few hours later, that strikes me as pertinent. Well?"

The blood had left his face, his host persona evaporating. "Astrid was . . . she could be a little bitch. I'm sorry. I know it's rude and you're not supposed to say such things. But she could be. A real bitch."

"Not to speak ill of the dead or anything."

Landry leaned forward. "She was a bitch to me in high school. When we broke up. We left it in a bad place. I felt . . . well, I knew she'd made something of herself. I know that people change. Mature and become . . . different people."

"But she hadn't, is that it?"

He shook his head, still frustrated. "I approached her, tried to congratulate her, said how we'd been kids then and made some bad decisions . . ."

"What kind of bad decisions?"

Dawn Landry, lovely as ever, utterly composed, said, "My husband has a drinking problem. He's had it a long time. And he keeps it under control. Right now he's doing well."

"Okay," Krista said. "Why do you mention it?"

"His drinking problem started young. His parents kept a lot of liquor around the house, and did not keep track of it. David was helping himself as early as junior high."

"Okay," Krista said again.

"David has always handled it well, by which I mean . . . he's not a nasty drunk. If anything, he's a charming one. But with enough in him, he can be . . . uninhibited. When he knew this reunion was coming up, and that Astrid Lund would be coming, he . . . he told me something, so that I wouldn't hear it from her, particularly in an 'unfair manner,' as he put it."

"Go on."

Dawn brushed some golden-brown hair away from her face. "When he was dating Astrid, they were alone at her house one night. And my guess is she was one of those girls who would let the boys do everything but . . . you know . . . everything *but*. The kids all said she put out, at least according to David . . . only she was a virgin. When David . . . had her."

"He forced her."

"That's not how he puts it, but . . . I think so. He was definitely freaked out, because she was a virgin. There was blood. She got hysterical. He was worried she'd tell, but she never did. They never spoke of it."

"The first time you talked to Astrid," Keith said to Landry, "after that bad experience, was here? At the reunion?"

David nodded. "She was cold. Nasty. She said, 'You think I'm a bitch? I'll tell you what's a bitch—*karma's* a bitch.'"

"Where were you and David," Krista asked, "the second week of August last year?"

"I was home," Dawn said. "Saw my mother several times in Dubuque. Had lunch with friends. I was around. Easily proven. But David's story about being busy here at the lodge? No. He was away for much of August. Drying out. He's not had a drink since, to his credit. But this is a fairly regular routine with David."

"Where is the rehab facility?"

"It's in Delray Beach. Addiction Solutions. South Florida."

While her father was interviewing Josh, Krista sat opposite Jessy, her oldest and best friend in the world, who seemed to consider all this attention, re: the Astrid Lund killing, a kind of betrayal.

"What is the idea?" Jessy demanded. "Josh told me you had him come over and explain his whereabouts in August! I told you we were with my sister and her husband."

"You didn't tell me you were in Florida," Krista said, not bothering to correct the impression Jessy's husband had apparently given her about who initiated last night's visit.

Jessy folded her arms. "I didn't say we *weren't* in Florida."

"No, but you led me to believe you were at their cabin on Timber Lake."

Now Jessy's hands flew in the air. "I can't help it if you got the wrong idea! Talk to Judy and Gary—they'll be able to run down everything we did with them. We cram a lot into those vacations."

"Somebody crammed a murder in, *in Clearwater.*"

Jessy bolted to her feet. "I'm not putting up with another second of this crap! You want to talk to me, you go through my brother, the lawyer."

"Please . . ."

Jessy leaned in, her upper teeth showing and it wasn't a smile. "Please explain why you're all over me and Josh and everybody else here . . . but where is Ken Stock and his little Mary, whose best quality is looking the other way!"

Krista frowned at the mention of the school newspaper advisor. "What are you talking about?"

Jessy came around and leaned right in Krista's face. "Everybody back then knew about Ken and Astrid, or anyway suspected those two were . . . you know!"

"I didn't know . . ."

"Well ask around! Ken Stock is a notorious hound! He's always taking a girl student under his wing, 'mentoring' her. I don't know how he even had the nerve to come to the reunion!"

TWENTY-FIVE

With everyone back in their chairs at their tables, and no one looking terribly happy about it, Keith and Krista conferred at the opposite end of the banquet hall.

Hearing about Ken Stock, Keith said to his daughter, "We need to interview that son of a bitch in depth. Now."

She gestured with open hands. "He was at that conference in Atlanta with Chris Hope and Tyler. Why would they lie to help him?"

He mulled that for a moment. "Would they have to lie to back him up? Clearwater is, what? Seven hours by car from Atlanta? That's doable. It was a big, well-attended conference. Chris Hope was taking lectures and classes in different disciplines than Stock."

She was already nodding. "I'll call him. We'll go right over there."

Keith raised a forefinger. "First call Chris. Ask him exactly how much he recalls seeing Stock at that conference. In the meantime, I'll chat with our guests—and see if anybody besides your excitable friend Jessy ever heard the rumor that your favorite English teacher had a hobby."

She was shaking her head. "Pop, he was a mentor to me, as well. Encouraged my writing. He never did a thing that was even vaguely out of line."

Pop gave her a barely perceivable half smile that Krista had come to think was exclusive to cops. "Why, are you insulted he didn't? Think about who your father was."

"Good point."

"He's looking like our man. Go make your calls. I'm going to interview Landry again—him being in Florida in August puts him up the suspect list, too."

She nodded and went out into the hall.

Krista got Chris Hope at home.

He said, "Well, Tyler and I didn't even get to the hotel where the conference was held till late Thursday—all we missed was early registration and a welcoming ceremony. We saw Ken there on Friday, the first real day. Had lunch with him."

"Tell me—how did he seem?"

"His usual self. Articulate. I've always found him decent enough company. He did seem . . . well, he looked kind of . . . ragged."

"How so?"

"Oh, just tired. Jet-lagged, maybe. No. Wait . . . you know, he didn't fly there. He drove, like we did. Had his own car down there."

And he would have spent a lot of time behind the wheel, driving from Illinois to Clearwater and from Clearwater to Atlanta, especially since he would have to be seen at the conference on Friday to shore up his alibi.

That was another detail they'd missed.

Irritated with herself, she called Stock.

He'd obviously seen her caller ID, because he answered, "Krista, hello. I have to admit to feeling a little insulted."

That threw her. "Why is that?"

"Bill Bragg told me at school that you're having a reunion of reunion goers this evening. And I wasn't invited."

"That's only because you aren't a suspect," she lied. "But I do need to talk to you. Would now be all right?"

"Don't see why not. Did you want to talk to Mary, as well? She's here with me . . . You kids quiet down! . . . Sorry. When can I expect you?"

"Soon. We've wrapped up our 'reunion' at the lodge."

"Fine. See you soon. You know the address?"

"Yes, I have it."

She clicked off. If Stock was their man, he was one cool customer.

Krista stepped inside the banquet room. Her father was over sitting at his table with a beaten-down-looking David Landry. She curled a finger at him and Pop joined her. They stepped into the hall.

She said, "Ken Stock's at home with his wife and kids."

"Good. Mary Stock's an important cog in this, too—she may be covering for him."

"If he's our man."

Her father thought about it. "I have to finish up with our friend David, then I want to ask the group whether anyone else has heard these rumors about everybody's favorite English teacher and his female mentees."

"I'll go on ahead," she said, nodding. "You can follow me in the Impala, when you're free here. Give me your phone and I'll put Ken Stock's address in. I've got his cell and a landline, too."

He handed it over and she entered the info.

Pop said, "Are you sure you don't want to wait, for us to go out there together?"

"I'll be fine. Get what you need here and join me. Interviewing Stock and his wife will take a while, unless he lawyers up. And then we'll really know."

Her father wasn't thrilled with this plan, but he finally nodded, and she left him to wrap up here.

Outside the night and a windy cold February were waiting. The overcast sky could not quench the nearly full moon, which persistently peeked around the edges of clouds. In the parking lot, zipping up her thermal jacket, she stood for just a moment beside the Toyota, her breath fuming, and looked toward the trees that guarded Lake View Lodge, naked pillars of wood bursting out of patchy snow, their spindly arms seeming insufficient to their mission. As the moon and the clouds fought, ivory would sweep over the bare trees, giving them a glow only to be swallowed by darkness again.

She got behind the wheel and started out. The seven miles to the highway were windy and demanded respect, particularly on a night like this. Fairways and forest fought their own battle and they too would glow, then disappear, as the moon and clouds clashed.

Krista recalled a poem Pop had read to her as a child:

> *The wind was a torrent of darkness among the gusty trees,*
> *The moon was a ghostly galleon tossed upon cloudy seas,*
> *The road was a ribbon of moonlight over the purple moor,*
> *And the highwayman came riding—riding—riding—*
> *The highwayman came riding, up to the old inn-door.*

Years later she had asked Pop why that poem—the romantic tale of a criminal, after all—had been something a policeman chose to share with his young daughter.

"It's the sound of it," he'd told her, "and it's an exciting story, too. I wanted you to think of reading as something enjoyable, fun, not just schoolwork."

The irony of this moment, this flashback to a poem she'd treasured as kid, was that Mr. Stock had once asked her English class if anyone had a favorite poem.

She had responded with: "'The Highwayman,' Mr. Stock. By Alfred Noyes."

He had laughed and now, in her memory, she detected a cruelty in his response that she'd missed as a student.

"'Noyes,' I'm afraid, is a misspelling," he'd said. "That's corny noise, Ms. Larson."

She'd stood up for herself but sold out her favorite poem doing so, saying, "I was only eight and didn't know better, but I liked the way the words flowed."

"Fair enough," Mr. Stock had said, bestowing upon her a smile.

Overall Mr. Stock had been a positive influence, encouraging her to write, enlisting her for *The Spyglass*, the school paper, and *The Ship's Log*, the yearbook. And, as she'd told Pop, he'd never done anything, during all that time, to make him seem a letch much less a sexual predator.

The Lake View Lodge road, this time of year, wasn't much traveled, except for a few stretches along which were condos and elaborate rentals tied in with the place. So the approach of headlights in the left lane, someone coming home from town or heading to the lodge, was nothing to be surprised much less alarmed by.

At least not until the driver hit the brights, all but blinding her, and those unrelenting headlights swung her way, washing the Toyota in glaring light, the vehicle bearing down on her, engine roaring.

She swung the wheel right and avoided being hit, but the ditch took her, not treacherously deep but enough for the weight of the Toyota to give way to gravity and then the car rolled and as it did her right hand on the wheel twisted at the wrist, almost breaking, and when the Toyota landed at the bottom of the mini-ravine, upright, airbag not deploying on rollover, she tried to open the door with her left hand, but the door was jammed, and when she got out of her seat belt to reach over to the rider's side door, her right wrist sprained and hurting like hell, she couldn't open it, not with her outstretched left, either.

Footsteps in brittle snow were crunching toward her, the brightness of the headlights gone, and yet she knew it wasn't help on the way.

Keith was finished with David Landry, who had told him of the strict locked-door policy of the rehab facility in Florida. Landry provided phone numbers and names and other contact info, so Keith could verify that the resort manager had been a virtual prisoner, unlikely to be able to slip out and make a Clearwater murder run.

Standing before the unhappy group of eight at their four tables, Keith said, "Mrs. Webster says rumor has it Ken Stock has had affairs with female students—perhaps with many over the years. Have any of you heard of that?"

Frank Wunder and his wife both shook their heads, and Landry said, "No. Never." And Dawn didn't react at all.

But the Braggs were exchanging troubled frowns.

"Bill?" Keith said. "Kelly? You wish to comment?"

The football coach said, "I don't pay much attention to rumors. Repeating them just seems . . ." He shrugged, unwilling or unable to say more.

The girls' gym teacher said, "I never witnessed anything. But the girls would talk. Still, it was all secondhand. Never did any of them say, 'It happened to me.' Always it was, 'I know a girl who . . .'"

Both Braggs had trailed off, and Keith could well understand that the couple, in their situation, would be sensitive about what harm a nasty rumor could do to a good teacher's life and career.

No longer the gracious host, Landry asked, "Are we done?"

"Wait here a moment," he told the group.

In the hall Keith tried Ken Stock's cell number; it went to voice mail. Then he tried the landline.

"Hello, Keith," Mary Stock's voice said. "What can I do for you?"

"Hi, Mary. Let me talk to Ken, please."

"He's not here, I'm afraid. He's over in Dubuque doing some library research. Can I help?"

A chill went through him. "Uh, interesting. Does he do that often? Library research?"

"Oh, yes. He's been working on a novel about the Civil War. That gets into everybody's blood, I guess, in Galena, General Grant and all."

"Was he researching last night, too, by any chance?"

"Why, yes. He's really getting into it these days."

"Thanks, Mary. I'll call again later."

He clicked off.

Stock was their killer, all right—and, on his cell, Stock had pretended to be home when he spoke to Krista, summoning her to come meet him. What exactly that portended, Keith did not know.

He only knew he had to move, and move fast.

He rushed back into the banquet hall, grabbed his jacket, and was about to speak, when Bill Bragg spoke up first.

"I don't know if it's important, Keith," the coach said. "But I asked Ken today if he'd been called about this meeting. And he said no."

Keith frowned and held up a hand. "Everyone please stay out here. Why don't you go to the lounge, relax and have a drink. Run a tab on me, David."

Everyone thought that was a good idea, but Keith was already gone.

Krista clambered over into and across the rider's seat and, using her left hand, opened the door. She climbed out, got her feet under her, and looked back toward the road. Down the drop-off came a figure, vague under the cloudy sky. Then the clouds moved and moonlight lit him momentarily, like a strobe light, just long enough to reveal Ken Stock, in a brown leather jacket over the tie and khakis he'd no doubt worn when he stood before his students at GHS today, telling them what poetry to like.

But in class the teacher wouldn't have been holding in his fist a butcher knife, which under another strobe of moon gleamed and reflected and winked at her. The blade wasn't long, maybe six inches, but it lacked the curve of most such knives, its point sharp.

He continued down the incline, not moving fast, because it was too steep to risk that, with clusters of snow here and there. She couldn't use her right hand, the sprain making it useless, the fingers uncooperative, and when she reached over with her left to her holstered Glock, she fumbled with the self-locking strap, couldn't work it, and then he was almost down the incline, knife in his fist held shoulder high, his eyes unblinking and zeroing in on her.

The trees were close. They didn't offer much brush for shelter, only occasional pines among the mostly naked oaks, but if she could get in deep enough, she might tuck behind a trunk with the heft for hiding. Her feet crushed frozen remainders of snow, her boots snapping twigs and crinkling long-dead leaves.

She could hear him behind her.

He wasn't moving as quickly as she was. The moon had found its way around the cloud cover, painting the world a blue-gray ivory now. She needed the clouds to win long enough for her to stop running and take cover and be able to get at her damn gun.

Into the woods she went.

Like Cinderella before her.

And she had been Red Riding Hood, hasn't she?

Keith, at the wheel of the Impala, had no idea what to expect. He only knew that Stock had lured Krista out this way, that Stock had not been home when she called but somewhere presumably close, since the bastard knew about the gathering of suspects.

And he hadn't been able to raise Krista on her cell. More damn voice mail.

He didn't have a weapon. He'd maintained his conceal-and-carry permit, but without a gun on his hip, he might as well not have renewed the damn thing. He should have gone back to his old habit of carrying even when he was off duty, only retirement had seemed the end of that—when Krista brought him on to this case, though, with a crazy goddamn killer loose, he should have been smart enough to use his gun for something other than self-pitying thoughts of suicide.

The hell of it was, he didn't know whether to drive fast or slow. His daughter was in danger and all he could do was swiftly scan the road and the left and right, and try to think through the pounding of his heart in his ears.

Then there it was.

Up ahead, at right, on the wrong side of the road, parked at a half-ass angle, a white Ford Edge. Keith pulled over, the two cars nose to nose, and got out and came around.

Banged-up some at the bottom of the ditch was the Toyota—had it rolled and landed upright? Nobody was on the steep downward slope, then perhaps a hundred yards leading to, and into, the trees, a thickness of forest made thin by winter. The ground was mottled with snowy remnants, but until the moon took hold of the cloud-streaked sky, and lighted the earth up for him, Keith hadn't seen the footprints—two sets of them.

Wide-spaced—running.

Closer-together—striding.

The tracks took him to the brink of the trees, where he stopped to call it in.

"Officer in trouble," he told the sheriff's department dispatcher.

Tucked behind a tree now, her back to it, she used her left hand, her good hand, to pat her pockets for the cell phone; but it wasn't there—she'd lost it in the rollover.

Never mind, she told herself. The gun. The gun is the thing.

She worked her left hand over and released the locking hood on the holster, which took pushing down on the gun butt and rotating the weapon to release—not easy with the left hand for a Glock holstered on the right hip.

But she managed it.

Breathing hard, yet in control, she turned to face the tree trunk. She peeked around. She listened.

She heard nothing.

Was he gone? Had he given up? Was he the fleeing one now? Surely Stock knew killing the cop looking for him would serve no rational purpose.

Or was rationality even a factor now?

Was he, as her father had put it, devolving and accelerating? Was madness all he had now? Or did he think by stopping her that he might buy himself a few hours to make a better escape?

She listened.

Could she risk moving out of these woods?

She thought of another poem, about deep, dark woods, and promises to be kept before sleep could come . . .

Now *that* was a poem Mr. Stock would have approved.

She listened for footsteps, heard nothing, nothing, nothing . . . then a crunch of snow and snapped twigs and she spun and there he was, his expression as blank as the blade he raised at her, unchanging as it came down.

She moved to her right, protecting her chest but sacrificing her left arm, somewhat, the blade catching mostly her thermal jacket, though she felt the wetness of the wound. The shock of it, though, had sent her arm reflexively to the right and the Glock flew somewhere, thunking in the night.

She ran, barely keeping her balance.

She could hear her pursuer behind her now, crunching along in the stocking feet she'd glimpsed. He'd taken his shoes off to creep up on her.

The better to see you with, my dear.

She ran now, back the way they'd come, some logical part of her mind saying rescue might be on the way by now, her car in the ditch, the parked Ford on the wrong side of the road . . . maybe help would come from that direction . . . but help might not come, so her route included where she'd unintentionally tossed the Glock . . .

Keith could hear the movement.

Feet on frozen clumps of snow, branches snapping, leaves crinkling, and he was so close now he could hear the heavy breathing, like an obscene phone call, two people participating, his daughter and the man after her.

He thought he'd misjudged but then finally saw Krista and the teacher, and found he was coming at them at an angle. His daughter seemed to be leading her attacker back toward the ditch and the road. Stock didn't discern the difference between the footsteps of stalked and stalker until Keith was almost on him.

Stock's blank expression distorted into rage and the knife was raised very high when Keith tackled him, taking him down between two trees onto brittle snow that cracked like little bones. Bigger bones within Keith, that busted rib and its bruised brothers, proved they could push their demands through even the best painkillers and he was screaming when the son of bitch squirmed out of his grasp.

Then Stock was on his feet, Keith on the ground, a few yards separating them. The killer, butcher knife high, began to close the distance.

Krista almost tripped over the Glock.

She knelt, grabbed it up into her left-handed grasp. That arm was slashed, not bad maybe, gashed at the bicep, and her other hand was a useless thing.

But when she turned, through the spaces between barren oaks, she could see Stock with the blade raised, moving toward Pop, who was on the ground, trying to get up.

"Stay down!" she yelled.

She fired, fired again, again, the shots irregular, her unsteady arm doing her no favors, carving chunks of bark from trees and missing her favorite teacher, who turned and with a ghastly grin charged toward her, circling a tree to do so, and the moon through the witchy branches let that high-held blade wink at her one last time.

She fired again and took off a chunk of his ear.

That froze him.

He stood wide-eyed, hand going to the mangled flesh hanging from the left side of his head, getting blood all over his fingers, his expression telling her that Ken Stock experiencing pain had never been part of the plan.

She had a millisecond before he could compose himself enough to complete his murderous onslaught and she fired one more time.

The bullet entered his forehead—not in the dead center, but close enough—the metal projectile emerging from the back of his skull in a stew of blood, bone, and brains. He tottered, not feeling anything, already as dead as the leaves under his stockinged feet, and then he fell flat on his back, between a pair of trees that didn't notice him at all.

She went over to Pop and helped him up.

He grimaced and groaned and said, "This pro bono work is hard."

She laughed. He did, too. She hugged him. Gently. She hadn't forgotten his broken rib. They looked at each other. Smiling. Tears streaming.

"Not exactly ambidextrous, huh?" she asked.

"You got the job done, honey. Right, Mr. Stock?"

But Stock—on his back, eyes and a dime-size hole in his forehead staring sightlessly up through a skeletal filigree of forest, under a ghostly galleon of a moon—had not a thing to say.

ACKNOWLEDGMENTS

My thanks to Police Chief Lori Huntington of the Galena Police Department, who welcomed my wife Barb and me into her office, answering many questions and giving us a tour of the station. Throughout the writing of *Girl Most Likely*, Chief Huntington responded to my ongoing questions about procedure and other Galena matters. Her help and her patience went above and beyond the call of duty. But liberties have been taken and any inaccuracies are my own.

I should also note that Chief Huntington is not the basis of Krista Larson—the plot and characters for *Girl Most Likely* were already developed when research revealed the happy coincidence of Galena's actual chief being a young woman who had risen through the ranks.

Other references included various issues of *The Galenian* magazine; *Galena, Illinois: A Timeless Treasure* (2015) by Philip A. Aleo; and *Galena Illinois: A Brief History* (2010) and *Galena* (Images of America, 2005), both by Diann Marsh.

Barb, who writes the Antiques mysteries with me (bylined Barbara Allan), provided vital editing and suggestions throughout. Also, my frequent collaborator, Matthew V. Clemens, answered a number of police procedure questions.

I'd like also to thank my editor at Thomas & Mercer, Liz Pearsons, and editorial director Grace Doyle for their support, belief, and patience. As usual, thanks go as well to my friend and agent, Dominick Abel.

ABOUT THE AUTHOR

Photo © 2013 M.A.C. Productions LLC

Max Allan Collins was named a Grand Master in 2017 by the Mystery Writers of America. He has earned an unprecedented twenty-three Private Eye Writers of America Shamus Award nominations, winning two for his Nathan Heller novels. That series also earned Collins the PWA Hammer Award for making a major contribution to the private-eye genre. He received the PWA Eye Lifetime Achievement Award in 2006. His other books include the *New York Times* bestseller *Saving Private Ryan* and the *USA Today* bestselling CSI series.

His graphic novel *Road to Perdition* is the basis of the Academy Award–winning Tom Hanks film, and is followed by two acclaimed prose sequels and several more graphic novels in the same series. His other comics credits include the syndicated strip *Dick Tracy*, *Wild Dog*, *Batman*, and his own *Ms. Tree*.

Collins is also a screenwriter, playwright, and a leading indie filmmaker in his native Iowa, where he lives with his wife, writer Barbara Collins; as "Barbara Allan," they have collaborated on fourteen novels. For more information, visit www.maxallancollins.com.